Books by Larry Woiwode

NOVELS

What I'm Going to Do, I Think (1969)
Beyond the Bedroom Wall (1975)
Poppa John (1981)
Born Brothers (1988)

POEMS

Even Tide (1977)

STORIES

The Neumiller Stories (1989)

THE NEUMILLER STORIES

THE NEUMILLER STORIES

STORIES

LARRY WOIWODE

Michael di Capua Books

Farrar, Straus and Giroux

New York

Library of Congress catalog card number: 89-61247

Published simultaneously in Canada by Harper & Collins, Toronto

Printed in the United States of America

Designed by Cynthia Krupat

First edition, 1989

The stories collected here were first published in The New Yorker,
with the exception of "The Suitor," which appeared in McCall's, and
"She," in Gentlemen's Quarterly

FOR MICHAEL DI CAPUA

Salud

Contents

Preface

The possibility of this collection first presented itself in 1975, when I set the galleys of my second novel, *Beyond the Bedroom Wall*, down on the desk of William Maxwell, then my editor at *The New Yorker*, and he began to page through them, slowly at first, and then looked up over his glasses, and said, "Goodness, you've changed almost every one of these." He had worked on a good dozen chapters of the book, originally written as stories and taken by the magazine, as I had gone over them, again and again, first in white proofs, then in pink, so I was aware of the generosity of his nature. But it never occurred to me that he might have portions of them all but memorized. That there was also possibly dismay in his voice didn't penetrate until later.

So it is only proper to acknowledge, first, his hand in these, in the form they take here, and in the same breath in which I do this, with all gratitude, to absolve him of any responsibility for my further relationship with the Neumillers; the variety of finished perspectives he opened up could have turned in any direction.

Of the baker's dozen stories settled upon, three of the largest, from the eighties, have not been collected before.

The remaining ten appeared, often in quite different form, in *Beyond the Bedroom Wall*, and certain of them, such as "The Suitor," underwent a transformation so complete they now appear, I feel, for the first time.

The stories are arranged in order of completion, indicated by the dates prefacing each section. I have regularized names and restored original titles, including "Beyond the Bedroom Wall," assuming that any confusion this causes with the novel will be offset by the confusions about the novel it clears up.

The first ten stories, spanning my working relationship with William Maxwell, until the time of his retirement from *The New Yorker*, are the work of a young man. I don't want the measured tread of middle age to intrude on him, so I've largely let these stories be. I could never reproduce, at this age, his youthful urgency or single-minded intent. "Oh, Colette, Colette, if I could kiss the calluses on your writing hand," he wrote, planning to purge every trace of falsity and rhetoric from his fiction. Not so, in spite of all those trips and calls to Maxwell, who, though he must have been driven nearly to distraction at times, never said, "That's enough." He knew that although it's permissible to meddle with a young man's prose, it's best, as I've learned since, not to meddle with a young man's ideals. I stand aside.

1964–1967

DEATHLESS

LOVERS

She lifts the earthenware cream crock from the dishpan, shakes beads of water from its oatmeal-colored sides, and sets it, upside down, on the drainboard. Her movements are dignified and precise. When she walks, she holds her tall body erect and glides along a straight line, as though her lovely soul were liquid and could spill. The boy beside her smiles. Her youth and grace enable him to forget she is not his mother, who has died the winter before, but his grandmother; her sure gestures firm the air, so that when he breathes deeply, as he does now, he breathes strength.

He stands, the dish towel draped over his open hand like a magician's silk, waiting. Her light-brown hair is plaited into two long braids coiled round and round her delicate skull. Lightened by sunlight, strongly angular, her face could be the face on a statue of a Norse goddess, and when it suddenly breaks into movement, he is both startled and pleased, and shivers, cold.

"Quit gaping," she says softly. "And close your mouth or it'll fill up with flies, sure as I live."

"It's not open."

"It is, too."

"You can't tell. You're not even looking this way."

"I can tell."

Her beauty unnerves her. She has never allowed her photograph to be taken, and when she combs out her waist-length hair at night, or when the boy combs it out for her, chasing blond and pink highlights down the ripples raised by the braids, she sits on the edge of the bed, away from the mirror, her head bowed.

Now she shakes water from a bundle of forks and gives them to him to dry, and as he takes them, his hand touches her skin. It is smoother than the silver, and so transparent the lilac veins and amber freckles glow beneath it. She smiles, and he looks down at his bare feet. More than watching her, her touch gives him strength.

"Lordy, Lordy! you're so bashful!" she says, almost sings, in a voice that pleases him because it is like a young girl's—full of teasing bravado and so thin and so pure it seems liable to crack, like fine china.

"Nobody knows you're bashful but me. They all think you're quiet or just plain dumb."

"They" refers to the other side of the family—the boy's father and paternal grandparents. She steals him from them each summer, and when she and the boy are reunited on her farm in Minnesota, as they want to be, she arms herself against any possible liking he might have built up for *them* over the year. She lets him know, sometimes not too discreetly, that love, which she feels for him (in contrast to the guardianship they take for granted), is more observant. But if she believes she has been unfair, or wronged them, or colored his emotion too much, she switches from criticism to breathtaking praise.

"I'm not bashful either," he says.

"You're not? You're not, huh?" She puts her fingers to his throat and raises his face. "Then why are you blushing? Huh? Huh?"

He pulls away, turning to put the forks in the chimney cupboard, and her "Huh?," which she repeats and delights in repeating, grows into laughter. She has nailed him down to a truth.

"Grandpa doesn't talk either," the boy says. "He just grunts."

Her husband is the sore spot, as they both know. He is a vain, meticulous man who wears high black hook-and-eye dress shoes and pin-striped shirts with bright arm garters, whether he's in the living room, listening to baseball on the radio, or in the barnyard with his favorite team of horses, Colonel and Queenie, feeding them cookies. The boy can't understand this love for the horses. If he were his grandfather, he would shoot them. Two winters ago, when the old man was gathering hay during a snowstorm, they bolted, and he was pitched headlong off the hayrack and broke his spine.

The accident has diminished him. Although he was always tiny, the top of his head doesn't reach his wife's shoulder now. And though she purposely keeps the cookies in the same place, where he can reach them, he believes he steals them without her knowledge, and is so pleased with his foxiness he chuckles the rest of the day, chuckles too much. She talks down to him more than she does to the boy and picks arguments with him, which almost always end with him cursing her and her in tears. He can't seem to bear remembering that she nursed him when he was helpless, and despises her for it. Which hurts her, because it seems unreasonable and thankless. Of his old passion all that remains is what once moved him to kick a fidgety milk cow so hard her rear legs collapsed and she sat down in her stanchion—his temper—and she scolds him for it with a temper of her own.

"Maybe your grandpa doesn't talk much now," she says, "but there was never a smidgen of bashfulness in that man ever in his whole life. He's a miserable, miserable, spiteful old crow!"

These last words were so harsh the boy has looked up. Beneath her high cheekbones red patches appear and spread toward her thin, graceful neck. If he hadn't seen her rock the old man in her arms, singing "So, so; so, saso; so, so . . ." on the nights when he wakes from his recurring dream of being shut up forever in a hospital, the boy would think she hates him.

She empties the dishwater into the sink, takes a dipper of hot water from the reservoir in the cookstove, swirls it in the pan, and splashes it over the wooden paddles of a butter churn she has washed. Her anger has already cooled, and in her clear musical voice she's humming a Lutheran hymn. Her detachment stirs the boy's jealousy, and he figures that to get through to her he has to go farther.

"Why don't you have hot and cold running water," he asks, "like other people do?"

"Because we're in the country. And plumbing out here comes too high." This is said almost to herself, as she dries the piece of crockery. The boy feels trapped; he must make her pay more attention to him than to dishes.

"When you grow up," she says, "and get to be a big strong man, you can build me a nice new house in town somewhere, with plumbing and all the conveniences."

"No I can't. You'll be dead by then."

"What!"

"You'll be dead by then."

"What kind of a thing is that to say to your grandma! Huh? Huh?"

She tilts his face up again. In her eyes there is hurt and stern anger, then disbelief, and then she laughs, and says, "If that doesn't take the cake! So I'll be dead by then, huh? So that's what you think. Is that what you think? Huh?"

"I just said that. I don't want you to be."

"Of course not," she says, and moved by his sadness she takes him in her arms. "So, so," she says. "I know you didn't mean it."

He is overwhelmed by his effect. He smiles against her dress that smells of dry pine needles, of freshly baked bread and wet clothes—a smell he will remember in its layers of detail, more than ten years later, when she suddenly dies. And, as he grows older, whenever he loves a woman, fears that he'll lose her, and his love becomes so smothering and possessive that she runs from him, the same smell will surprise his senses, leaving him breathless and weak.

BEYOND THE
BEDROOM WALL

At the age of nine I wasn't afraid of the dark. When I ran down a deserted street at night, I knew the chilling pursuer I felt at my back was put there by my own act of running, and would disappear—like any creature of the imagination when put to a test—the second I slowed to a walk. The gray hands that reached for me as I lay in bed were of my own creation, too, and once I had proved my power to summon them up, for the sake of a safe, enjoyable scare, I could destroy them.

When the change came, it seemed to come in a moment, but I believe I was being prepared for it. I believe it began one morning when my father read a letter at the breakfast table. The letter was from his father, a prosperous contractor in Illinois; a new school district was being formed in the town he lived in, and they were looking for a high-school principal. For the large and muscular, leathery-faced man my father was—strong-minded about his beliefs, uncompromising in carrying out school policies—he was surprisingly unaggressive when it came to family matters. He seemed to dread the possibility of making the wrong decision. He turned to my mother.

Wasn't he satisfied with the job he had, she wanted to know. Of course, but there wasn't much chance of getting ahead in North Dakota. Wasn't he the superintendent of a high school now? Yes, that was true, he said, speaking as calmly and as reasonably as she did. And didn't he make enough to keep them happy? More than enough. Then would it be wise to give up the job he had, and sell the house, and move to Illinois, where it was so hot and so humid, when a job hadn't actually been promised to him yet? Didn't she like Illinois? Not especially. Well, they had only been there in the summer, and he imagined that was why. His father hadn't liked it at first, either, but now he called it God's country. Then why did he so often come back to North Dakota? Well, probably because North Dakota was his home state. And wasn't it theirs? Yes, but his father had done so well for himself down there, and maybe he could, too. Wouldn't she like a nicer house? This was the house she had always wanted—how could there be a better one? Well, his only reason for considering the idea at all was that his father was getting old and wanted the family reunited. She knew that, didn't she? Yes, she said, and leaned to him and kissed him. He took both her hands in his. Wouldn't she like it if they were in a bigger town where he could make more money and she could have more friends? She bowed her head, as she did only when she was sad or very ashamed.

And so, in the early summer of that year, we moved from North Dakota to the small town in central Illinois where my grandfather lived. While my father was waiting to hear about the appointment, he bought and started remodeling a duplex that had originally been a gasoline station. He ripped up the twelve-inch baseboards and tore stucco off the inside walls, knocked down a small enclosure in one corner of the living room (what it was, no one knew), sawed a long rectangular hole in the kitchen floor and put up a partition in front of it, creating a new stairway to the basement, and converted the concrete island that had once held the gasoline pumps, a car's breadth from the front door, into a flower planter. Setting aside his usual calm and reserve, he went at the place with such a passion that I was inspired; I learned to use a hammer like a man and started to have at the old house, too.

The bedroom I was given had no window. It was a small upstairs room with a ceiling that took its sharp slant from the pitch of the roof. There wasn't any floor in the rest of the attic, so the room was surrounded by bare ceiling joists, and felt as isolated as I did in this place we had moved to. There was no daylight and no light fixture in the room, no smell but the smell of dust and old lumber (the previous owner had used it as a storeroom), no color, no company; the seasons outside were merely changes in temperature. When my father first showed me the room, he said he would add a dormer and fill it with daylight as soon as he finished remodeling the downstairs, but, for the time being, all he did was move a dresser into the room and set up a narrow cot against one wall.

Lying on the cot, I learned the secrets of the dark. A wooden catwalk with a banister ran from the door of the bedroom to the head of the stairs. If I got out of bed, feeling my way to the steps, and went down them, I entered a house deep in sleep. A low hallway (I could hear it!) led from the foot of the stairs in one direction, to the left, past the bathroom, and ended at the living room. If I snapped the wall switch, the whole living room was caught off guard—the windows blinked, rugs stretched out flat, and chair backs straightened. To my right, in the far wall of the living room, the door of my parents' bedroom guarded their sleep; to my left, an arch leading to the kitchen—a high, wide arch—yawned. Utensils on the stove and the glass knobs on the doors and drawers of the cabinets, picking up the light from the living room, were like half-opened, protesting eyes.

Back in bed, hearing the whole house creak and sigh in its heavy sleep, I also learned about the one element that stays awake: the air. Long after the house was asleep, and long after I should have been, the dark air was alive with excitement. Because there was never any light in the room, from the sun or the moon, the air was my gauge of time and events. A disturbance outside—a passing train, a car, the lashing of a tree—caused it to ripple. When the sun rose, the air became angry, agitated, and some nights, for a reason I could never understand, it thickened and pressed against me.

Before the state of Illinois officially certified my father as a teacher, all the administrative and even the teaching positions in the new school district were filled. He had to start working for my grandfather, as a carpenter. My father wasn't one to go back on a promise or leave a job unfinished, but his remodeling of the house slowed to a stop; gray rock lath rose to shoulder height, and above that the bare studs, black with dirt and age, stood exposed. My room remained without a window.

My mother did not like the house we were living in, and was troubled that my father had to give up teaching, the profession he loved, and become a common laborer. She was also in her last months of pregnancy. She became silent and secretive, and kept her eyes lowered. My father watched her from the time he came home from work until he went to bed. How was she feeling today? Fine. Was there anything he could do? No. Would she like to go out—to a movie or somewhere? No. When her answers turned from single words to shrugs, and when his smile and his time-honored burlesque of the schottische, with the broom as his partner, failed to cheer her up, he became silent, too.

One afternoon I stood near the top of a stepladder and nailed lath to the partition in the kitchen. My mother sat at the table, paying little attention to the noise I made, and embroidered on a dish towel. Once when I missed the nail completely, and the stud, too, sending a circular hole through the rock lath with the head of the hammer, I cursed. Still she didn't look up. When I had first started using foul language, she had washed my mouth out with soap. I had never heard my father swear, and now she was letting me get away with it. I felt manly and arrogant, and made even more noise.

But then I realized how much she must have changed, to ignore what she had once disapproved of, and I studied her from the top of the stepladder. Her face had lost all its beauty. It was dry and chapped, and her dark-brown hair, which usually hung loose, was pinned back behind her ears. At her temples, just above her eyebrows, I could see the bones of her skull. She had paused in her sewing, and was looking at her hand—first the palm, then the back.

"Mom? Are you okay?"

Without looking up, she said, "Yes," and quickly continued sewing, as if I'd caught her at something. "Don't worry about me," she said. "Do your job."

Her manner upset me. I came down from the stepladder, marked a piece of lath, and cut across it with the razor knife, shakily curving off in the wrong direction a couple of times. I snapped the lath across my knee, broke off the hinged endpiece, and started up the ladder, when an emotion spread from her and pressed on me like a hand. I stopped, my eyes on the grooves of one of the steps, and tried to figure out what she was feeling. Then I turned to look at her, and the grooves seemed to lift with my eyes, stretch through the air, and link us. She raised her face and I felt weak; I'd never been so close to her. At any other time she might have smiled, or told me, with a blush, to quit staring, but now she stared at me until I was the one who blushed, and so badly I had to start hammering again.

"Don't," she said.

"Don't what?"

I turned to her and she was running her fingertips over the embroidery.

"Don't work anymore."

"The hammering bothers you?"

"No. I don't want you to work."

"Why not?"

She wouldn't look at me. "Go and play."

"Who with?" I took a nail out of my mouth and pounded it in place. "Dad told me to do this wall."

"I don't want you to work with your hands! You're too young to work."

"No, I'm not!"

"Don't argue. Go outside."

With her head lowered, her voice didn't seem a part of her. I came down the ladder angrily, determined to make her look at me, and saw that the length and breadth of her cheeks were wet with tears.

I went out the back door and sat on the steps. It wasn't right of her to go against my father's word, and she never had. She was even going against her own! She wouldn't talk to you, and when she did she wouldn't look at you, and then she cried. If something was wrong and she didn't want me to know what it was, I wished she would simply leave me alone. Then I remembered the long, unguarded look she had held me with.

One January night I woke, for no apparent reason, and felt the air above my cot had thickened. It was denser than it was when the sun rose, and some sound was trying to make its way through the denseness. I listened so intently my eyes joined in the effort, searching the volume of dark air, and then I heard (coming from the ground floor? from somewhere above the roof?) a sound like the breathy creak of a pigeon's wings, rising and falling, reaching for me and then falling away again. I rolled over and my shoulder struck the wall.

Light switches clicked downstairs, there were footsteps, the telephone jingled as it was cranked, and I felt the heavy throb of my father's bass voice. After a number of throbs, punctuated by silences that seemed humming question marks in the dark air, the receiver slapped into its holder, my father's footsteps crossed the kitchen, and another switch clicked. A white rectangle, its top end bent up against the foot of the wall, gripped the floor; he had turned on the light in the hallway downstairs. He made several quick trips from the bathroom to their bedroom and back again. I went to the banister, looked down the stairwell, and saw his shadow cross the bottom steps.

"Dad?"

After a silence, a pause in the footsteps, his head appeared around the corner. "What are you doing up at this hour?"

"Nothing."

"You'd better go back to bed."

"Who were you talking to on the phone?"

"The doctor. Do you realize it's three o'clock?"

"Is somebody sick?"

He stared up at me, and finally said, "Go to bed. Please."

I did, but I couldn't sleep. The birdlike sounds rose up again, his footsteps crossed the house, in long strides this time, and the jingling of the telephone was harsh. I got out of bed and was nearly to the bottom of the stairs when I heard my father's voice: ". . . realize it's practically a half hour since I called? You can't be more than a block away, and . . . *What?* How in the world can a man read at a time like this? . . . Well, I don't give a damn about your— your *damn* family doctor's book! . . ."

The profanity, so wrong on my father's tongue, scared me. And his voice was usually under control; I had never heard it like this. I went to the kitchen doorway and saw that he was trembling, holding on to the wooden box of the wall telephone to steady himself. "Are you listening? You get over here this minute or I'll come and get you!" He hooked the receiver into its metal cradle, leaned a shoulder against the wall, and whispered, "Oh, God! What next?" Then he gathered himself and drew his body erect, and when he turned his face to me it wasn't my father's face. It was so white it looked as if his day's growth of beard had caved it in, and his large eyes were glazed.

"I thought I told you to go to bed."

"Are you sick?"

"What are you *doing* down here?"

"I have to go to the bathroom."

He bowed his head, gripped the bridge of his nose, and let out a moan of someone deathly ill. "Go," he said.

"What's the matter?"

"Do as you're told."

I decided I would go to their bedroom before I went

back upstairs, to find out from my mother what was wrong, but when I stepped out of the bathroom he stood blocking the hall.

"Hurry up," he said. "I'll turn out the light."

"I want to see Mom."

"Not now. Not tonight."

"Why not?"

"She's too sick."

"Let me *see* her!"

"Maybe tomorrow. Go now."

"She's sick?"

He nodded his head with such finality I wasn't able to ask anything else, or disobey—run past him to their bedroom—but as I climbed the stairs I was sure I had done something wrong. Because I didn't know what it was, and at the same time realized it was my *mother* who was ill, I started to tremble, and when I settled into bed and the rectangle on the wall vanished, darkness pressed on me as it never had before. It took my entire imagination, and closed eyes, to keep it away, and just as I heard strange voices—several of them, it seemed—I gave in to the dark.

I dreamed I was walking with my mother through a department store. The walls and ceiling were white, and the floor of white marble, with low display cases set at great distances from one another. My mother held my hand in a firm grip. She wanted to go upstairs, and I wanted to stay where we were, on the ground floor, and look in the display cases. I pulled away from her and ran to one. *Don't. Don't look!* she called after me, and her voice echoed through the empty store.

The case was filled with blue china figurines. There was a blue swan, similar to the one in our kitchen, with a hole in its back, so that it could be used as a flowerpot, blue angels, and small blue busts of children. My mother put her hand on my shoulder and said, *Come away.* I turned to say no and couldn't breathe. She stood far above me, taller than she had ever been, her face made of blue china and her eyes alive and staring at me as they had in the kitchen. She pulled her coat close around her throat, turned and walked away, and when I tried to run after her, my feet wouldn't move.

I woke to darkness, twisted in the blankets, my heart beating hard against the cot. I had to see my mother. I started to get out of bed and struck the wall. I was stupefied; the wall was on the other side of the cot. I tried again. I knew there was no wall there, and not all the logic in the world, or the wall itself, could convince me otherwise. Nothing as simple as getting reversed in bed occurred to me. I tried again and again, and finally fell back onto the cot, and my left arm extended into open space. If there was a wall where I was convinced there was none, I couldn't imagine what waited for me in that emptiness where the wall should be. I pulled my arm back and held it over my chest, afraid to move, afraid of the dark.

•

In the morning, without having to be told, I knew my mother was gone. My father, who had had no sleep, said she had been taken by ambulance to the hospital. Without being able to confide in him, or in anyone (once the sun has risen, the dark seems partly our imagination), I knew I would never see my mother again, and started preparing myself for her death.

THE

VISITATION

From the time he was first able to remember, all the way back to when words weren't words but colors and images of states of mind, what he remembered most of all was the quality of the stories his mother told at night. He would lie on his back, looking up at the circle of light cast on the ceiling by the lamp, and she would sit beside the lamp, her face in shadow, her lap flooded with light, her folded hands in her lap, and tell him about a time before he was born.

Her stories were as simple and as pure as the circle of light on the ceiling, and they seemed to become part of the light itself, distinct from him and even from her, so that when he turned on his side or on his stomach as she spoke, or when he turned to look at her lips forming the words of the story, widening into a smile when there was a scene that pleased her, pursing in anger or indignation, relaxing and drooping at the corners when she was recalling sadness, even then the location of the story didn't change. Its source and substance, its beginning and end, was the circle of light.

She seemed a medium through which a spirit was passing, and that spirit gathered itself on the ceiling and hung above him, a life in itself, a form he could absorb or look at impassively but whose substance he couldn't ignore. Even when she left the room and shut off the light, its presence remained. He would breathe shallowly, feeling its heaviness above him, the heaviness of a mood or emotion more than anything particular she had said, and then, just as he was dropping off to sleep, he felt it descend and enter him. Here it became a part of his dreams.

The mixture of colors, pictures, a phrase rising from the center of a landscape, her voice; stories about her childhood, her mother and father, about the farm they lived on in central North Dakota when she was a child; stories that her grandfather, one of the first to homestead in the state, told her—of grass fires, miles wide, coming toward him over the plain; of being snowed in for a week in a one-room shack, while drifts of snow rose closer and closer to the top of the stovepipe; of men wandering a few miles from their homesteading shacks and getting lost because the plain, with its russet covering of grass, looked the same in every direction.

With a note of amusement in her voice she recalled that her grandfather ended each story of his homesteading days with the phrase, "Ya, sure, that was before they had windmills or trees." And there were the stories of her brothers, Conrad and Elling. Elling, the oldest of the three, was a prankster. He searched out a swallow's nest and a magpie's nest and then switched the two sets of eggs; put a baby mouse in his father's riding boot, and could have got away with it if he hadn't bragged about it to Conrad, the youngest of the three. For the scare the mouse gave his father (he threw his boot across the room and broke out the glass door of the china cabinet), and for beating up Conrad, Elling had to live for a week in the hayloft. He also unearthed a shovelful of arrowheads while he was breaking up a new piece of land with the horse plow, and had sense enough to dig deeper, discovering the site of an Indian village, which was deeded to the Historical Society of North Dakota, and was now a well-known land-mark.

After reading a magazine article on crop rotation, Elling started telling his father how to run the farm, and was so persistent and condescending about it that the old man finally gave him such a whack across the backside with his cane that its end broke off. Elling was the star of the high-school track team, and set the state record, still unbroken, in the hop, step, and jump. For touching up the statue of the Alma Mater with red barn paint and for antics at sororities (these remained obscure) he was dropped from college after his first year. And then, after such an unpromising start, Elling surprised everybody by leaving the farm and becoming a prominent businessman—the state distributor of Hart Parr tractors and farm machinery.

Conrad was accident-prone. He fell off the Shetland pony, Midge, so tame it was almost a house pet, and broke his collarbone, fell through a hole in the hayloft and broke three ribs, fell off the corral and broke his wrist, and once, when he was being chased around the barnyard by a turkey gobbler—looking at it in horror over his shoulder—he ran into the metal corner of a hayrack and broke open his head. He was the quiet, retiring one, who seldom got angry, but when he did he picked up whatever was at hand—a branch, a length of pipe, a pitchfork—and chased Elling all the way to the front porch and into the house with a look in his eyes like he meant to kill.

Conrad wanted a puppy from the day he learned to speak, and on his fifth birthday, his father finally gave him one—a black water spaniel only a few weeks old—and said, "If I ever see that thing in the house I'll take down the gun and shoot it."

Conrad named the dog Curly and carried it in his arms all morning and afternoon—on a Monday, when his mother was doing the washing. He wouldn't even come into the house for lunch, but toward evening he went in for a drink of water and, remembering his father's warning, left the puppy on the porch in the safest place he could find—a bushel basket of clothes sitting on the wash bench. During the time he was inside, the dog scrambled out of the basket and jumped onto the lid of an oval boiler standing on the floor, tipped up the lid, and slipped into the scalding water. When his father heard the dog's agonized crying and ran out to the porch, he saw Conrad trying to lift it out of the boiler with his bare hands.

In the end, his father had to shoot the dog after all, and he wouldn't believe Conrad hadn't put it in the boiler on purpose, because a few weeks before he had caught Conrad trying to drown a baby duck in the horse tank. From that day Conrad became even more shy, and this was the reason, it was said, that he never married and never left the farm.

Each of her stories about Conrad ended on the same note: "Your Uncle Conrad, I want you to know, has been terribly misunderstood his whole life." And there was a shading in her voice that implied, "I, too, have been misunderstood, and when you grow up you can expect the same."

And there were stories whose details the boy couldn't remember but whose moods he retained. The next day, or weeks later, as he was sitting in the sunlit alcove of the bay window, playing with the toys he had gathered there, one of the moods would rise in him, and he would pause with an abstracted look, testing the quality of what he felt—whether its source was a story or an incident from his actual life. One afternoon as he sat like this, looking past the windmill he had built from Tinkertoys, conscious only of a hot brocade (the result of sunlight streaming through the window's lace curtains) spread over his cheek and ear, he heard, coming from the end of the hallway off the living room, the sound of his mother's voice in surprise, the sound of other voices, and then a burst of laughter.

He stood up and the windmill tipped over and struck the floor. He saw that one of the blades of its fan—a piece of violet paperboard—had come loose. Then the door to the hallway swung open and the boy's mother walked into the living room with a heavyset man, a stranger, following behind, bringing with him a cold fragrance of spring air. The man smiled at him, then said, "And this must be Jerry. It's hard to believe he's this big!"

This stranger walked to the bay window, the floor trembling under his strides, and held out some pamphlets. "Here," he said. "I brought you these. Go ahead, take them! Don't be bashful."

The boy looked at his mother, to see if this was all right, and she frowned.

"Jerome!" she said. "What's the matter with you? Don't you remember him? Don't you know who that is?"

Jerome remembered a stranger with the smell of cold air clinging to him who came to the house and gave him a package of Sen-Sen and then tickled him until he turned blue, couldn't catch his breath, and had to have cold water thrown in his face. Was this that man? He looked to his mother for confirmation.

"Shame on you!" she said. "That's your Uncle Elling!"

Jerome stepped back. Could the Elling of his mother's stories be standing above him, a real person, so old and so fat?

"Here," Elling said, and offered the pamphlets again. "They're yours." Jerome took them, and Elling removed his hat, placed his hands on his knees, and bent over until his face was only inches away. *Sen-Sen.* "What's the matter?" he asked. His blond hair, cropped close to his skull, sparkled in the sunlight, and his long ears glowed orange, rendering him almost luminous. "You're not scared of your Uncle Elling, are you? You're not an old fraidycat?"

"He's probably just bashful," a deep bass voice said. Jerome looked up and another man came through the doorway and stood behind his mother. This one was so tall that his face, tanned brown to the hatline (the rest of his high forehead was pure ivory) and his shoulders, too, showed above the top of her head. She said, "Well, if you don't remember your Uncle Elling, who's been here to see you once before, you certainly don't remember *him.* That's Conrad."

"How do you do," Conrad pronounced in his bass voice. "I'm Conrad."

Jerome looked at the pamphlets in his hand. On the cover of one was a picture in color of a tractor, with a man sitting on it, and there was printing under its wheels. Somehow the picture related the phantoms that formed the circle of light on the ceiling, the Elling and Conrad of his mother's stories, to the Elling and Conrad before him in the flesh. If they were still there. He looked up and found them smiling at him. He was in the same room with figures out of the past. Ghosts.

"If he's just going to stand there and not say a word, come on and sit down," his mother said.

The three went to the couch on the other side of the room and sat facing the bay window.

"This is too good to be true," she said. "I was just talking about you last night!"

"The hell," Elling said.

"I was telling Jerome about the time you went to the Metzler place to bring back those sheep that got out—"

"And traded a lamb for old man Metzler's .22?" Elling asked. "That time?"

She nodded.

"Dad whaled the daylights out of me. I thought he wouldn't miss the lamb, but I'll be damned if I knew how to account for the rifle. You told him that?"

She nodded again, more energetically, and Elling frowned at Jerome, and said, "Don't believe a word of it. I wasn't ever that dumb."

The adults laughed in a way that excluded Jerome and at the same time released him; he was free to do what he wanted. He sat back on the floor and began paging through an illustrated pamphlet.

"Why stop by on today of all days?" she asked.

"Well," Elling said, "to tell you the truth, it's almost by accident. The concatenations of circumstance, you might say." He looked aside at them, but they continued to study him with affection and interest, as if they expected to be dazzled by him. "I had to make the drive over from Bismarck to Valley anyway," he said, setting his hat on his knee, "to see my district representative there, and since I'm breaking in my new car and wanted to get some extra miles on it, what I did was first I swung up north to home to say hello to the folks, and when Brother here saw the new Pontiac and heard I was tired of driving it—you can't take it above forty miles an hour and, God, that gets on my nerves—he offered to drive all the way into Valley for me. And since—"

"You're driving his new car?" she asked.

The grin Conrad gave in reply—with his teeth and the whites of his eyes appearing in striking contrast to his tan—indicated that nothing could get between him and his pleasure as long as he knew he'd soon be back behind that wheel.

"Well, you be careful with it!" she said. "You hear? Still the grin, growing broader.

"And since he's been wanting to go to Valley for months now," Elling went on, "but can never seem to get away, so he tells me, this was convenient for the both of us. Well, he was driving along, happy as can be, until we got down around Bordulac. Then he mentioned that he hadn't ever seen Jerry, or your new place here, and he wondered if maybe we couldn't make a little side trip and drop in and see you. So I said, 'Sure! Why not!'"

"I can't understand why it's never occurred to you before," she said. "It's been almost two years."

"Oh, it can't be *that* long!"

"It most certainly is! You were just mentioning how big Jerome is. He'll soon be five. He was three years old the last time you were here."

"Really? That was two years ago?"

"Two years this June."

"I'll be damned. Two years is a long time. By God, it's a good thing Brother was with me this trip or I likely wouldn't be here now!"

"It's plain to see that he cares about others and you don't."

"Oh, now . . ."

There was a distant rumbling sound, as of someone moving furniture in an upstairs room, so faint and short-lived that by the time they had listened to make sure they'd heard right the sound had stopped. Jerome put aside one pamphlet and began paging through another, trying to attract as little attention to himself as possible.

"Jerry!" Elling said. "Jerry, don't you want to ride my pony?" He lifted his hat and patted his knee where he expected Jerome to sit. "Pony boy, pony boy, won't you be my pony boy!" he sang, jogging his knee in time to the beat—"Don't say no, here we go . . ." Jerome kept glancing at the pamphlets, and a look of perplexity came over Elling's face. "Can he read?" he asked.

"A little. He won't start school till next fall."

"How are the pictures?" Elling asked.

Jerome looked up and smiled, honored that he was being spoken to as an adult, but since he didn't know how to respond to the honor, also embarrassed.

"Can't you talk?" his mother said. "Do you like them or not?"

"Yes."

"We got a word out of him!" Elling said. "That's something! When strangers come to our place, the kids run and hide in the bathroom!"

"But you're not strangers," she said. "And if he doesn't know how to behave with his own uncles, he can sit there like a dunce."

"I know how he feels," Conrad said. "I was the same way once."

"Oh!" she exclaimed, turning to Conrad. "Do you remember the time you saw those nuns? Mother had taken you into town, into the department store, and was looking through the linens and white things. You didn't know it, but the reason she had you with her was to buy you a new jacket. You had never seen one in your life, and when you turned around and saw them there, right behind you, you pointed your finger and started yelling, 'The black ones! The black ones!'"

She and Elling laughed, and Conrad's ivory forehead darkened. He lowered his eyes and murmured, "I vaguely remember."

"Talk about being scared!" Elling said. "Remember the night the folks went over to the Metzlers' to play pinochle and left the three of us at home alone? We were wondering what we could do, without getting into a lot of trouble, when one of you—I think it was you, Alpha—brought me this book and asked me to read a story in it, and we all sat down on the couch, just like this, one of you on the either side of me. What kind of a guy wrote that story is what I'd like to know! It was about a man that stabbed his sister, tied her in chains, and as if that wasn't enough, buried her in the basement. And then this friend of his comes to visit, and the sister revives or rises from the dead and decides to get even, so, sure enough, while they're upstairs talking, up she gets out of the coffin, blood all over her and everything, up the stairs she comes, and walks into the room where they are. Well, just as I got to that part, there was this big boom on the front porch. None of us could move. Much as I wanted to close that damn book, I couldn't. There was all kinds of scratching and pattering out there, too—*chains!* I thought, but I suppose it was just a chicken—and I swear I even heard the knob turn and the door open and close. So I sat there, hardly able to breathe, thinking, Any minute now, we're going to have a corpse coming through that door. We sat like that for a half hour."

"A half hour at the least!" she said. "When the folks came back we were still sitting there! They figured we must have done something awful, we were so quiet. We never did tell them, did we? I think we were too ashamed to admit we were so scared."

"Ashamed?" Elling said. "My God, I was in my teens!"

"I was nine then," Conrad said. "I remember."

"There was an old man who lived across the road from us," she said. "In that little shack beside the granaries. Do you remember him? The old man with the long mustaches who poured his coffee out in a saucer before he drank it. What was his real name? We called him 'Uncle,' but I know he wasn't our uncle. Was he even related?"

"I think he was Dad's uncle," Elling said. "He spoke some foreign tongue. Finnish, I think. But I don't know what happened to him. One day he was gone. Wasn't somebody living there with him?"

"Some woman," she said. "But I don't think they were married."

"Sounds like Dad's uncle," Elling said.

"Do you remember seeing the buffalo wolves?" she asked.

"Didn't I take a shot at them with that ill-fated .22?"

"Or the time Dad got in a barroom brawl?"

"Somebody hit him over the head with a bottle of gin," Elling said. "A full one. You could smell him a mile off."

"Do you remember the sheep dog, the collie who ate cigarette butts?"

"Duke," Conrad said.

"Do you—"

"Whoa!" Elling said, and held up a hand. "Right here's where we stop. This happens to me all the time—going over the past—even when I'm away from the two of you, and every time it happens, it's like I'm stepping out of who I don't want to be into what I really am. And that's bad. It scares me. It's not who I am, not *really*. I'm me.

That person's gone. I have to stop myself and say 'No, no, that's all over! Here's where you stand now. Look! You're grown up! You have a wife and kids to attend to. You have an important job.' That's what I say, and sometimes it helps, but it doesn't change things much. The Metzlers still mean more to me than any millionaire client. The smallest detail from then is clearer in my mind than what I did yesterday, or the day before that, and the older I grow and the farther I get from those days, the more important the details seem. Will the present ever be like that? I don't know. I'd hate to think something has to be dead and gone before you can appreciate it. That's why I don't like to think about the past or talk about it much. It either makes me feel like a fool or like my heart's going to break. Those days are gone and that's it! Well, now I've made a fool of myself for talking so much. You mustn't misunderstand me, though. I don't believe in going backwards. A person has to go forwards. He's got to do what he's got to do and he's got to grow up! But it does seem a shame that the things I feel the strongest about aren't here anymore. By God, it *is* a shame. It's not right, it's a crime! That's the way I feel about it and the way everybody else feels, too!" He paused for a moment at their silence, then said, "Isn't it?"

"Well, if—" she began.

"Oh, yes!" Conrad said. "Those days were beautiful. I keep going over them again and again, over them and over them, just like they were the only part of my life I really lived. And, you know, it doesn't make any difference how many times I go over them. They never get tiresome, and I never run out of things to think about. Oh, I couldn't begin to tell you half of it. The hay fields, the grain fields, the old silo, the way the sun was then, the way we were. There's been so many times I've—"

Tears brimmed in his eyes and he bowed his head. There was a strained moment between them, and then Elling said, "Why, look, if we were separated then for an hour, we started a small rebellion, or went looking for one or the other, and now we've been apart for two years, two whole years, and none of us even noticed it."

"Maybe you didn't," she said. "But I did. I've missed you both. I *miss* you."

"Oh, I'm sure you have," Elling said. "I know you have. And I've missed you, too. But it's a different kind of missing. We don't throw fits like we used to, or sneak off to one another's room, or drop everything to make sure one or the other is where we think he is, doing what he should be doing. Hell, we get by. We get by somehow, and that's the worst part of it—that we get by."

"Yes," Conrad said, his bass voice blending with the rumbling sound that had begun again, "and every year it gets worse."

The bay window darkened and it started to rain. She looked at Jerome with a frown, as if he were responsible, and Conrad and Elling glanced at one another, then looked out the window. Jerome got up and stood at the curtains and listened to the rain falling onto the roof, the lawn and sidewalk, the leaves of the lilacs; and then, without a warning flash of light, the first clap of thunder rattled the panes of the window. Jerome lowered the curtain, went to his windmill, and sat on the floor beside it.

"He might be afraid of his uncles," Elling said. "But he's not scared a bit by the wrath of God. Good!"

Looking out at the darkening sky, Conrad said, "I was thinking I heard some thunder before. Well, it'll be good for the crops."

"I don't suppose you can stay on for the night?" she asked.

"Oh, no!" Elling said. "No, I have to be into Valley by supper. No, just the roads from here to Bordulac are bad. After that, we'll be fine."

"Was there a thunderstorm predicted?" she asked.

"Not that I know of," Elling said.

"I wondered," she said. "I didn't hear anything on the radio."

"This isn't a thunderstorm," Elling corrected her. "This is a cloudburst."

"Maybe," Conrad said. "But it's not going to let up just yet."

"How do you know?" Elling asked.

"I can feel it in my knee."

"I thought that meant trouble."

"Sometimes it means a good hard rain."

"You knew it was going to rain?"

"I figured it might," Conrad said.

They all turned their attention back to Jerome, nervous, and for the first time since they'd sat down, a silence, which contained in it only the sound of rain and of water running off the eaves, spread through the house.

"I'm glad I got to see him," Conrad murmured.

Jerome didn't hear. He was trying to reinsert the trapezoid-shaped violet blade into the slit at the end of the Tinkertoy stick. The piece of paperboard had been used so much its edges were frayed. He wiggled it at the top of the stick; it wouldn't go in. He examined the end of the stick, and then placed it against a top tooth and pushed up on it, trying to flare the slit, and the buzzing sensation at the roof of his mouth reminded him of attempting that one other time; of splitting the stick and running the pointed end into the roof of his mouth. He rubbed his tongue along the ridges of his palate (which was itching now), removed the stick from his mouth, and looked at the violet blade. He put it between his lips, compressed them, drew it out, and repeated this several times, copying what his mother did with thread before she speared the eye of a needle. He aligned the dampened edge of the blade with the slit in the stick, stopped, and looked up.

All three of them were staring at him. They shifted their weight on the couch and looked at him uneasily, as if to say, *Go on, please. If you get it together, we'll be back on the right track. Go on. We're counting on you.* He felt responsible for causing their conversation to stop, and he wanted to fix the windmill so they could pick up where they'd left off, but as long as they were staring at him like that he couldn't move.

Then the three of them locked into place, as if he were viewing a photograph that had been snapped of them at that moment, and began receding into his mind, growing smaller and more faint, retreating like spirits he had taken by surprise (as indeed they were; that same afternoon brochures and pamphlets for Hart Parr farm machinery were scattered in the wet grass from an unmarked railroad crossing down the tracks for a hundred yards to where the train—dragging with it a Pontiac that held the remnants of two dead men—finally came to a stop; and five years later his mother died in childbirth) until the three of them disappeared entirely, and the boy, encumbered with the full weight of his twenty-seven years, now an intern, finds himself sitting under lamplight in the small sleeping room that will be his home for the next year, staring at a pamphlet in his lap opened to the first page:

Emergency Room Procedures
Garfield Park Hospital
Chicago, Illinois

PHEASANTS

For the tenth time she went to the window in the pantry off the kitchen, lifted back the curtain, and looked out, down a dirt street three blocks long. No sign of him—only moonlight on the deserted walks. Cold fall air radiated through the glass and cooled her face, which was flushed with the fever of anxiety and impatience, and then, two blocks down, a streetlamp went on, lighting a patch of the building beside it, and a prowling cat bolted for cover. Late with the lights again tonight. It was nearly nine o'clock and her children were in bed.

She watched Maynard Labor leave the shack under the water tower, where he had thrown the switch for the lights, and start toward Main Street, passing under the streetlamp, trailing vapors of spent breath, his head bowed, his hands in his pockets. On his way to the tavern for another drink. Now when Martin did come, she would be able to see him turn the corner and start up the street, and could have everything on the table and ready for him. She sighed, and her eyes fell to a card inserted in the crack between windowpane and sash. On the side facing her was a picture of Jesus, Mary, and Joseph—the Infant standing on Mary's knee like a balanced statue—and on the reverse, facing out, she knew there were instructions for an act of perfect contrition, followed by a list of life-insurance policies and their yearly rates, and, at the bottom, in the blunt type of a hand stamp:

HOLY FAMILY LIFE INSURANCE
Martin Neumiller
Your agent here in central North Dakota
"Honest as my policies"

Surely one of the children, not Martin, had put the card there, she thought, and blushed for her husband. Then, feeling exposed to the whole village, she jerked the curtain back in place.

Anger and indignation rose in her, and she was ready to defend him against anybody who would belittle his work or say a word against him. She would tell them how the home office had been so pleased with his sales they had offered him the area around Fargo-Moorhead, which he had refused, saying he was honored, but if it was agreeable with them he would rather his children grew up close to the country, as he had. She would tell them how, on a suggestion from someone at church, he would drive off thirty miles or more to where a new tenant was supposed to have moved in—a man starting out in farming who might need a policy—and get there to find the place deserted, and drive all the way back with no complaints.

And in the first place, he didn't have to be selling insurance. He had a college education and could go back to teaching, his real profession, any time he wanted to. Again this fall, the president of the board came to the house and tried to persuade him to take back his job, but he wouldn't. She doubted that he ever would, and that disturbed her. She was proud of his education. He was the only person in the village, other than the two high-school teachers, with a college degree, and he had a gift for inspiring young people. Nevertheless, at the end of the school term the year before, he said to her, "I'm never going to make a decent wage teaching school, and you and the boys deserve a better life—a happier one than this. I'm going to find a job that makes real money."

"No! No!" she wanted to cry out, but held herself silent. She didn't believe in interfering with his decisions. She never had, and wouldn't now. So, on the advice of Father Schimmelpfennig, the parish priest and Martin's best friend, Martin started selling insurance.

She turned from the window, walked into the kitchen, and held her hand over the oven vent at the back of the stove. Warmth was still rising from it. She went to the table and smoothed the plaid oilcloth, which was already smooth, and straightened the silverware beside Martin's plate, and then, as though this had emptied her of her usual energy, she sank into his chair and propped her head in her hands.

For a long time she had been angry at Father Schimmelpfennig and other of Martin's friends—Evan Savitsky, for instance—because she believed they were responsible for causing him to quit teaching. But the anger was unreasonable, she realized, and turned in the wrong direction. She was to blame. Since their second child she had been unhappy in a way she hadn't been before; it was an unhappiness with no limits, no bottom to touch or height to rise above, and it remained all the time. She felt that they would never get ahead, that they could never afford to have another child, a girl, and she started thinking of how it would be to have new clothes, the bedroom set she wanted, a bigger house—she had only thought these things, she'd never spoken them, but somehow, perhaps through her touch, they'd been communicated to Martin. Money and possessions would never free her from her unhappiness, she knew, but the thoughts had come, bidden or unbidden (it made no difference) they had come; they were a part of her.

In her mind she saw, stretching off to infinity, a plain with no visible sign of life, nothing but a small dark shape off in the distance, interrupting the straight line of the horizon. The image had been returning all day, and by now she felt haunted by it. She knew it was the view from one of the houses where she had grown up, but couldn't remember which house. Her family had moved so much when she was a child. She most likely wouldn't have remembered the scene at all if it hadn't been for the photograph. She put that business out of her mind.

Martin got on well with other people, and had the necessary enthusiasm for a salesman, but he was too considerate; he made sure a farmer understood a policy completely, its strong points and its weak points, before he sold it to him. He would spend an afternoon explaining, clarifying, advising, and in the end the man might decide that he wanted more time to think about it, or maybe didn't need a policy at all. So Martin was making less money now than when he was teaching. For a while he even had to take part-time jobs to keep them in food, and since the beginning of the summer he had been working as a farmhand for Evan Savitsky. Mrs. Savitsky picked him up at six in the morning and then Evan brought him into town at night and drove straight to Main Street and went into the tavern, and Martin, who didn't drink and wouldn't set foot in there, had to walk back home. Once she asked if Evan couldn't practice a little restraint and take the time to drop him off at home first, and Martin said, "A man should be thankful for what he gets and not expect to get one thing more."

The worst part, to her, was that he was working with his hands. Her father and grandfather had been farmers, dirt farmers like everybody else in this part of the state, and both had died broken men, bitter and penniless, without even owning the land they had worked all their lives and died on. This country was so identical from mile to mile, it was the same as the sky above—not meant for men. An education was the only way to rise free from it, and for two years she went to college herself, working her way through, until she received her certificate to teach. But she'd never been able to really test herself. She taught for one year in a country school—and all that time was engaged to Martin and had that support—before she married.

She was ashamed of the smallness of her thoughts and afraid Martin would sense their further trend. She was holding herself at a distance from him, and lately felt relieved when he left for work, but then the children made her lonely and she couldn't wait for him to get back. She wanted him here now. More than ever, she felt expendable and desolate, because of the photograph.

She seldom looked on her past with pleasure, but that morning she had been imagining her mother as a young woman—working at the cookstove, carrying water from the well, lighting the kerosene lamps, turning down the covers—and of the way these insignificant acts assumed a dignity under her mother's hand. And then she remembered her mother's favorite photograph of her, taken when she was a child of five or six, which her mother had had enlarged and given to her as a gift when she married Martin. In the photograph she is standing on the prairie, knee-deep in buffalo grass, wearing a pair of baggy overalls and a straw hat that's too big for her (probably her mother's) with the ties hanging loose. She is smiling into the camera, and in her hands, which are clasped over her belly, is a black-eyed Susan. The only other element in the picture besides the plain and the sky is a small black shape just above her shoulder—probably the crown of a tree.

The more she thought of her mother, the more vivid the picture became in her mind, as if the sun were emerging from behind a cloud, and just when it seemed that everything had returned to the state it was in at the moment the picture was snapped, she, the girl in the overalls, turned and walked out of sight. All that was left was the plain and the dark shape. It had to be a tree.

•

She sensed the nearness of Martin and stood up from the table, listening, then went out of the kitchen, into the living room, where the oil furnace cast an orange oval on the linoleum, and had just stepped into their bedroom when there was a knock at the back door. Who? Martin, when he returned from work, came through the side door, into the entry, and left his work clothes there. She lifted the bedroom curtain and looked out. The street here was empty, too. Again there was the knocking, harder this time. The back door, like all the others, was unlocked. She assured herself that it was only a neighbor, that there was nothing to fear, but as she walked into the kitchen the strength left her limbs. It was Martin, standing below her, at the bottom of the steps, a broad grin on his dusty, sweat-streaked face. She opened the door wider.

"What on earth are you doing back *here?*" she asked, and was surprised at the alarm in her voice.

"This," he said, and raised his arm. In his hand he

held a brace of pheasants, their green heads and gold breast feathers glowing in the light.

"Where did you get those?"

"Hunting! Where do you think?"

"You've been hunting?"

"Evan took me. Aren't they beauties!" he said, his deep voice compacted within the confines of the windowless, lean-to porch. He went to the edge of the swath of light that fell through the door, reached above his head, located a strand of wire dangling from the low roof, and wrapped the wire around the legs of the birds. They swung noiselessly from side to side, the tips of their outstretched wings slicing into the light. "For tonight, I'll leave them there. I'll clean them in the morning."

"You should do it now."

"They'll be all right. It's cold enough. Well, maybe I should bleed them. No, it's too late for that. Oh, they'll be all right the way they are. We'll have some for supper tomorrow, and I'll take the rest to the locker."

He came up the steps, and she started forward to embrace him, but he held up his hand. "Let me wash first," he said. "I'm filthy!" He went to the washstand at the side of the kitchen and tossed his cap down on the counter. "How are the boys?" he asked.

"Fine."

"Good!" He dipped water from the bucket into the washbasin, and she stood watching his back and broad shoulders swing from vessel to vessel. It worried her that he had been hunting, and she wanted to tell him about the photograph. She tried to impose a rational order on her feelings. But at that moment he looked at her over his shoulder and smiled. Then his face turned serious. "Are you all right?" he asked. "Is everything all right?"

"Yes."

"Are you sure?"

"Yes."

"What a day!" he said, and plunged his hands into the water and rubbed them with vigor over his face, causing his skin to squeak. She stepped to the stove, took the food out of the oven, placed it on the table, and sat down in a chair facing his.

"Just after lunch, when Evan and I were out in the yard getting the tractors ready," he said, still washing his face, "Evan's neighbor—Frank Crimmins—drove up in his car. I figured something was up. Crimmins doesn't usually get out of bed until noon, and then he sits around the house all day while his wife does most of the work—he's only got a half section of land, and he hasn't even got his hay in yet! Well, he came up and said he heard the pheasants were thick as grass over by Pingree. He said we deserved the day off—that was some way of putting it when you consider Evan has six sections to get ready before the freeze, and that I have no say in it at all—he said we deserved the day off and should take it off, by Lord, and go get some of those pheasants for ourselves before the sportsmen came up from all over and took them from us. Oh, he can talk a stream. Evan asked me if I'd like to go, which was kind. I know he's afraid of falling behind this year, even with me helping. But there's a split in that man," he said, and turned his glistening face to her. "As conscientious as he is about work, work takes second place if there's a chance for some sport. I saw that, and Crimmins saw it, too, and started talking as fast as he could. I told Evan I didn't have a license or a gun. He said I didn't need a license and he'd let me use his old 20-gauge. I could see he was already convinced."

He picked up the towel and turned toward her, wiping his hands. "But he wouldn't simply leave that easily either, not Evan. We were out by the gas tank, as I said, greasing up the tractors, and he pointed out a chicken over by the garden, a good fifteen feet away, and said, 'See that? Watch. I'll check with the powers that be and see if my aim's on. If it's on, we go. If it's not, we stay.' He picked up a grease gun, held it at his side—didn't even aim, mind you—and gave a good hard pump on the handle, and the chicken took off squawking, flapping its wings, with a big spot of grease on it. It just goes to show you the luck that man has! So we got out the guns, took off in separate cars, and drove over to Pingree, and within an hour we had our limit, all three of us. And that's not all. I got something of my own done, too," he said, and came to her and kissed her forehead along the hairline. "But you," he said. "What about you? How was your day?"

"Fine."

"You sure?" he said, passing his hand over her hair. "You're sure everything's all right?"

"Yes," she said, and looked up and saw that he was staring at the clock on the wall.

"Is it that late?" He sat down and helped himself to the peas, the potatoes, and the roast. "I better get a move on," he said, already chewing. "I'm going to be late the way it is."

"Late?" she said. "What for?"

His fork stopped halfway to his mouth, his large luminous eyes turned up, and his eyebrows rose. "What for? It's Friday night!"

"Oh," she said. "Oh, I forgot." On Friday nights he played pinochle with Evan, Maynard Labor, and other parishioners, at Father Schimmelpfennig's.

"As I said," he went on, "I got some work done on my own, too. On the way back from Pingree, Evan dropped me off at the Spragues' and the Hyerdahls'. I've told you "about them," he said, his voice growing more concerned and deliberate. "They're both still turning some policies over in their minds. I talked to each of them for a while, and Evan waited the car for me. That's why I'm so late. I don't know about Sprague, but I'm positive Hyerdahl's going to buy. That'll be the third policy this month. Won't that be good?"

"Yes."

"Well," he said, pushing his plate aside and standing up. "I better change clothes and get going."

He went into their bedroom. She cleared the table, went to the sink, dumped the oily, grayish water out of the dishpan, rinsed it clean, refilled it, and started washing the dishes. Hands, strong and warm, smelling of aftershave, gripped her shoulders, and she swung around, startled and irritated. As she stared at him, the irritation stayed, sharpening her awareness of his chest, shoulders, lips— and of herself; of how, in spite of her anger and confusion, she could respond to his nearness.

"Are you sure you're all right?" he asked.

"Yes. Fine. You just scared me."

"I'll be going, then."

Their eyes met and held and he narrowed his, then leaned down, and she turned her face, grazing his close stubble with her chin, and fitted her lips to the shape of his. He drew away, holding her at arm's length, and studied her face. She looked down, and he turned from her to the door and opened it. "I'll be back soon after twelve," he said, and snapped the lock. "Wait up if you want."

She breathed out and eased her weight against the sink, and her tears formed a nimbus around the light bulb above the table. Then she drew up, wiped a cheek with the back of her hand, and straightened her dress. She would not be weak like every other woman she knew, all of whom she hated. She went into the living room, switched on the floor lamp, sat in the easy chair, and took a book—*The Ordeal of Richard Feverel*—off the table beside it and opened it at her marker, a scrap of dress material. Adrian, the wise, fat, complacent philosopher, was giving a long-winded speech. He annoyed and depressed her so much she couldn't follow what he was saying.

There was a knock at the back door. Martin. He had decided not to play cards and had come back to her. She hurried into the kitchen, unlocked the door, and threw it open. A lean, hook-nosed man with a shock of curly hair showing in front of the raised bill of his baseball cap was on the top step, only inches from her—the young man who had recently moved in next door with his new wife— but she was so sure it would be Martin she might as well have embraced him.

He raised the bill of his cap in greeting, then added, "Hi."

"Hello." She stepped back a step.

"Is your husband in?"

"No."

"Oh. Well, I was out hunting today and got my limit of pheasants. It's too many for just my wife and I, so we were wondering if you folks wouldn't like a couple."

"Yes, we would, usually—any other time—" Glancing up, she saw that his brown eyes, moist in the light, were studying her with interest. "You see—" She pointed over his shoulder and he turned. "Martin was out, too. He got his limit."

"Oh, good," he said, and faced her again, sliding his

hands into his back pockets, his elbows turned out and swinging back and forth. "Good for him. You sure won't need any more from me, then, will you?"

"No. No, I don't think."

"My wife said I should come over and ask," he said, and shifted his weight and made an amused sound at the back of his throat. "So, here I am, asking."

"Thank you."

"You're welcome."

He lingered on the step, and she tried to think of something to say, conscious of his eyes traveling over her hair, her lowered face, the rest of her.

"Maybe I'll go see the Eatons," he said. "They might want one or two."

"You could ask."

"I will ask."

"Well, thank you again," she said, and as gracefully as she could, but with her eyes still lowered, she shut the door. She went back to the living room, her heart beating against her dress, and sat in the easy chair, picked her sewing basket off the floor, placed it in her lap, and worked a light bulb down into the toe of a sock, then threaded a needle with trembling fingers.

"Mom?"

The voice came from the boys' room; it was Charles, the younger of the two, and she waited to make sure he was actually awake.

"Mom?"

She set the basket down and went to the doorway.

"Yes," she said. "What is it?"

"Is Dad back yet?"

"No. Now go back to sleep."

"I thought I heard him talking."

"You couldn't have. He's not here."

"Was somebody else here?"

It was simple enough to explain, but she said, "No. Nobody. Sleep now!"

"Turn on the light. I want to see your face."

"I can't," she said. "It'll wake your brother."

"I'm awake!" Jerome's voice said. "Tell us a story, and maybe by the time you're done Dad'll be back."

She was relieved not to be alone. In the semidarkness of the room she located the pinup lamp on the wall, and a half circle of light fell across the foot of their bed. "Now then," she said. "What is it?"

"Tell us a story!" Jerome repeated.

"Where's Dad?" Charles asked.

"At Father Schimmelpfennig's."

"What's wrong?" Charles asked.

"Nothing's wrong."

"Is something wrong with Dad?"

"No," she said. "There's nothing wrong with your father." She sat down on the edge of the bed. "Which story would you like to hear?"

"The one about Grandpa Neumiller and the billy goat!" Jerome said, and started laughing over the story, which he knew by heart.

"No!" Charles said, moving next to his brother and raising himself up to see her better. "No, tell about yourself. Tell about the time you went to town on a pony. When it was snowing!"

"Since you can't decide which you want to hear," she said, "I'll tell them both."

In a noisy uproar of covers they struggled around until they were sitting with their backs against the head-board, and then, in a gesture similar to one of hers, Jerome brushed the hair from his forehead. Both of them needed haircuts, she saw. Their eyes, as large and luminous as

Martin's, studied her for the sign that meant she would
begin, but an unexpected emotion took possession of her
and she leaned and put an arm around each of them and
pulled them against her. "Oh!" she cried, and drew them
tighter.

"What is it, Mom?"
"Mom! What's the matter?"
In her mind she saw those birds, lovely, dignified,
their gleaming bodies and bright plumage catching the
light from the kitchen as they swung from the wire, and
at the sight of them she felt dangerous, capable of doing
serious harm to her sons.

THE BEGINNING

OF GRIEF

From the way his five children gathered around him at the dinner table Martin could tell something was wrong. He put his silverware beside his plate, leaving untouched the food he had prepared and heaped there, and leaned his forehead on clasped hands as if to say grace. Beneath his closed eyelids, inflamed by lime burns and bits of sand, he saw pulsing networks, as though his vessels were of neon, and then the substance of his muscles and limbs appeared to move upward, pulsing, and he felt out of touch with the bulk of his body, reduced to less than he'd ever been, imprisoned within the sphere of his eye. The size of his world now.

He would quit work late, drive from whatever part of the county his job, plastering, had taken him to that day, back to Forest Creek, and pick up the little ones, the two girls, at the baby-sitter's, and then drive back home and cook dinner and call the boys in to the table—now that it was summer, they spent the day at home alone—only to see in their attitudes that they were trying to conceal something. Then another circuit, as familiar as the first, began. He would have to travel through the events of their day, prying his way into them, find out what the trouble was, find out who had caused it, then set right the one who was at fault, or, if there had been fighting, punish him. He hated it. It was difficult for him to pass judgment on anyone, much less his own children, and even more difficult to see them hurt. Alpha had always handled the discipline.

She was prudent and judicious, and had no patience with wrongdoing. For years she tried to persuade him to give up his job, because she felt his employers were taking advantage of him. They went on long vacations and left the business in his hands. They showed up for work irregularly, at their leisure, assuming that he would keep matters in order, and never increased his wages. But they were well-meaning and young, and he stayed on with them, in spite of her disapproval, because he liked them and knew that without him they wouldn't have a business. The memory of it, along with dozens of others, tormented him now. A year ago she had died. The torment was more than grief. It grew, linking one memory to another, linking networks of them together, and would not let her go.

"Dad? Are you all right?"

He let his arms drop beside his plate. "Yes. Just tired."

She was at the periphery of every thought, closing in on his mind like a second conscience. His ideas, before he could speak them, were observed by her and he gave them up. The sheen of her hair was in the hair of the older girl, who was only five, and to run his hand over the girl's hair was excruciating, almost a sin. Her indignation was in his voice when he began arguing with his employers and when, ten months ago, he gave them final notice. He mortgaged the house, sold the car, hired a laborer, and started a business of his own. *M. Neumiller & Sons, Plastering,* he hand-painted on the doors and tailgate of an old pickup he bought.

All they had for transportation was the pickup. In winter and when it was raining, the six of them rode in the cab, the boys holding the girls on their laps, a smell of acrid rubber and gasoline enwrapping them, the bags of plaster color breaking and spilling and staining the floorboards in a merge of muddy gray, and in better weather the boys rode in the bed of the truck. At first they liked it so much they sang and shouted, they stood and made wings like birds, or held their arms like Superman, and he had to keep knocking on the rear window and signaling them to sit. But lately when they went anywhere the boys huddled down with their backs against the cab, and Martin could see, as they climbed out over the tailgate at their destination, her gestures and her averted eyes when she was suffering silent humiliation.

He would have taken his life, merely to end all this, and perhaps be with her (who could say?), if it hadn't been for the children. And when they were disobedient or unhappy, he felt there was no use. He looked across the table at his middle son, Charles, aged ten, who sat with his elbows on the tabletop and his eyes lowered, forking food into his mouth as fast as he could. Charles's large skull had a bluish tint to it. A few days ago, for some unaccountable reason, he'd taken out the electric razor and shaved off all his hair.

"Well, what kind of trouble did you cause today?" Martin asked, and with the words he felt weary and resentful. He was being unjust. He couldn't help himself. It seemed Charles was always the guilty one. He had a bad temper, a savage energy, and was unpredictable. When Alpha was alive, she seemed to favor Charles, yet he was the one she most often lost her temper with. Once she caught him striking matches along the foundation of a house and came up behind him, grabbed him by the arm, grabbed up a bundle of the matches, set the matches ablaze, and held them under his hand until he understood what it felt like to be burned.

Charles couldn't stand to lose. When the simplest game or argument didn't go in his favor, he started a fight, and if he was left alone with the younger ones he set up strict rules, such as no singing, no talking, no TV, no dinner, or he made them march in unison around the room, and if they violated his rules he hit them or shoved them into a closet and held the door shut.

Now Charles looked up, gave an impatient scowl, and said, "What did I *do?* Nothing." His bright-blue eyes looked larger now that he had no hair, and his long eyelashes, catching the light of the bare bulb overhead, sparkled as he blinked several times. He was also a practiced liar.

"*Nothing?* Then what's the matter? Why do you act so guilty? Why are you all so quiet?"

"We're eating," Charles said.

Martin turned to his oldest son, who sat next to Charles, and said in a restrained and altered tone, as though speaking to an arbiter, "Jerome, what is this?" Jerome was twelve but could be left with the girls, the youngest of whom was only three, in entire trust. He sensed their needs and anticipated their whims, and was gentle, and so could care for them better than most adults. He was truthful enough, unless he was protecting one of the others, in which case, with his intelligence, he could make himself a blank.

"Jerome," Martin said, placing his fists, broad as saucers, on the tabletop. "I asked you a question. What's going on here?"

"I don't know."

"You don't know?"

"I don't think I really saw it."

"Saw what?"

"Anything that happened."

"Then something did happen."

"I don't know."

"You just said it did."

"I didn't see it."

"Ach!"

It was futile. The two girls, sitting along the side of the table to his left, their wide eyes fastened on him, had paled at the sound of his voice. It angered him to keep at this in a way that gave it such importance, but his interrogations and lectures were becoming harder to control, more involved and emotional. He rarely lifted a hand against the children, as she had; he believed it was unnecessary and wrong, and besides, he feared the strength of an adult against a child, especially his own strength. He stared at the open lime burns on his knuckles, clenching his fists, angered even more by his indecisiveness, and then reached for his fork. He stopped. His youngest son, Tim, who sat across from the girls, alone at that side of the table, looked anxiously at Martin, then at his brothers, and then at his food, which he'd hardly touched.

Tim, so changed by her death, had become Martin's favorite. The boy was no longer exuberant and cheerful, as he'd always been, and he often woke at night and wandered through the bedrooms trailing a blanket, asking for her, and if his wanderings didn't wake Martin so he could take the boy into bed with him, Tim searched through all the rooms of the house, went out the door into the back yard, went to the plot where she had had her garden, and lay down there and slept until morning.

Tim was old enough to know her as his sisters never

would, but too young to be a companion to Jerome and Charles, who grew close after her death. When he approached them, shy and ill at ease, they sent him to play with the girls. For a while he had been bringing home his own playmates—a procession of the most reticent, underfed, tattered, backward boys in his class. He invited them in for meals, offered them the pick of his toys, and attached himself to them, feeding off their presence, devoting himself to them, until they became bored with his worshipful attitude and let him drop. Now the boy's eyes, light green, large and seductive, were traveling around the table with a harried look.

With his lime-burned hand Martin reached out and touched Tim's shoulder. "You didn't do anything, did you?" he asked, and the boy, shrugging off his hand, turned around and took hold of the back of his chair and broke into tears.

"Jerome! What's this about? Answer me!"

"I don't know how to," Jerome said, and looked aside at Charles, who was still eating as fast as he could.

"Did he hurt Tim?" Martin demanded. "Is Charles the cause of this?"

Jerome lowered his eyes.

"Tim, you can tell me," Martin said. "You don't have to be afraid now."

"I'm done," Charles said, and scraped back his chair. "I'm going out."

"You sit right where you are till I'm through with you!"

Charles sat, piled more food on his plate, and started eating again.

"And if we have to sit here all night till I find out what's been going on," Martin said, "we will."

Tim shifted his weight, his eyes made an anxious circuit of the table, and then, shrinking back in his chair, he cried, "He kicked Marvin!"

"Who did?"

"Charles!"

"*Kicked* him?"

"Then Marvin went home! He was crying!" Marvin, a frail boy who had just moved up from Kentucky, was Tim's most recent and enduring friend.

"What is this? Jerome?"

Jerome kept picking at his food, then murmured, "We were having a track meet over at the school and Marvin was on Charles's side. Tim and I were on the other. Marvin got tired toward the end and didn't want to run, so maybe Charles did something. I don't know. I didn't see it. I was running."

Realizing that Jerome had said all he was going to, Martin moved his eyes to Charles. "Is this true?"

"No."

"Don't lie to me."

"Marvin just started crying, then wanted to go home, that's all. He's a baby."

"Quit eating and look at me when I speak to you! Now nobody just starts crying for no reason—I know that and you know it, too."

"I told him to play right. He wasn't playing right."

"Wasn't playing 'right.' What's 'right?'"

Sensing he had exposed himself in a way that had caused trouble in the past, Charles looked breathless, as if he were running again, circling something dangerous. "We were way ahead in points," he said, "and then Marvin faked like he was tired. He wouldn't do anything anymore. Then when we were all running the mile he just walked along. He could have got second or third, at least, and we score 5, 3, 1. He didn't care whether we got those last points. We needed them."

"You mean you hurt him just because you were worried about losing?"

"Who says I hurt him?"

"Tim said you kicked him."

"If I had to run every race, Marvin could run at least one. He was only in the field events."

"How could you do such a thing?"

"What?"

"Whatever you did."

"Well, what would you do if you were all tired out and came around the track about the third time and there your teammate was, walking along like an old lady."

"So you kicked him."

"I brushed against him. Maybe I nicked him with my foot."

"Can't you leave other people alone? Don't you realize he's one of the few friends Tim's got? Let him run or walk or crawl or sit on his can or do what he wants, dammit!" Silverware jumped as Martin hit the tabletop. "What's the matter with you? What makes you think you're a judge of others?"

"I know I was running and he wasn't."

"He's not you. He's—"

"He was on my side!"

"Will you *listen* to me!"

Martin started to rise and his belt caught on the edge of the table, upsetting his coffee and a carton of milk. Charles pushed himself back from the table and tipped over his chair, and the slap that was intended for him carried past and struck the youngest girl. She went off her stool like a bundle and dropped to the floor, and when she realized where she was, she started wailing, then her sister joined in.

"Now look what you've made me do," Martin said, and started around the table with the galling details—the girl on the floor, the puddle of coffee and milk beside her, Tim with his hands over his face—streaming along his vision, sharpening his outrage. Charles hadn't got to his feet yet and was maneuvering among the chairs on his hands and knees, trying to make it to a safe spot, his rump raised. Martin stepped up behind him and kicked and struck bone, and Charles, his limbs splaying out, hit flat on his stomach. Martin lifted him to his feet. "Now get upstairs," he said in a hoarse voice. "Get upstairs before something worse happens."

Charles gave him a furious going-over with his eyes before he turned and ran up the stairs, and then Martin realized what he'd done and started trembling. He sent Tim and Jerome outdoors, took the girls, one in each arm, and carried them into the bedroom and tried to comfort them. Their eyes were wide with terror, and the youngest one didn't want to be touched.

When they were calmer, he undressed them and put them to bed, hardly aware of what he was doing; the presence in the upstairs room demanded all his attention. He went into the kitchen and sat at the table, his knees giving with an ache from balancing on a springy scaffold the whole day, carrying a hawk of heavy plaster in one hand and reaching overhead with the other to skim finish coat on a ceiling. He felt too old to go on with the work. Tonight brought it to an end. No, there was book work to do, orders to call in, material to get, his lunch to pack.

He wanted to go upstairs but wasn't sure it was the right thing to do. He was too afraid of what he'd done to allow his thoughts to focus. He started eating, but the food was cold and he had no appetite.

He gathered up the dishes, took them to the sink, shook detergent over them, adjusted the temperature of the water, and let it run while he took a rag from the S-trap under the sink and wiped off the table. Then he got down on his hands and knees, and as he was mopping up the milk and coffee his vision narrowed, darkening the patch of wet linoleum, and he felt faint. He stood up and leaned with a hand on the table. An even, abrasive sound was traveling through his consciousness as though it meant to erode it. He hurried over to the sink and shut off the water, but the sound stayed.

He dipped a plate in and out of the water, rinsing off the grease, and his sight fastened on the soapy rainbow sliding along the plate's rim. He let it slip beneath the suds as he pictured her turning from the sink, inclining her head to one side and lifting the hair from her cheek with the back of her hand, her face flushed, her eyes traveling around the room as though there were no name for what she was searching for.

He went up the steps. Charles was lying face down on the unmade bed, his exclamations and sobs smothered by a pillow he held over his head. Martin eased himself onto the edge of the bed and lifted the pillow away. "Listen, now. I've tried—"

The boy grabbed at the loose bedclothes and shoved them around his face.

"How many times have I told you—" Martin began, but stopped at the thought of being sanctimonious. He looked away and saw the bed, with Charles's body half covered with a sheet lying on it, and part of his own shoulder in a dresser mirror, and it was as though he were seeing through to the past. The scene, scaled down, dimmer than in hospital light, was one he had lived through with her: those close to you seemed solid and understandable, fixed in your mind for good, but their real selves were off in the distance, a part of the world, and the world opened and took them without reason; was opening up as before, the body beside him falling away, while he sat off to the side, his shoulder held in a mirror, as helpless as with her.

Then he felt himself being drawn down, too. He searched for something to hold to. Wadded socks lay on the floor, gathering tufts of dust. Tubes and coils of a dismantled radio were strewn in one corner along with a model pistol of plastic, model ships, and a Boy Scout neckerchief. Dirty clothes were piled on a dresser, trailing down its front, and more clothes were draped over the back of a chair.

"If your mother—" The words only took him deeper. He put his hands on Charles's shoulders and tried to raise him up, but the boy struggled free and dropped back onto the mattress.

"Don't now," Martin said. "Don't carry on so. Please. Sit up."

"I'm sorry!"

"I know. Now don't."

"I can't stop!"

"Try to look at it—"

"My head hurts! It feels like something wants to come out of it!"

Martin passed his hand over Charles's skull, and the sensation of stiff stubble rubbing over the palm of his hand—what had led the boy to do this? what did this hark back to?—increased his sense of helplessness.

"Don't now," he said, and sensed the words encircle him. Father, mother, nurse, teacher, arbiter, guardian, judge—all the roles were too much. He no longer had the power to reach through to his children as their father, the man who loved them above all else, and that inability, more than anything, was the fault breaking him.

He heard a muffled sound, regular and tense, and at first thought it was a summons, a last revelation he would have to face, and then was sure it was the labored beating of his own heart. He turned. Charles was lying in the same position, face down, but his hand was tapping over the covers; it touched Martin tentatively, backed away, and then came down, damp and hot with perspiration, on his thigh. He took it in his and an order came over the room.

"I'm sorry," Charles said in a muffled voice. "Forgive me."

"Did I hurt you?"

"No."

"Do you want to come downstairs?"

"No."

"Do you feel any better?"

"Yes."

"I've sent Tim and Jerome outdoors. The girls are in bed. I'm sorry they saw this."

"I didn't mean to do it. He wasn't playing right."

"I know. Here," Martin said, and raised Charles and arranged him so they were sitting next to one another. "Let's go downstairs and do the dishes. Then we'll both feel better." He put his arm around Charles's waist. "Will you come downstairs and help me do the dishes?"

1968–1972

THE SUITOR

He dreamed he'd been sleeping in the catacombs, those tombs he'd heard of only out of history books and from nuns' lips. The shuffling of a pair of slippers traced a series of paths and passageways through his sleep, the sound of a dropped object struck deep into his dream, and somebody in the kitchen (who?) whispering to somebody else rapidly, rapidly, like rain, had washed out a great cave, the hollow where he now lay.

At the border of wakefulness, he became aware of the cold, a numbness in his ears and fingertips, and then conscious that his body was constricted, as if encased in an unnatural skin. And then he remembered that he was still fully dressed.

There was a sound of coals being shaken down at a cookstove. He opened his eyes and saw a pattern of cracks, intricate as a web, in the leather back of the horsehair sofa, and January 1, 1939, registered in his mind. He closed his eyes. The date could mark the beginning, not only of a new year, but of a new life. Oh, let it. He sighed and covered his head with the quilt. Until he knew Alpha was up out of bed and downstairs, he didn't want the Joneses to know he was awake. He'd never faced her parents alone, without Alpha present, and that prospect made him more uneasy than ever. The night before, sitting in front of the Joneses' fireplace, he had asked Alpha to be his wife. Now he lay in the front room of her house, where she, at this moment, was most likely still asleep. A smile of pleasure appeared on his face.

Time and the elements themselves, as if conspiring toward his purpose, had rendered the setting for the proposal almost perfect. First, the New Year. Then the weather; yesterday, when he left home after lunch, the sky was pale blue against the white of the plain, the air still and brilliant, but soon snowflakes started falling, a wind hit, and by the time he pulled into the Joneses' drive, a distance of five miles, the white stuff was up to the axle hubs of his Model A.

The blizzard blew the rest of the afternoon, wrapping the house in blackness, while the windmill clattered and shrieked in the distance because no one could go out to shut it off, for fear of getting lost. Kerosene lamps were lit, rags stuffed under doors, logs brought in from the back porch, along with two lumps of coal, precious coal, and blankets hung up over all the windows.

Except for telling God, in variations of His name, what He was doing to the livestock with this storm, Alpha's father maintained an uncharacteristic silence. It was her mother who finally spoke. When there was no letup in the blizzard and it became obvious that he, the suitor, would have to spend the night, she sighed from the cookstove where she was making supper and then shrugged her shoulders and, without turning to him, said, "The couch will be yours." And Alpha, who was at her back, attempting to help, turned and winked at him.

Then the fire. In front of it on the hooked rug, their faces fevered from its heat. Popcorn and divinity in bowls between them. Their fingertips touching. The whine of the blizzard outside and the sensation that they had been spared and set down, privileged beings, on an island in the sea of it. Alone. On the oval of the hooked rug, the O of love with them at its center. Lowering their voices when her parents, after several good-nights and a great deal of commotion, at last went to bed. A transfixing silence as they stared at the fire, and then the question, present in him for two years, rising of its own accord.

"If you ever asked," she whispered, "I knew it would be tonight."

"How?"

"I knew."

"I've been afraid," he said.

"I know, *I've* been afraid."

"Of what?"

"Me. You." A glance toward her parents' bedroom. "What makes a man afraid?"

"I don't know. Everything. What you?"

"I'm not, really, now that you asked."

"Then will—" It was impossible for him to repeat it. The wind rose, and the flames swayed toward the dark bricks to his left.

"Yes," she whispered.

Or did he imagine it? At that moment, her mother, wrapped in a robe, appeared in the doorway, and said, "Alpha, it's past time you were in bed." Then to him she said, "Here," holding out bedclothes at arm's length, so he had to rise, go to her, and, since she kept a firm grip on a quilt, look level into her eyes as she said, "This is to keep you warm."

Alpha's footsteps went retreating up the stairs while her mother, ignoring his offers to help, saying, "Shoo! Shoo!" in a tone that sounded almost playful, piled more logs on the fire. Then she stood with her back to the flames, facing him, her palms open at her sides to catch the heat. He couldn't see, from the couch, the expression on her face or know whether she'd overheard them.

"I sleep light," she said, and left the room.

The floorboards above him groaned and creaked and he tried to visualize Alpha upstairs, and when he did, so vividly, he tried not to. He said a half dozen Hail Marys, and then his boyhood bedtime prayers went through his head at the speed of a Soo Line express. He discovered that there were five buttons on his shirt, and pausing at each button, gripping it tight, he ran his fingers down his shirtfront (five Hail Marys), then ran them up it (a decade of the Rosary) and held his Adam's apple for an Our Father.

What did she do for so long, moving around up there, to prepare herself for bed? Then there was a sound of springs as she settled into the bed itself, and that was worse. He lost track of the times he'd touched his Adam's apple and rolled on his side to say an Act of Contrition.

Had she said yes, or was it the wind and fire? Her hand had said yes; the angle of her head, bowed so that her dark hair concealed her features, exposing only her brow bronzed by the fire; the fold of her legs beneath her dress, her bare feet, her tipped shoes lying beside them—all this said, *Yes*, *Yes*, but did she?

Alpha Neumiller. Alpha and Martin Neumiller. Their names settled in that conjunction. But if it were so, if she said yes, then it would be difficult for them, he knew; their families lived on neighboring farms but neither parents had been in the others' house, and that was not common in this country, not a good sign.

His mother was on the way to the mailbox three years ago when she saw a stranger walking down the railroad tracks, and hurried back inside to describe him. "He was so little I thought it was a kid at first, also because he wasn't wearing a hat, not even a cap, mind you. His hair was gray on the sides, mussed up like a madman's and flying in the wind, and his eyes were like an old billy goat's. He was making a beeline for town like there was a train behind him!" She wondered who it could be—a bum, or somebody she should know about to watch out for?

"Oh, that's Ed Jones," his father said. "He just moved in at the old Hollingsworth place."

That night their household woke to the sound of someone singing obscene songs, and looked out to see a man staggering along the tracks in the moonlight: Ed Jones on his way home.

Why did his mother have to be so pious and straitlaced and use her religion as the gauge to measure others? They were all adults, and some of the songs were amusing. After a few weekends of more of the same, she started calling Alpha's father "the devil Jones" or "that insane atheist down the road." She demanded that the men of the house, her son or her husband, one of them or both, go tell that drunk to use the roads like everybody else, so Martin and his father walked to the tracks one night and intercepted the dapper little man.

"I haven't got a car," Jones told them, "and I'll be damned if I'll waste the wear and tear on a good team just to go into town and get soused, and that's where I'm bound. These tracks are the straightest shot I know from those two sections of quack grass back there, which some piker pawned off on me as a farm, to the front door of the closest gin mill. And after farming quack grass for a week straight with no help, no sons at home, I don't mind saying I like a snort or two. For the nerves. What do you folks do about quack grass? I've never seen it grow so thick. I beat it with a hoe, I keep the wife and daughter after it, pulling it up by hand—roots, runners, and all—and even burn the crap. That's right, you laugh, but, by Christ, I burn a hayrack of it one day, and the next it's up as thick as ever, choking my wheat."

The Hollingsworth place was one of the last pieces of land in the area to see the plow, Martin's father told him; the sod was turned under barely ten years ago, and only a couple of crops put in before the Depression.

"So that's it. It'll take me five years, then, or more, before all the buried stuff comes up where I can kill it. Damn! Well, I'll keep at it till I win. It's partly my fault I got took. I wanted this Hollingsworthless place because of the barn. Have you ever been in it? It's a beauty, built better than a brick— Well, it's the best barn I've seen in my life, and I've always said that if a man can't sleep in his barn, it's not a fit place for livestock. We make use of the poor beasts their whole lives, we beat them—I do—we make money off them, we don't let them run wild the way they used to, so the least we can do is not lock them up inside some drafty, stinky, dirt-floored, jerry-built shack that's never warm and you can't keep clean, isn't it?"

They nodded.

The three of them talked a long time, or rather Jones talked while the two of them, taciturn by nature, stood blinking at the outpour, until they heard from the house: "Charles! Martin! *Dinner!*" Jones shook their hands, saying he hoped they had a chance to visit again, and then the two of them went in to dinner, where his father said, "There's nothing the matter with that man. He can walk where he wants."

So his mother quoted back at his father one of his father's favorite maxims, "You are judged not by who you are or what you are but by the company you keep." And his father tried not to be unkind about it, but from that day he kept his distance from Ed Jones.

Jones seemed to sense this, but was always friendly to Martin, the suitor, "the big hulk," as Jones called him—or was almost always friendly, anyway. Alpha's mother never was. All her mother said to him, it seemed, was hello and goodbye, and if he was in the same room with her, she managed to keep her back to him most of the time.

And when he finally finished college, working his way through for five years, and took a job with the state, an accomplishment he was sure would soften her mother, she instead became, at the least, ironic. "It's the *educated one*," she would call to Alpha, and walk out of the room. Then he learned from Alpha that her mother had been raised a Missouri Synod Lutheran and believed that every Catholic was up to no good. Lord in heaven, angels and saints, look with mercy on us!

·

He listened for her footsteps upstairs, but there was nothing. Silence.

Alpha's father liked him, though, or at least pretended to. Every time the Model A appeared in the yard, he was like a welcoming committee in one, exuberant and garrulous, calling him "Martin" and "boy," clapping him on the shoulder and going on, as if Martin were his equal, about Roosevelt and Landon, the repeal of Prohibition, horses

(Jones's passion) as opposed to mechanized farming, and, with a quick wink, skating near the subject that caused Martin to blush.

Inside the house, though, he was often as silent as Martin's father, remote and morose, and spent most of his time at the radio. So outspoken on any topic, around anyone, even his daughter, and then this silence in the house. Alpha couldn't explain it. She knew little about her father's past, was uncertain about his behavior—"I don't know if he's mean. I don't know if he's kind"—and spoke as though he were an enigma to respect and beware of.

And there had been the incidents. Two summers ago, Martin had driven over to the Joneses' and taken Alpha to a baseball game (5 to 3; home team lost) and on the way back Alpha asked him to stop the noise of the car so they could talk. He pulled off the road, into a stand of ragweeds, and killed the engine. "What is it, Alpha?"

She leaned her head on his chest and wouldn't speak. He settled himself in the seat and put his arm over her shoulders. It was starting to turn dark, and a dove was mourning in the distance, in a dove's three notes, the first two as if to proclaim the two of them together, *You* and *You*, the last so stretched out and desolate it was like the plain, an *Oooo* that traveled in a curve as solitary and final as a falling star. Heart, heart, does it have to end here? No. Yes. Holy Mary, sanctuary of— His fingertips under her chin, lifting her face close, her pupils enlarged and dark, and then kissing her on the lips.

Something hit the windshield, and they jumped back. Thirty feet away, high above them on the railway embankment, stood old Ed Jones. He tossed some pebbles from one hand, put his fists on his hips as he stared at them, and then turned and kept walking down the tracks toward town.

Alpha was terrified, in tears, holding him by the arm all the way to her place, and she made him promise to stop by the next day to help her explain, or protect her if need be, no matter what happened. When he arrived the next day, shaking at the wheel, Alpha walked out with a look of wonder on face; nothing had happened.

They kept suspecting it would come out after one of Jones's return trips from the tavern, but it never did. Apparently, Jones never told anyone, not even his wife—certainly not his wife. Unless that incident explained the other. Once, when Martin came for Alpha, Jones was talking to a neighbor, Ray Peterson, in the front room. Martin waited for Alpha in the kitchen, standing in the door next to the cookstove, observing Alpha's mother at the kitchen table in a familiar attitude, her back to him, as she wet her fingers and paged through the new Sears, Roebuck catalogue.

Then he caught a phrase from the front room—"damn mackerel snappers"—in Peterson's voice, he thought, and started to cough and clear his throat, to let them know he was in the house.

It was Ed Jones, and he was saying, "Show me a Catholic and I'll show you a hypocrite. They're the most lying, sanctimonious bunch of—" Were they drinking? Drunk? Martin coughed harder and shuffled his feet, and heard a rise in volume from Jones in response. "They could maim or kill a man and call it okay, because they're the chosen, and there's no way around it. They know how to pray right, you see, and we don't. They got the little stalls where—" And if those don't work, they got the *beads*.

Alpha's mother stood and went into the front room, to put a stop to this, he thought, but her footsteps carried on to the bedroom. "Like rabbits, the way they breed. You wonder when they got time to go to church! The daughter here is going with one, you know. Oh, he's all right by me, a fine boy, but someday if she doesn't watch it, I say"—a change in tone, as if he'd lifted his face to her bedroom— "I say, 'Alpha! One of these days you're going to have a dozen kids running around in the same room with you, none of them over the age of ten, and all of them swinging those beads like lassos. "Whoop-ee, Ma! Let's get to church!" ' "

Martin made it through the door on weak legs, out the back porch, and into fresh air, sure that Jones was drunk. He went to the pump and wet his head and wiped his face and wrists with his handkerchief, then got into the car. When Alpha finally came out, her face was flushed and she wouldn't look at him. She was silent most of the afternoon, wadding and squeezing a kerchief in her lap, and later on, when he tried to bring up the subject, she said, "No. Don't. He didn't mean it. He's bitter because he has no sons at home to work with."

·

There was a sound of logs rumbling into the woodbox, and Martin rose from the luxury of half-sleep, aware now of the morning coldness in his bones and a filmy sensation on his skin from sleeping in his clothes. He heard whispering again in the kitchen, a bang of the back door, and then the sound of a kettle set on to boil as its wet bottom started stuttering on the stove top. He strained to hear Alpha, but the floorboards above were silent, the bedsprings still. The back door opened, it closed, and footsteps came across the kitchen, cold snow screaming under them on the linoleum.

"Ed!" A piercing whisper.
"Yes?" He could whisper?
"What do you think you're doing?"

"Taking this in there."

"No you're not."

"He should be up by now."

"I mean, not like that, with those snowy boots."

"Oh, that," he said, rising out of the whisper. "It's clean snow. To hell with it."

The footsteps carried into the front room, passing so close Martin could smell ice on foreign clothes, and then logs tumbled onto the hearth. There was a squeak of rubber, the crack of a knee joint, and grunts and muttered curses as the wood was stacked in place.

Martin waited through a silence, expecting the fire to start, anticipating its warmth, and then sensed that Jones was staring at him.

"Hey, boy, aren't you up yet?"

Martin uncovered his head. "Yes."

Jones stood in front of the fireplace in a sheepskin coat and fur cap, and when Martin rose on an elbow he started stomping his felt-booted feet as though dancing and clapping his leather mittens together. It was so cold in the room Martin could see his breath. Couldn't they afford a fire in here before night? Alpha must be freezing.

"Well?" Jones said. "I finally got that windmill shut off before it rattled its metal brains out. The wind let up at four, and I ran out then. It's a good thing you're going into business and not farming is all I can say. Do you know what time it is? It's almost eight o'clock."

"Oh."

"You're damn tootin! And it's twenty below out."

"Oh."

"Oh, oh.' Didn't you hear what I said?"

"Yes. I mean, *what* that you said?"

"It's almost eight."

"Oh." He was baffled by this cheerful household talk,

and then Jones moved closer, a scowl on his face, his black eyelashes fringed with beads of ice that were beginning to melt, and Martin shivered at how cold it must be.

"You're sure you're really awake?" Jones asked.

"Yes."

"Then you better get up and give me a hand."

"The stock?" Martin asked, and shoved off the quilt and sat.

"Stock, hell! That was done hours ago. We have to get your car out of the snow."

"Oh." Puzzled by this, in a daze, Martin reached for a shoe with his toes, pulled it close, slipped his stockinged foot into its cold sheath, and as he bent to lace it discovered his bladder was as big as a pumpkin.

"Model A's!" Jones exclaimed. "I tried cranking the son of a—"

"Ed!" From the kitchen. "Watch that tongue."

"I tried cranking it for a half hour and couldn't even make it go poot. How do you adjust your spark?"

"A quarter down."

"No wonder!"

Then Martin started to shake, and it wasn't from the cold; the Joneses were turning him out before he had a chance to see Alpha. He finished tying his shoes and looked up at Jones's excited eyes, trying to find the words to explain to him that he'd proposed.

"Come on, boy, what's up with you this morning?" Jones said, and clapped his mittens close to Martin's head. "I've never seen a man move so slow in my life!"

"I wanted—" Martin couldn't go on.

"Are you positive you're not still asleep?"

"No."

"No?"

"I mean, I'm not."

"Then let's get going!"

Martin followed him into the kitchen, where Mrs. Jones was waiting; her gray eyes, usually as vague and glazed as a convalescent's, were direct and merry this morning, Martin saw. She gave him a brisk nod, and said, "Good morning. Sorry you can't have breakfast."

She'd heard him propose.

She pulled his overcoat from the shelf of the cookstove, shook it out, and held it for him by the shoulders, and he turned, feeling his lips start to quiver. Please, God, couldn't Alpha appear now?

"Come on, come on," said Jones, "quit acting like a sheep! Get a move on!"

Martin extended his arms behind his back, and the sleeves of the overcoat, heated from the stove, slipped up his arms. He pulled it on and started to button it up, the warmth inside drawing the chill from his bones, and turned back to Mrs. Jones. "I want—" he began. "I—"

"No need for thanks," she said, and handed him his cap. "And no time. Goodbye."

Jones grabbed him by the elbow, opened the kitchen door, pulled him onto the porch, and kicked the door shut. The windows of the porch were covered with tar paper, and it was nearly as dark as night.

"My overshoes," Martin said.

"Right there, beside the separator. Hurry it up."

The rubber of the overshoes was frozen, stiff and difficult to bend, and they were icy against his ankles. If he had to bend once more, he thought, and then his fingertip froze to a buckle. He jerked it loose, leaving a strip of skin, angered at his humiliation, and then pulled his gloves out of his pocket and drew them on while the old man clucked his tongue, and said, "What's the matter, boy? You know you should have had those on first."

Martin rose from the overshoes, standing tall above Jones, and decided that now was the time to speak, but Jones swung open the outside door, and it was as if two objects as sharp as icicles had been driven home into Martin's eyes. He could barely open them against the brilliance of the snow, and when his vision had finally adjusted, he saw his car standing in a drift up to its running board with a team of black Percherons, nodding against the traces, blowing frosty plumes below their decorated blinkers, their backs steaming, hitched with eveners and hayrope to the car's front bumper.

"I know it looks bad here," Jones said, and took hold of his arm, dragging him through the heaped banks and drifts, "but I've walked up to the main road, and it's already been traveled, so there won't be any trouble once we get there, or if there is, I'll pull you all the way into town. And right there is the team that can do it!" Jones turned to him with a grin of pride that changed to consternation. "Damn it to hell," he said. "A tie. Do you need one?"

"Tie?"

Jones stepped back a step, and his eyes narrowed, but not from the glare. "What's the matter with you this morning, boy? Aren't you well, or didn't you sleep either, or what? I'm not up on all your rigamarole, but today is Sunday, for God's sake, and I know you've got to get to church. Do you need to borrow a tie or not?"

"Oh, no. No, I—"

"The wife, she was a regular churchgoer once, you know, so she's been on my tail since before dawn's light to get you there on time. I guess she wants to keep you pure, now that you've proposed to the daughter. Oh, I know all about it, and I'm proud to say I was the first to know. Alpha finally gave out, or I suppose she'd be here helping us, that's the kind of person she is—she was so excited she couldn't sleep the whole night, so she came downstairs about five, right after I got the gag on that windmill, and told me the news, and I want you to know that both of us, the wife and I both, realize you've got a fine mind and body, and figure everything else will work out from there. But do you want to know something?"

Martin was afraid that if he spoke it might come out in a howl.

"Hold on, now," Jones said. "I'll tell you. With all the churchgoing and whatnot the wife has had—this is on her—and the praying for my soul and so forth, she went and forgot it was Sunday. *I* was the one who remembered."

Jones nudged Martin, winked an ice-fringed eye, and said, "Now, what do you think? Do you think I might be Christian?"

PNEUMONIA

Alpha's spirit was crippled by the injustice of it. Her son had just turned six and was dying. After a winter of prolonged illnesses, Charles had developed double pneumonia, and when he was rushed by car to the hospital in McCallister, a young doctor, starchy and officious, who perhaps felt that his first duty was to be candid, told them the boy had about a fifty-fifty chance of pulling through. His condition had worsened.

In this underpopulated area of this underpopulated state, it was almost impossible to get penicillin, the new antibiotic they were using on the boy, and if there was another blizzard like the one last week, the shipment wouldn't get through. Already the roads to McCallister were nearly impassable—the plowed banks piled higher than a car top most of the way, with only a single lane opened up in the worst places—and there was no airport at McCallister, which was the only town in a three-county area with a hospital. The hospital's only oxygen tent had to be shared with other patients. Charles had received the last rites of the Church.

The probability of his death had invaded her, weighted her, moved into the marrow of her bones until she was so heavy with it she hated the details of each day, beginning with the appearance of the sun. She didn't want to get out of bed, or fix meals, or take care of her other children, and she couldn't eat. The crying of Marie, her baby daughter, or the sound of children's voices when the parochial school across the street recessed, infuriated her to the point of tears. All she wanted was to stand at the bay window, as she did now, and stare out at the snow.

It was mounded four feet high in the lilac bushes. The wind had eroded the snowbanks piled along the foundation of the house, and streamers of snow were traveling at an angle across the yard and filling in a cave one of her sons had dug. She'd like to go there and hide.

Charles had been the easiest to raise, and the most difficult. He seemed hardier and less vulnerable than Jerome, who was seven, or Tim, three. He was less prone to crying or tantrums, though if either overtook him it was a day before he recovered. He was fearless, but led to do frightening things; he climbed the water tower when he was five, a hundred feet to its top, and peed from there, Jerome said. He was inquisitive but quiet, and carried out his investigations in an orderly, secretive way, preferring to assess a subject on his own, to observe and listen and read, rather than bother her with questions.

There were times when he seemed to be considering everything and everybody about him while merely going through the motions of play. It was the quality in him she was most attentive to, and respected the most, and the one she feared most, too. What was he thinking then? Could he have known this was coming? Impossible. An impossible, horrible thought. Hers.

His face was more mature than other children's, the

future person he would become already evident around his lips and in his eyes. Every day his eyes deepened with their own secrets. So bright blue.

All she'd been able to do before he was taken to the hospital was feed him orange juice and ice cream and aspirin mashed up in honey, change his bedclothes when they grew damp with sweat, cool his face with a washcloth, give him alcohol rubs, or help him with the bedpan. Jerome and Tim were as silent around him as around strangers. What did they sense? Lately she'd been so distant and abrupt that they kept to their room or moved around the house looking guilty and apologetic, as though they were to blame. She had no words to comfort them. All her energies were turned inward, on Charles, and to expend them on even the other children seemed to diminish his strength.

She was able to visit the hospital only once a day, if that often; McCallister was fifteen miles, and there wasn't always a sitter available for Tim and Marie on two or three occasions each day. Martin, her husband, visited the hospital that often, and she resented his freedom; he was the principal of the high school and could come and go as he pleased. She resented his resilience, that he was a male, his patience, his faith, his strength—everything that he was. She could hardly bear to speak to him. Unless they were talking about Charles—painful conversations when they couldn't look at one another—their talk had become flat and monosyllabic:

"Eggs?"

"Two."

Or, "How was your day?"

"Fine. Yours?"

"Fine."

"The kids?"

"Fine."

Or, "Good night."

"Good night."

He would take her hand and stare at her in silence, his large eyes beginning to widen—with what? commiseration? helplessness? guilt?—until he looked so imploring that even if she felt like unburdening herself, she had to turn and walk away.

The first time she went to the hospital and saw where they'd put Charles, in an oversized, metal-slatted crib covered with a plastic tent, he looked so frail and dehumanized she had to leave the room. Did Charles know that? In a recurring dream, she saw him in his own crib, the one he'd grown out of three years ago, as an infant. As she stood above him and watched he grew smaller and smaller, and then at the second before he disappeared into death, she felt him return to her body. And then she would wake rigid on the bed, sweat crawling through her hair, convinced that if she moved she'd kill them both.

One afternoon when Charles was still at home, he suddenly became more distant and feverish, and began talking with glazed eyes about nuns scrubbing him in a washtub and men made of wire chasing him with a flying boat—while she wiped at his face with a washcloth, wanting to shake him or slap him until he talked sense, or hold him so tight he couldn't speak, or throw on her coat and leave the house. When Martin came home from school, she told him that she couldn't go on with it, that Charles was ill beyond her abilities to nurse or comfort him, and if this kept up she'd go insane.

Martin went into Charles's room, sat on the edge of his bed, and took his hand. "Charlie," he said. "It's Dad. Are you awake?"

"Uh-huh."

"How do you feel?"

"Pretty good."

"Do you want to go to the hospital?"

"Oh, no, I don't need to. I'm better now."

"You're sure?"

"Oh, yes."

But about twelve o'clock that night they heard him calling, "Dad, Dad," and hurried into his room.

"I'm here," Martin said. "What is it?"

"I think I was wrong."

"What do you mean?"

"You better take me to the hospital."

She stepped to the bed and placed her lips on Charles's forehead, to test his temperature, and the fever radiated against them like a sun. She prepared a thermos of coffee for Martin while he warmed up the car—he would have to go alone; she couldn't wake the other children or risk having the baby in the car with Charles—and then they wrapped the boy in quilts and rugs, and as she was tucking him into the front seat of the car she said, "Now, hurry up and get well, so you can come back home."

"Am I coming back?" he asked.

"Of course you are!"

But the way he asked the question would be imprinted in her for good: straightforward, without fear or self-pity, as if he simply wanted to know the truth. And what could she say to him but "Of course, of course, of course"—it was all she could say.

In the hospital his condition became so critical that the doctor called Father Schimmelpfennig, the only person in the village with a telephone, and the priest picked up Martin at school and then came to the house in his black Chevrolet and drove the three of them into McCallister.

The boy's skin was bluish ivory, and he seemed to be

passing in and out of consciousness. They tried to talk to him, and then Father Schimmelpfennig, a ruddy Westphalian who was on friendly terms with every child in his parish, removed his black overcoat, took a purple stole from his breast pocket, kissed the Cross sewn at its center, put it on, and stood over the crib.

"Charles? Charles?" he kept repeating in his heavy German accent, so that the name sounded nearly like "chalice." "Charles?"

"Yes." Finally. A dry whisper like the rustle of paper.

"Have you been a good boy, Charles?"

"What?"

"Have you been a good boy? Have you done any bad tings, committed any bad sins?"

There was an unintelligible response.

"Do you have anyting you'd like to tell me, confess to me? Like in da confessional?"

"Hnn?"

"Do you have anyting you'd like to tell me?"

"Uh-huh."

The priest held his ear close to Charles's face. "You can say. Nobody will hear."

"I'm not ever happy anymore."

Father Schimmelpfennig glanced at Martin and Alpha to see if they'd heard, and then took out a prayer book and a leather kit, and bent over the boy and began murmuring in Latin and applying the oil of extreme unction, and she walked out to the hall, half blinded by a prism of tears, blundered into a rest room, the wrong one, and was sick to her stomach in a urinal.

If she could believe in a religion, like Martin, that defined the character of God and gave Him substance, perhaps she could believe in God Himself, and bear this with more equanimity and self-control. Martin carried a rosary everywhere, even to school, in his suit pocket, and there were nights when she'd seen him take it to bed. He came from a family of eleven, where everybody was attuned to the needs of one another and had grown up to feel protected, not only because of the size of the family but because of the religion they shared; all of them were devout. She and her brothers seldom went to church, and then often with relatives. Her mother hadn't been in a church since she was married, and the only time her father, a farmer, referred to any deity was during a natural disaster, a personal setback, or in a moment of terrible anger, when he cursed God as though He were a hired man, a foolish, incompetent one, sitting in the same room with him. Which was as reasonable a thing to do as any, by God. God. Ha! You clumsy, ignorant, unfair sonofabitch.

There.

Her tears opened paths to the residue of feeling left in her.

When she was a child, she used to sit in the open door of the haymow and watch as it began to get dark, while below her, in the barn, she could hear the calves baaing almost like sheep, cows lowing to them, the clash of a bucket, footsteps, and the muffled voice of her father as he did the chores. The chicken coop was below her, across the lane from the barn, and suddenly, at a certain stage of darkness, chickens, white blurs, would appear from the brush, from the wheat field, from the pasture on the other side of the road, and begin moving toward the coop as though drawn to a magnet, some of them running, catching up to others and frightening them into a run, some of them moving slowly through the darkness, alone. Watching them, listening to her father murmuring to the animals below, she was filled with peace; and, for some reason, a great sadness. Why? Then the windows of the house lit, her mother stepped onto the porch and called, "Alpha! Supper!" There was such calm and simplicity in it, yet an urgency, too, and she ran toward the house as though pursued. Then the yellowish light from the kerosene lamps, a light with the added dimension of smell, and the serenity of her mother as she moved about the kitchen, testing the food on the cookstove, setting plates and silverware at their places around the table, reassembling the sterilized sections of the cream separator so the separator would be ready when her father came with the milk.

Why didn't she, her mother's daughter, have the same serenity? Why didn't she have a soothing effect on her children? Her son. It seemed inconceivable that she was a mother.

It was even more inconceivable that one of her children could die.

Could he? What were the reasons for death, what was its cause? Where was such a decision made? Could it be altered? If it could, for whoever might be listening, she was willing to give up her life for her son's.

Outside, beyond the window where she stood, the yard drew into focus. It was growing dark. The wind had risen and snow was swirling upward in ascending sheets. There was a gray shape beyond the lilac bushes. It moved toward her, growing larger at the edge of the window, and then she looked up, her eyes adjusted, and she was staring into a reflection of Martin's face.

"Alpha?" Martin said tentatively, testing her mood.

"It's time I made supper."

He watched her walk into the kitchen, and then stepped up to the window, which faced east, in the direction of McCallister, and was frosted at the level of his chest from her breath. He couldn't blame her for avoiding him. All of his thoughts were base and vile. He had never, even as an adolescent or a young man, been so horny. Throughout their marriage he'd been a dependable husband, he'd hardly looked at other women, which was not so much an indication of his moral character as of his passion; he was devoted to her, immersed in love, so involved in pleasing her he hardly had time to look.

But lately, at school, he'd begun to notice the varieties of development in his female students, the delicacy of their hands and fingers, the shape and size of their breasts, the breadth of their hips, their bare legs, the curve of buttocks beneath their skirts. Once when he was at the blackboard, mechanically writing out an algebraic equation while most of his mind hovered around an image of Alpha, of her at home alone, attending to Charles, trying at the same time to keep up with the other children and her everyday chores, he found himself in the center of a dead silence, the entire class staring at him while he stared between the parted legs of Carol Hahn, a redhead whose skirt had slipped above her knees. Her face was crimson. He announced that he wasn't feeling well (and after catching himself at that he did feel ill) and dismissed the class.

The graver Charles's condition became, the more his own needs narrowed to sex. And Alpha apparently sensed it, because there were times when it seemed she wanted to talk, but as soon as he went up to her she turned and walked away, out of the room, as if in disgust. He'd tried everything he could think of to keep his mind off her body—novel-reading, prayer, meditation on the Blessed Virgin and the Trinity, cold showers, chopping wood, no pepper on his food—everything. Good Lord, he'd even started taking a rosary to bed with him!

The night he returned from taking Charles to the

hospital, after he'd told her what the doctor had said, and they'd talked and tried to comfort one another, they got into bed and lay on opposite sides ("I don't really want to be touched now," she told him), sleepless, tossing under the covers, and then by accident their legs touched, she turned, and he fell on her like an animal.

Since then, it seemed to shame her to have him close.

This morning, before the children were awake, the two of them were at the breakfast table and he was picking at a grapefruit, trying to decide whether to mention what had happened at the hospital yesterday evening, when she said, "The crisis should come today, shouldn't it?"

"Or tomorrow."

"He'll let us know?"

"He'll call Father."

"And we'll leave right away?"

"Yes."

And with those words he knew he could never tell her, no matter what. She was across the table from him, staring at her cup of coffee, and it was as though he were seeing her for the first time, anonymously, seated across from him in a train or a bus, and he noticed again how frail she was, and how this enhanced her beauty. The boy had her same cheekbones, her small nose, and her lips, sharply outlined, the upper one curved like a crossbow, the lower full and sensual—his desire for her began to rise, and then, in a moment of horrible revelation (her eyes were cast down, revealing violet lids, and her face was pale), he saw her as the corpse of Charles.

"Alpha!" he said. "You have to eat!"

She got up and left the table.

Her grief was dynamic, even when expressed in anger, and she was always busy, angrily busy, working to ease her grief. His sat in him like a stone. He hated to speak or eat or perform the simplest task in her presence, not only because he was afraid his actions would expose his true feelings, as hers did, and reveal his guilt, his lack of hope, his base desires, and a worse flaw he'd discovered in himself and was trying to cover up by carrying a rosary everywhere—his growing conviction that there was no God—but because he knew it angered her even more, now that the boy seemed so near death, to see the usual effortless interest in life of anybody else. Because he'd carried Charles into the hospital and had left him there, he felt responsible for the way she was acting, and so, in the entrapping logic of emotion, he felt responsible for the boy's illness.

And what if Charles died?

He chewed on his upper lip, which was cracked from the dry heat of the house, pushed up his glasses, and gripped the bridge of his nose. He was sure he heard the baby crying. He listened for her, for Alpha's footsteps hurrying into her bedroom, but he'd imagined it. He massaged the bridge of his nose until the sound disappeared, and let his glasses fall back in place.

Whenever anybody asked him who his favorite was among the children, he always said, "Whoever is sick or in trouble, that's my favorite; that's the one who needs me the most." But he was in such fear for Charles's life he could hardly bear to think of him, much less lend him emotional support, and the minute he walked out of the hospital he couldn't even picture the boy's face. Sometimes he would see for an instant, as if stopped in a vivid flash of light, a detail that caused his breath to catch: a nose with a plastic tube in one nostril; a white profile with its eye rolled back in death (an image intertwined with the hospital smell of alcohol and ether); a buttock honeycombed and bleeding from hypodermic needles; a bony forearm resting on the velvet of a coffin— That was how he saw his son.

And once in a moment of terrible stress, when the tension threatened to deprive him of his power to reason, he found himself calculating how much more money they would have if Charles died.

He looked at the oval of his face reflected on the window, into its eyes, then beyond them to the outside, and felt a chill branch through his back. Loose snow was rising in columns and pillars that swayed and bent, collapsed, rose up in another spot, then went whirling toward the southwest out of sight. If one of those hits this window, he thought, Charles will die, and at that moment a white sheet taller than the telephone wires, with lacy streamers coiling along its trailing edge, headed toward the house, and in the second that he readjusted his thought to No! it means he won't, it swept past the lilacs and hit the window with such force the house seemed to rock. He put his hand in his pocket and clutched his rosary.

What was he doing?

He saw a sheet being drawn over a body, a mound of dirt on snow, an ivory head levitating from the bottom of a grave, and heard two voices, his and the boy's, laughing in a closed space.

Yesterday evening he'd visited the hospital alone, and Charles had at last seemed lucid; they talked about the rest of the family, the snow, the new sled the boys got for Christmas, some of Charles's school friends, and then Charles said, "Dad, what do I have?"

"Pneumonia."

"What's that?"

"Sort of like bronchitis, only in the lungs."

"How do you spell it?"

"P-n-e—"

"P?"

"That's right."

"It doesn't start with N?"

"No. P-n-e-u-m-o-n-i-a."

"Pneumonia, pneumonia," the boy kept repeating, as though mesmerized by the word. "It starts with a P?"

"Yes, a P."

"Peeeee!" Charles cried, giddy.

"You're right," Martin said, and winked.

Charles laughed so hard he started to cough and the cough wouldn't stop; it went on until he was choking and fighting for breath so badly Martin ran for a nurse. When he found one far down the hall and they hurried into the room, Charles's face was blue and he was unconscious, having convulsions.

If Charles died, it would be his fault.

He heard rapid steps behind him—Alpha's when she was determined or in a fury—and turned. She halted farther from him than usual, her eyes glazed and feverish-looking (was she also getting sick?), and empty of expression.

"Father Schimmelpfennig is here," she said. "He says it's time to go."

•

When Charles thinks of his parents, which is seldom now, he thinks of them as the monarchs of a kingdom he once visited in a dream. His mother wears a full-length dress, flaming red, whose color increases the humming in his ears, and reveals only her profile, like the queen on a playing card. His father wears a fur cap with the earflaps turned up like half-moons, and carries a broom in one hand. When he speaks, his voice has lost its usual timbre and sounds like the squeaking (the boy observes this with interest, but without puzzlement or surprise) of a rubber mouse. What is it he's trying to say?

When his real father, looming over the bed, speaks to him from his real face, it's as difficult to understand; the boy's ears seem covered with cellophane that vibrates with every outside sound.

"Herzz veritizz swowoza bee."

"Brrodja deeezz."

His lips, split by fever, taste like nickels. His bones are of ice and the ice is wrapped with layers of hot flesh. His head is filled with fluid that exerts pressure at the base of his nose, and his eyes are dry as paper. The band of pain constricting his chest strangles the air he breathes, and the shallow breaths he has to take, to keep it from breaking, are becoming shallower and more rapid.

He has no center. When he opens his eyes, he might be looking up from his stomach or a knee. Sometimes he's the size of a thimble and at other times so enormous his toe could cover a city. One day his arms, which are either too heavy or too light, were gone. Where?

His illness is a sea and others live on land, unreachable. Coming from a great height, they materialize beside his bed and he stares up at them from beneath rocking water; their images sway with the movement of the water (as their mouths move) while his body rocks beneath. A nurse appears with a hypodermic the size of a pine tree, turns him on his stomach (wasn't he on it?), and as she drives it through his back the white-haired man across the hall screams again. Or was the hypodermic for him? Charles turns, or imagines he does, and it's night once more.

His father appears, his mother appears. They float and rock outside the bright, burning layers of fever that enwrap him like tinfoil, in a fragile, metallic grip, and a cold wet hand spans his forehead. Yes? What is it? They disappear in a brightness like the sun, and he sees a player piano, shining, crystalline, composed of ice or glass. Jingle ping tink-tink. Jingle *ping*. There is a pain above his right eye like an embedded ax. His father and mother reappear and confront him with a phenomenon that makes no sense; there are, after all, other people in the world, real people, and they are alive. They are his parents. Why are they so happy?

They smile and talk, showing their teeth, and now are high above him, elongated, blurred and haloed with yellow, and smaller, as if seen through a tube. Their voices buzz and vibrate in his ears and then go away. A blue figure 2 bends and unbends where they were. They appear again, smiling and talking, jingle *ping*. To reach their distant land, he has to lift himself up, rising on an elevator of his will, and hold his body on the surface of the sea with his entire strength. He grips the bedclothes and turns his parched corneas on his parents. Only his father is there.

Coming from such a depth, it's as if he's entered a strange house in the middle of the night, has found his way to the living room and in its brilliant light has come face to face (*Dad!*) with the right man. Why is his father there? Startled, he feels his strength leave as he falls beneath the sea of sickness, deeper than before. He raises himself again, for the last time, it feels, and holds himself on the surface until his father says something that causes him to laugh. The laughing turns to a cough that splits his chest open, breaks the ice of his bones, and drives splinters into his flesh. He would rather be alone.

Above his left eye (the other eye remains closed), a bright disk, which might be the ceiling light, trembles and burns. It seems the last power he has to contend with, and he pleads with it to move, or go out, but it won't. Even when he closes his eye, the disk clings to his lid, changing colors, expanding into a profile, then a circle of piano keys. If he could deal with the light or the profile (now a figure 2), he understands that he would be at peace, because there has been a change. He can feel a heaviness, like honey and salt water, rising in his nose, and although it hurts him to breathe it more than any phase of his illness has, he breathes deeply and evenly, trying to drown.

Then he is chewing bubble gum. His jaws move from side to side in a soft, erotic mastication. He is home again, in bed, asleep yet not asleep; his eyelids are transparent. He sees that there is nothing beyond the bedroom curtains, no yard or hedge or houses or countryside, only a shading of light blue, like sky. As his jaws move, he hears a sound between his ears like a waterfall heard from a distance, rising in volume each time his mouth opens wide. He begins to chew the bedclothes. The curtains blow in and cover the bed. He chews them. The jaws move farther apart with each bite, becoming more rubbery, speeded up, and voracious, chewing everything within reach—a dresser, a nightstand (both of which turn as elastic as the bedclothes), a closet, a wall. And when the sunlight, as blue as night, enters the room, the jaws begin chewing it.

Then the jaws move off and change, otherworldly, but remain a part of him and continue to chew with increasing violence, rising high as the house, slamming down hard, higher, and then they turn as if seeking direction, turn again and start toward him. He tries to get out of bed but the curtains cover him, and now they're heavy as sand. The jaws, flying apart in bites so wide they disappear for a while, get the edge of the mattress. A bite of it. He makes a final effort to move, using the last of his remaining strength, the ration he's held in reserve, and breaks free into an icy brightness, borne on a chilly current of blue air, and sees a mirror image of his body, tiny as a doll, heading toward a hole in the shining universe.

•

As the doctor drew away from the crib and straightened, Charles's reflection disappeared from the round mirror on his forehead.

"His fever's broken," the doctor said. "He's going to be all right."

THE OLD
HALVORSON PLACE

A family of fourteen had lived in the house before the Neumillers. Their name was Russell. Mr. Russell, who was the sexton of St. Mary Margaret's Catholic Church and the janitor of the parochial school, had seven sons and five daughters ranging in age from eleven to thirty-six. Two of the sons were ordained into the priesthood and three of the daughters became nuns. One daughter was said to be an accomplished musician and another had literary leanings, and together they composed the music and lyrics of the school song that is still sung in Hyatt, North Dakota.

Martin Neumiller, the principal of the high school, had been annoyed for years by the stilted words of the old song (sung to the tune of "On, Wisconsin!") and he persuaded the Russell girls to write the new one. It begins

We'll raise a lofty, mighty cheer for you,
Straight from the hearts of students fond and true

and its concluding lines are

The parish owned the Russell house and everybody in the parish had expected the Russells to live out their lives in it, a monument to the faith. But one day old Mr. Russell went to Father Schimmelpfennig and said that he was giving up both jobs and moving out of town. What?

He was grateful for all the parish had done for him, but he felt there were better opportunities in South Dakota for him and the children who remained at home. Father Schimmelpfennig offered him the house rent-free.

Mr. Russell said he couldn't accept charity. Hyatt wasn't growing and would never grow, he felt, and he wanted to take advantage of the boom down at Rapid City, maybe even go into business for himself, and hoped the younger kids could attend bigger schools.

Two months later the Russells were gone. They were a cloistered, close-knit family, and other than the song, they left little trace of themselves behind when they moved. Father Schimmelpfennig let their house stand vacant for a year, as if he found it impossible to admit their absence, and then the Neumillers needed a place.

Martin Neumiller, who was devoted to home life and ambitious for his family, but without guile, nearly biblical in his purity of motive and character, was Father Schimmelpfennig's friend and confidant, and Martin had three bright, promising young sons.

The Neumillers had lived in several other houses in Hyatt, none of them satisfactory. One they rented from a widow, who continued to live on in a separate wing and promised to make herself "so scarce you won't know I'm here," but didn't. In another, the furnace never worked properly, and a smell that originated in one of the kitchen walls was amazing in its rankness. Rather than break into the wall of a house that didn't belong to them, they kept wondering, What could it be?

In their present house, the basement flooded to the floor joists in the spring (bringing up buried salamanders that went floating out into the yard), and the foundation eroded so badly several walls began to part from the ceiling. And all of these places had contained noisy populations of mice and rats, driven indoors by the bitter, drawn-out winters, and none of the houses had been large enough. At this time, the Neumillers' three sons—Jerome, Charles, and Timothy—were sharing the same room to sleep and play in, and although Jerome, the oldest, was only five, Alpha Neumiller was pregnant again.

There were ten rooms in the old Russell house—three bedrooms upstairs, plus a large attic, and three more bedrooms downstairs; a living room, with a big bay window, and a dining room; a kitchen; a pantry as large as the kitchen; a basement with vegetable bins and rows of shelves for canned food; an indoor bathroom (a rarity in Hyatt— there was no running water in the village and only the drains were plumbed in) with all of the fixtures; a front porch, with turned posts and gingerbread trim; an enclosed porch on the south side; and, attached to the rear of the house, a lean-to porch which had once been used to stable a pony and was now a coal shed. The rent was twenty-five dollars a month.

Alpha Neumiller was ecstatic. She pirouetted through the rooms of the empty house, saying, "The space, the space, the space!" And several months later, on Charles's fifth birthday, she leaned against a wall with her arms folded, smiling as she watched a dozen birthday guests play Red Rover—*Red Rover!*—in her living room. The room was so large that her upright piano, which had always been in the way, seemed to have shrunk three sizes. Her piano! She sat down and began playing "Clair de Lune," and all the children stopped their game and stared at her as she played.

Martin could appreciate the depth of her satisfaction; there were articles close to her heart, family heirlooms and wedding presents, that they hadn't unpacked since their marriage, and some of their furniture—a dining-room set with inlays of bird's-eye maple, a handmade gateleg table—had never been used. But around town and at the Friday-night pinochle games at Father Schimmelpfennig's, Martin was heard to say, "Sometimes I can't understand that woman. She loves the place, sure, how could she help it? But it's always been like this. The happiest times of her life are when we move."

•

Martin's father, who had settled in Illinois several years ago, was in North Dakota visiting relatives and friends, and he drove up to Hyatt to help them move. Somehow he got stuck with the job of bringing in the basement things, and toward the end of the day he turned to Alpha with a solemn face and said, "I've carried nine hundred and ninety-nine empty fruit jars down these stairs." He was a building contractor. He made minor repairs around the house, and persuaded Martin to pour a concrete slab that began at the outside wall of the lean-to, went in a curve around the corner of the house, past the enclosed porch, and abutted against the bay window. It was a full day's work for five men, excluding Martin and his father, and when the slab was finally poured, and Martin's father had finished troweling it by the light of a floor lamp Martin held above him, he said, "There. Now the boys have a place to ride their tricycles."

While they were still getting settled into the house, Martin took Jerome and Charles upstairs and led them into a room overlooking the street corner. Against one wall was an enormous rolltop desk of oak. "Look!" Martin said, and turned to them as though offering a gift. The boys looked at one another with questioning frowns, and Jerome shrugged. "Well, don't you see what's happened here?" Martin asked.

They didn't see.

"First of all, you can tell by looking that it couldn't have come up by the stairs. They're too narrow. The door to this room is even narrower than the stairway, and the windows are narrower yet."

He squatted at the desk and rapped on it with a knuckle. "That's solid oak, you hear? The corners have been dovetailed and then trimmed over. You can feel the dovetailing here in the back. Right here. Now, nobody could take this apart, once it was built, without damaging the wood somewhere—especially where it's dovetailed—and they certainly would have left a mark on the finish. But the finish is practically perfect—the original, I'd guess. Isn't it beautiful?"

They nodded, impatient to get their own hands on that feathery dovetail stuff.

"There's only one possibility," Martin said, and smiled at them in conclusion. "When this place was built, an elderly cabinetmaker came to the house, carried his hand tools and materials up to this room, and built this desk on the spot where we're standing. But why? Why would anybody want to build a desk way up here?"

Mysteries, for Martin, were a source of delight; there was nothing unnatural about them, as he saw it. They were a major ingredient of life, meant to be explored and marveled at, but never feared, and seldom explained. Where others overlooked mystery, he could find it, and this kept him in a state of childlike wonder, exuberance, and joy.

·

Alpha was surprised that the interior of the house wasn't more beat up. From the outside it appeared that it would be; paint was flaking from the second story, the roof of the lean-to was beginning to sag, and the hedge that bordered the yard on three sides had been allowed to grow to a height of seven feet. But Martin's father said that the house was structurally sound, surprisingly so, and the interior was in excellent condition, even though fourteen people had lived in the place for a decade.

The hardwood floors didn't need refinishing. The baseboards at toe level were battered, but otherwise the original oak woodwork, the sliding oak doors to the master bedroom, the turned posts beneath the oak banister leading upstairs, the bookshelves around the bottom of the bay window, also of oak, had hardly a scratch on them. And there were no ink stains or adolescent carvings on the rolltop desk.

The Russells had even left a new-looking chair at the desk. The Neumillers couldn't understand why, unless it had been standing there when the Russells moved in, because the Russells left nothing else behind to provide a clue to their life in the house—no old receipts, letters, or notes, not one stray sock in the bottom of a closet, not even a drawing or a set of initials on the walls, or, as Alpha put it, "not a speck of themselves or their dirt."

The attic, however, was packed with valuables, so layered with dust it looked as though the Russells had never touched them. Was it because they belonged to the family that had built the house and lived there originally, the Halvorsons? Their name was everywhere in the attic, on the backs of daguerreotypes and photographs, in the flyleaves of books, underneath chair seats; even written, along with a set of measurements, across the bosom of an old dress form.

In a large and decaying leather-bound volume, *A Century End History and Biography of North Dakota*, Martin found an engraving of a daguerreotype of Mr. Halvorson, a twin to another picture of him in the attic, along with this information:

ALVARD J. HALVORSON. This gentleman, of whom a portrait will be found on the opposite page, occupies a prominent position as a real-estate dealer in Hyatt, Leeds County. To his influence is due much of the solid prosperity of Leeds and Ecklund Counties.

Our subject was born in Hamlin Township, Michigan, Aug. 1, 1839, and was the only son of Selmer and Dora (Waldorf) Halvorson, the former of Scandinavian and the latter of German descent. Mr. Halvorson was raised on his father's farm and attended country schools and at the age of nineteen went to Indianapolis, Indiana, in company with his father and later was engaged in business and also in farming with his father in Indiana for about twenty years.

Our subject moved to Valley City, North Dakota, in the fall of 1879 and became interested in Leeds County lands in 1881, since which time A. J. HALVORSON CO. has added as much as perhaps any other firm in the development of the possibilities of the agricultural and stock-raising interests of North Dakota, and he now conducts an extensive real-estate business in Hyatt, where the family located in 1895, two years after the founding of Hyatt.

Our subject was married at Indianapolis, Indiana, in 1865, to Miss Catherine Maxwell, who is of Scottish descent. Mr. and Mrs. Halvorson are the parents of three children, who bear the following names: Olivia C., Alice N., and Lydia. The two older children were born in Indiana and the last named in North Dakota. Politically, Mr. Halvorson is a Republican and has taken a highly active part in affairs pertaining to local government.

Nobody living in Hyatt at present could remember the Halvorsons, much less say why they'd moved and left so much behind. This fascinated Martin. He went to the library in the county seat, McCallister, and conducted his own research in the record books there. He didn't find many allusions to Mr. Halvorson, but he discovered how it was possible for the Halvorson family to be forgotten; the village had changed that much.

It was plotted by Richard Hyatt, an English lord, and began as a settlement of wealthy and cultivated Englishmen and Scots (one of whom constructed an artificial lake and a nine-hole golf course at the edge of town), and then it turned into a trading center for the German and Scandinavian and Irish immigrants who homesteaded in the area, and for a while was the county seat. And finally, after the county building was hauled off by the tradesmen of a neighboring town in the dead of the night, and after suffering the effects of the Crash and the Great Depression, besides being missed by the main line of the railroad, it became what it was now—a poor village, largely German and Roman Catholic, with only the lake remaining as a reminder of its past. Its present population was two hundred and thirty-two. This figure Martin knew before he began his research; he'd taken the 1940 census.

Although several other families must have lived in the Neumillers' house since the time of the Halvorsons, it appeared that no one had touched the Halvorsons' belongings in the attic, as though to tamper with them or to remove them were to tamper with the heart of the house. Or perhaps their possessions had been so numerous (wasn't the desk theirs?) that people had merely taken what they wanted without much diminishing the original store. Martin, for instance, as he walked around the attic, said that when they left, if they ever did, he was going to take those candlesticks, that teapot, the horse collar there, and a wheelbarrowful of these books.

Alpha said that just to stand in the place made her temperature drop ten degrees, and she'd rather he left everything the way it was.

"But what about these?" he said, and held up a set of copper bowls with silver medallions on their handles. "These are collector's items."

"I have more bowls than I know what to do with already."

"What about a book? Wouldn't you like to read some of these books?"

"I would if I'd bought them." She picked up Timmy, who was putting fluffs of dust into a china commode, and started out the door.

"Let's have an auction," Jerome said. "Let's sell all this stuff and make a bunch of money." He and Charles were sorting through a stack of dusty phonograph records.

"Leave those alone," Alpha Neumiller said. "They're not yours. I don't want you two playing in this attic—ever, you understand? I'm going to keep the hook at the top of this door latched. I bet that's what Mrs. Russell did. You don't belong in here."

The boys turned to their father, who was rummaging through a round-topped trunk bound with leather straps, and Jerome asked if they could move this—he rapped on an ancient Victrola with his knuckles—and the records into their playroom. The door was plenty big, Jerome said. Martin looked up, his eyes bright and abstracted, unaware that Alpha had spoken, and said, "Sure. Why not? Let's get it in there and see if it works."

·

The Victrola sat in a corner of the second-floor room designated as the boys' playroom, near the door that led to the attic. It was such a tall machine they had to stand on a stool to place records on the turntable. On the underside of its cover, beveled like a coffin lid, *Lydia* had been scratched into the wood with something sharp, and the name, foreign to them, seemed strangely appropriate there. No needles had survived with the machine, so their father fashioned one from the end of a safety pin. Among the old records from the attic, they found only one they really liked; the rest, thick Edison records with hymns on them, they sailed out a second-story window.

They played that same record over and over, in spite of the scratches on its surface—years of them, layers of them—that made the metallic tenor sound as though it came out of the center of a gale, and they never tired of hearing the man sing about Sal, his maiden fair, singing Polly Wolly Doodle all the day, with her curly eyes and her laughing hair . . .

They stood on the stool and worked the crank, staring at the name scratched on the lid. "Fare thee well! Fare thee well!" the tenor sang. "Fare thee well, my fairy fey!" And no matter how many times it rose up, tinny and frail from the ancient grooves, the image of a grasshopper sitting on a railroad track (singing Polly Wolly Doodle all the day) always made them get down, laughing, and roll around and slap the floor in hysterics.

They had their own library in the playroom; they had clay, blocks, marbles, and mallets, dominoes, Lincoln Logs, an electric train, and a handmade alphabet with wooden characters five inches high which they kept in dull-green ammunition boxes an uncle had brought back from the war. But none of these possessions were of the same caliber of interest as the Victrola, and when they weren't playing it, they spent their afternoons at the rolltop desk.

Their father had appropriated the desk. Here, he said, was where he intended to sit when he wrote his book—a project he talked about often, especially after any unusual or moving experience, or whenever he sat down and told them a story from his past. He referred to the book simply as "the book of my life," and if he'd been up in the room for the evening, Jerome and Charles would go to the desk the next day, slide its slatted cover up, and search through its drawers and cubbyholes for evidence of the book, in which they hoped to be included.

There was always a neat pile of white paper in the center of a green blotter, with a pen and a bottle of ink, plus a bottle of ink eradicator, standing ready. Next to the blotter was the large, leather-bound volume their father had found in the attic. Searching through the pigeonholes of the desk, they found old letters, scripts of dramatic and patriotic readings their father had performed in high school and college, a rubber stamp that reproduced his high, tilted signature, a watch fob braided from his mother's hair, a broken pocket watch, some rocks from the Badlands, and a plastic tube they could look into and see a monument of stone and the inscription *Geographical Center of North America, Rugby, North Dakota.*

In one of the drawers was a half-filled box of flaky cigars with IT'S A BOY! printed on the cellophane wrappers, and in another a metal file that contained insurance policies, birth certificates (their own and their parents', too, which was unsettling), government savings bonds in their names (money!), and their father's baby book. In the center drawer were pens and pencils and a ream of that same white paper, which never seemed to diminish.

Once, they discovered this on the top sheet:

CHAPTER I
—*My father's influence on my life*
(Mom's too)
CHAPTER II
—*The Depression Years*
CHAPTER III
—*I meet Alpha, my wife-to-be*
CHAPTER IV

?

Other than some notes to himself and a Christmas-card list, they never found anything else their father had written.

They could not resist the temptation of the attic, although they knew this upset their mother. She disliked the attic, disliked even more the idea of anybody's being in it (she never entered it herself), and was so adamant and humorless in her dislike that their father teased her by calling North Dakota "the cold-storage box way up at the top, the *attic* of the United States!"

They would put their record on the Victrola, move a stool over to the attic door, unlatch the hook, ease the door open, and step inside, and sunlight, coming through a pair of windows in the far wall, fell over them with a warmth sunlight had nowhere else. Old cobwebs powdered with dust, and shining filaments that spiders had recently strung in place, sparkled in its light, imparting a summer radiance to the air. The personal effects of the Halvorsons—the dress form, a brass bedstead, the boxes and trunks of memorabilia, a wooden wardrobe with a dress sword and sash hanging from its top, chairs, books, an oval mirror that held their reflections—stood around in solid eloquence.

Charles tiptoed over to a settee, upholstered in red velvet badly damaged by moths and nesting mice, and sat down. He bounced his weight on its springs. Who had sat here? What had they talked about? Had anybody cried on it, as he had on their couch? Or done a flip on it? He looked up at Jerome, who hadn't moved since they'd stepped into the attic.

The surrounding objects were as real and as awesome as a roomful of strangers, and more compelling; they belonged to a world removed not only by time—by half a century, as their father said—but by convention and law: the world of adults. Here they could handle and examine that world in every detail (and only through touch would it give up its mystery), without interference or protest, as they could not examine the world of their parents.

Since any wholehearted examination of the property of others was forbidden, they held back, hesitant, but all of the objects seemed to strain toward them, as if to give up their secrets. Jerome and Charles were not the only ones who sensed this. Only moments after they'd unhooked the door, they would hear, coming from the foot of the stairs, "Are you two into that attic again?"

"No!" they cried at the same time, a dead giveaway.

"You stay out of there when your father's not around! You hear?"

"We're not in here," Charles said.

"Don't lie to your mother!"

They looked at one another, and then Jerome went over and began to examine the object that had held his attention, and Charles picked up a wooden doll with most of its limbs missing, while the dented and tattered dress form—composed of varnished strips of paper that were lifting up in orangy translucent curls—stood above them, as unmoving and silent as a second, more permissive mother.

Jerome studied a wooden box with wires and disklike electrodes dangling from it. Its lid swung open like a little door, and from what he could understand of the instructions, which were pasted on the inside of the lid, it was a device for giving shocks to the head and feet.

"Look at this," Charles said. He took a lace dress out of a trunk and held it in front of him. "This is what they wore then. What would you think if you saw somebody wearing it? What would you think if I was a girl?" He wrinkled up his nose and giggled like one.

"Quit it," Jerome said. "Put it back." He was more cautious than Charles, more like his mother, and a dress seemed too personal to disturb.

He picked up a candlestick and pictured the dining room in a different setting, at night, deep in shadow, with candle flames lighting the faces around a table, a sound of silver scraping on plates, the rustle of skirts, and then a man's voice, gentle as the candlelight, rising from the shadows: "I have decided—"

"Hey, look at this," Charles said. He'd slipped on the rusty jacket of an old suit of tails that was many sizes too large for him.

"Take it off," Jerome said. "Put it back."

"All right. But I'm going to take this." It was a book, *Children of the Garden*, that personified the common species of flowers, giving them human features and appendages and names such as Betsy Bluebell. "We'll keep it in the playroom."

"Oh, all right. But don't leave it where Mom'll see it."

Jerome went to a box that contained daguerreotypes and old, fading, tea-colored photographs. There were pictures of rural families lined up in front of farmhouses: the farmer, bearded or with long side-whiskers, often sitting in a kitchen chair; his wife, her hair pulled back, standing beside him in a long-sleeved black dress, apparently old enough to be the children's grandmother; and all of the children, even the babies, looked big-headed and mature.

There were pictures of houses they recognized, of Main Street as it had once been, with a horse and carriage parked in front of Reiland's Tavern, and several views of their own home. Jerome motioned Charles over, and with an air of solemnity pointed to a rear view of their house, placing his fingertip on the attic window.

There were pictures of the Halvorsons, with the subject's name, the year the portrait was taken, and the person's age at the time written in an artistic hand across the back of each.

"Look at this," Jerome said, and wiped his forearm across a picture. A plump man in muttonchop whiskers stared up at them with the sparkling eyes of an unrepentant roué. Jerome frowned. "It's Mr. Halvorson. Do you like the way he looks?"

"I don't know."

"I don't," Jerome shuffled through all the pictures of Mr. Halvorson and his wife, who was broad and square-jawed and looked enough like her husband to be his brother. Two of the daughters looked exactly like her. In a portrait of the third girl, however, Jerome saw what he had hoped to see in the rest of the family. She was reclining at one end of the settee, an open book in her lap, a finger placed along her cheek, her lower lip, with a shine on it, shoved out. Light-colored hair fell to her waist, and her dark eyes were staring off at a scene, apparently a heart-breaking one, in the distance.

"See," Jerome said, pointing to the lace dress she was wearing. "That was probably hers."

"What about it?"

"You shouldn't be messing around with it like that."

"Why?"

"If it was hers— You shouldn't, that's all. Look how pretty she is."

"Not anymore."

"What do you mean?"

"She's probably old and ugly by now."

Jerome turned the picture over: "Lydia, at the age of thirteen, in the year of our Lord 1901."

"See," Charles said. "That's even before Dad was born, and look how old he is. If she—"

But the girl had Jerome in her possession. He saw her running through the downstairs hall on a day as sunlit as this one, running up the steps, her hair streaming behind, and rushing into the playroom to the Victrola. He turned. His mother stood in the doorway, flushed and out of breath from climbing the stairs in her condition.

"What did I tell you two? Get out of here! Get out, get out, get out!"

In August, Alpha Neumiller gave birth to a daughter, whom she named Marie, after Martin's mother. Jerome and Charles were envious of the attention the girl received, and embarrassed by her. They spent more and more of their time outdoors. But Tim, who was constantly left out of their projects and play, would stand at Marie's bassinet with his hands clasped behind him, sometimes for an hour, as if she were his only hope. Martin was proud of her as only the father of a daughter can be proud, and Alpha, who had always wanted a girl, associated this stroke of good luck with the move into the house. Before the baby arrived, she had decorated a downstairs bedroom in pink and frills.

It was becoming Alpha's house. Over the first winter, she had closed off the upstairs to reduce the heating bills and her own work, but now it was open and a major piece of framework in the home she was building within the house, not merely a place where the boys went to get off by themselves or make trouble. She put a sleeping cot, white organdy curtains, and glassed-in bookshelves that she'd bought at an auction, and thought she'd never use, in the room occupied by the rolltop desk, which she referred to as Martin's office. In a battered box of junk, she unearthed the shell of a painted turtle that Martin had once found, empty, along the railroad tracks and had filled with cement—a mislaid, long-forgotten talisman, which he used to use as a paperweight. She placed it on the pile of paper on his desk.

And she had her own room upstairs, a sewing room with an easy chair and a lamp for reading, when she wanted to relax and read, large closets that accommodated all their winter clothes, and so much space she was able to keep her curtain stretchers permanently set up.

She painted, with white enamel, the cupboards in the pantry and the kitchen, and Martin put down new linoleum in every room. He trimmed the hedge around the house, all of it, down to four feet, and got blisters and sores and then hands as hard as horn from the project, which took weeks. He bought and installed an oil heater in the living room, so they could keep the chill out of the downstairs on fall days without starting the furnace in the basement, and when school dismissed for the summer, he hired a neighbor, William Runyon, as a helper, and they scraped and wire-brushed and painted the outside of the house. It was the color Alpha had always wanted her house to be—warm yellow, with white trim.

She was unpacked and had found a place for every-thing, from the rocker she'd inherited from her grand-mother to her everyday soup spoons, and all of her furniture was being used. Then Martin bought a bedroom set of solid maple she'd dreamed of owning for five years ("\$210," she noted in her diary, "but so what?"), with a tall dresser for him and a vanity with a mirror big enough to satisfy her. And still the house looked underfurnished. Which to her was perfectly all right; nothing or nobody was underfoot.

She had helped Martin lay out a garden, and as vegetables came into season she canned and preserved them, along with fruits from the market, jellies and jams, berries picked from the countryside during picnics and outings, and some capons Martin bought from a neighbor. The shelves in the basement were beginning to fill up. The potato bin was full. There were parsnips, kohlrabi, turnips, and rutabagas, all dipped in paraffin to preserve them, in the other bins. She brought out the winter clothes and began to mend them.

.

One afternoon in late October, she was sitting in her rocker in the alcove formed by the bay window, absorbing the last of the season's sunlight before winter, and knitting a heavy pink cardigan for Marie, when she thought she heard a knock at the front door. She paused in her work and looked up; nobody ever used that door. The knock came again. She put her work in the seat of the chair and went to the boys' bedroom and found all three of them there, up to no mischief. She went through the living room, down the long hall to the front door, and opened it. A tall, youthful-looking priest stood on the porch.

"Hello. I'm James Russell. Just call me Father Jim."

"Oh. Hello."

"You must be Mrs. Neumiller."

"Yes."

"I used to live here."

"Well, come in."

He stepped inside, and his bright-green eyes traveled over every area of the entry and stairway, as if following a familiar course, and stopped; her sons, who had trailed after her through the living room, were standing at the end of the hall. "Ah," he said, "I see you have three fine young boys."

He strode past her, his cassock smelling of cologne and cigarette smoke, and went up to them and ruffled their hair. "Your father's a fine gentleman," he said. "He taught two of my brothers and two of my sisters, and they have nothing but praise for him. You can be proud. Have either of you—not you, little fellow—made your First Communion yet?"

"Me," Jerome said.

"What is God's loving care for us called?"

"God's loving care for us is called Divine Providence.'"

"What do we mean when we say that God is almighty?"

"When we say that God is almighty we mean that He can do all things.'"

"Is God all-wise, all-holy, all-merciful, and all-just?'"

"Yes. God is all-wise, all-holy, all-merciful, and all-just.'"

"You've learned your catechism well. Good, good." He turned to Alpha. "Do you have others?"

"A daughter, two and a half months."

"Is she asleep?"

"Yes."

"Ah, that's too bad. I'd like to bless the little tyke. Is your husband here?"

"No."

"Will he be back soon?"

"Later today. He's gone to McCallister."

"I'm afraid I won't even have a chance to see him, then, I'm so awfully rushed. That's a disappointment. He's meant a lot to us, you know, the younger ones especially. I haven't been in the area since I was transferred to Minneapolis, nearly three years now. I'm with the Jesuits there. I believe it was thought best that I not visit the family. We were all quite close." He rubbed and wrung his hands as if washing them as he looked around. "But the family, God bless them, is gone from the area now, and a conference came up in Bismarck that the Monsignor couldn't attend—one that might be quite important to the laity, by the way; it deals with sacramentals—so the Monsignor delegated me to go, and loaned me his car (I left the engine running; I'm already late), and since I was so close, only twenty-five miles off, I couldn't resist. I had to see the old place. Isn't it a lovely house?"

He began to pace around the living room, displacing the air in a way that Martin never did, his eyes moving with such speed and restlessness he kept changing direction, turning to look behind, staring up or to the side, turning again. "You've done very well by the old place. It's decorated with taste and is as neat as I can remember. The outside looks fine also—the new paint job, I mean—and the hedge; I think Father let that go the last years. I can't understand why he felt compelled to leave. The hardware store certainly hasn't worked out as he expected, not in that location, and he just suffered a second stroke. Edward and Jackie have left, of course, but Dennis is still at home to help. Dennis is a good lad. Enid has decided to take her vows—a surprise to us all, she seemed so involved in the arts—and Margaret graduated valedictorian this year. That makes five in the family so far." He stopped at the bay window.

"Isn't this a beautiful view? I've always liked to stand here and admire it. So did Mother. She would look out and pray the Rosary here at night, when most of us were in bed, and the whole house fell quiet. The lilac bushes there, the garden beyond, that nice oak down the road next to the Runyons'—somehow the arrangement is so pleasing and serene. I hope nobody ever builds on these lots to the corner. It would ruin the view. You can see past the state highway to that far-off Indian mound, or whatever it is. I think it's never been decided for sure, though it certainly couldn't be a hill—not in this territory. Hawk's Nest, it's called. Did you know that it stands nearly in the next county? I used to love to study it and wonder what it could be. Here's where I decided to become a priest."

He removed a white handkerchief from the sleeve of his cassock, blew his nose hard, then folded the handkerchief square, still staring out the window, and replaced it in his sleeve. Then he started to pace again, glancing into the dining room, the kitchen, the boys' bedroom, and through a gap in the sliding doors into the master bedroom.

"I'm sorry I'm in such an unneighborly rush. I'd like to sit down and visit, have dinner with you all—I can tell by your healthy boys you're a wonderful cook—and I wanted so much to see Martin." He stopped. "I'd love to run up and look at my old bedroom. But I'm afraid that would be imposing."

Alpha started to speak, but he held up his hand. "Also, I don't know if I could face it. Too emotional. Patrick and I used to share the room, and we lost him in the war." He crossed himself in a hurried way that appeared involuntary. "Well, boys, remember always to honor your father and mother, don't forget your morning and evening prayers, and keep yourself pure, for there's nothing more honorable in the eyes of God than purity. Now, come here, kneel down, and I'll give you my blessing."

Jerome and Charles knelt in front of him with their hands clasped and eyes closed, and Tim, copying them, did the same. Father Jim sketched crosses in the air above their heads and spoke the Latin in a clear voice, three times, without hurrying the familiar words. He thanked Alpha for her patience and hospitality, once again apologized for his rush, reminded her to give Martin his greetings, and then strode to the front door.

Jerome and Charles and Tim stood at the end of the hall and watched while he said goodbye to their mother and, as she bowed her head, quickly gave her his blessing. Then he walked across the porch, across the lawn, and out of sight, and they heard the sound of his car engine echo off a building and grow faint.

Their mother closed the door. She stood with her forehead against it and her hand on the knob, as though examining her thoughts with an intensity that held her there, and then turned to them. She looked thinner and older than a moment ago, and her expression, distant yet resigned, was an expression they'd never seen. But they knew what she was feeling; now the Russells, as well as the Halvorsons, would always occupy a part of their house. And although their mother might resist it, they knew it would only be a matter of time before they moved.

MARIE

Now all of the family was home for Christmas. When Marie returned from an afternoon of last-minute shopping with an aunt in Peoria, Jerome and Charles had arrived and were sitting at the kitchen table, playing a game of pinochle with Tim and her father. They were away at college and hadn't been home since Thanksgiving, and she was so happy to see them that she almost sang out "Joy to the World!" in a loud, clear voice, as she'd been singing it all the way home in the car.

"Mrs. Claus returneth," Tim said, and Marie wondered, since her hands were full of packages, how Tim pictured the name: Claws?

Charles looked up from his cards and said, "Hey, hey, Marie," and Jerome said, "How have you been?"

"Fine," she said, smiling and studying her older brothers with affection. They were wearing the sweaters she'd sent them for their birthdays—it was like them to be so thoughtful—and Jerome had on a new pair of horn-rimmed glasses that gave his hollow-cheeked face a fuller, more direct look.

She was relieved that they didn't get up from the table to greet her. She felt awkward enough already. They were much older than their ages, it seemed, and both so intelligent she was sure they'd learned things she couldn't possibly learn in her lifetime. She blushed, embarrassed and at the same time comforted by the emotions they aroused in her, and put her packages on the kitchen counter.

"Oh!" she said. She'd tracked in snow and it was melting around her shoes. She went to the sink, took a sponge from its drainboard, and blotted at the water. The house had to be perfect for Christmas, correctly arranged and immaculate, so the spirit of the season could move unhindered through the rooms. It had taken her two weeks to clean and decorate the house, and now, as usual, she was the first to track it up.

"Have you joined the Thespian Club yet?" Charles asked. He'd been the president when he was a senior in high school, and he acted at the university now; his hair was long, halfway down his neck, and she remembered hearing that he was in another play, one by Shakespeare, with "night" in the title. She'd often wanted to go to the university with her father to watch Charles perform, but she was afraid she wouldn't understand the play and then wouldn't know what to say to Charles afterward. He was that sensitive.

"Oh, no," she said. "I'm just a freshman."

"So? I joined when I was a freshman."

"But you're so good. I can't act."

"Sure you can."

"I'd feel too dumb standing in front of all those people."

"Get into makeup or props."

"Maybe next year."

Her father, who'd been staring at Charles, said, "Will it be necessary for her to grow her hair as long as yours in order to act?"

"Oh, for God's sake," Charles said.

"I used to act in school, too, you know," her father said, "but that doesn't mean I ran around looking like a bum. I'll give you five dollars right now if you'll run uptown the first thing tomorrow and have that cut off."

"It's supposed to be long."

"Wear a wig!"

Charles's face flushed and he turned to his cards.

Marie put the sponge in the sink and noticed that Tim and her father, who were paired off against Jerome and Charles, were secretly passing the signals that Tim had devised over the fall. Did Jerome and Charles have their own signals? She hoped so.

Tim crossed his eyes and said through clenched teeth, "Rack 'em up! Wrap 'em up! Rip 'em up! Whip 'em out!"— he plucked a card from the neat fan in his hand and lifted it high in the air—"Ah, ha! Ah, ya-ha-ha! *Winny*-beat! *Winny*-beat! Whoo, whooooooo!" His eyes uncrossed. "Feast on this, fond bluver Jerbloom," he said, and flipped the card, an ace, down on the table. "Shazam! Screwdini takes another sizzling trick!"

Jerome, whose play was next, kept staring at his cards and said, in his dispassionate, gravelly drawl, "You're a hebephrenic schizophrenic."

"Oooo!" Tim said. "Large words stream from one so mightily educated."

"Come on, come *on*," her father said. "Either play cards or act the fool, one of the two, or let's just quit right now."

"I choose the former of those, kind sire," Tim said, and tossed down another ace.

"Hmm," her father said, glancing at his cards. "That helps."

"You betchum, Big M," Tim said.

"Play!"

At her father's elbow was a beanbag ashtray filled with cigarette butts, orange peels, peanut shells, and the butts and chewed bits of her father's cigars. She'd have to remember to empty the ashtray before it gave off that awful odor of old cigars she'd grown up with most of her life; and she'd have to remember, too, to set out more ashtrays. Jerome and Charles smoked in the house now, instead of going for a walk.

Jerome closed one eye, pushed out his lips, drew back from his cards like a farmer, and said in a farmer's voice, "Looks like you two are gonna git trounced agin!" And then threw down a trump.

Marie laughed. Jerome, the oldest, was solemn and reserved, and never acted in such an absurd manner unless he was embarrassed. He must be happy to see her. She smiled and the light around the edges of her eyes turned rainbow-colored from tears. She picked up her packages and went into the living room, dimly lit and aromatic of pine pitch from the ceiling-high tree. The television was playing, staining the front wall and half of the ceiling gray-violet, and above the back of the easy chair she could see a half-moon of big hair curlers. Without taking her eyes from the television, without moving the curlers, Susan said, in her rapid, matter-of-fact voice, "What'd you get me, Mare?"

Her younger sister was as intelligent as the boys—a straight-A student who seldom had to study. Although Susan had never taken an algebra course, she was able to solve Marie's algebra problems (how could anybody add x's, letters of the alphabet?), and Marie sometimes felt that she'd been born into this family to remind the others to be grateful.

"You'll have to wait till Christmas to find out," Marie said.

"You never wait."

"I know."

"You see everything everybody's got a week before they get it."

"I know," Marie said.

She couldn't bear the uncertainty. She rewrapped the packages as carefully as she could, sometimes adding touches of her own—a larger bow, an arrangement of bright tape, or a design cut from colored foil or an old Christmas card. Unless they were gifts for her father. She had to rewrap his exactly as she'd found them or he'd realize they'd been opened, and he couldn't stand it if anybody knew what he was getting before he did. She arranged the gifts she'd brought in (she'd redo them later), along with the others already under the tree, to balance colors and display to the best advantage the most artistically wrapped. Then she reached to the stand at the center of the tree and put her finger into it; she'd filled it with water this morning and added a spoonful of molasses for food, and the level was still high.

She realized that she was singing "O Little Town of Bethlehem" under her breath and stopped. It irritated Tim and Charles that she was always singing and humming songs—Tim, especially—and when they were younger Tim had named her Hum-Hound. Lately, whenever a song unconsciously rose from her, she'd be jolted by a punch to her shoulder. "Hum-Hound! Hum-Hound!" Tim would say with eyes so angry his pupils appeared red. "Dirty damn-ass Hum-Hound!"

She rearranged a few of the foil icicles hanging from

the branches. She'd used eleven packages on the tree. Instead of draping handfuls of icicles here and there, or tossing them at the tree, as the boys usually did, and letting them fall where they would, she had suspended each icicle separately, as she'd seen somebody else (a friend's mother?) do, and now the tree looked like a waterfall of silver. The colored lights were reflected everywhere off the icicles, along with the ornaments (she moved a blue globe with a gold sunburst in its center to another branch), if they were hung in the right places.

Something was missing. She stepped back and looked up. The star at the tip of the tree was lit, casting a red streak across the ceiling. She'd arranged cotton snow around the stand before putting down the packages, the manger scene was set up, and this year she'd repaired a shepherd that hadn't been used as long as she could remember, and had included him in the group of night visitors at the stable. Every room in the house but the one she shared with Susan was clean, the floors were waxed, and the Christmas-tree lights were reflected in the sheen of this one like colored stars at her feet.

A miniature sleigh filled with candy and nuts sat in a circle of pine branches on the coffee table, and she could see the wreath on the front door, through the venetian blinds. An angel in an attitude of prayer kneeled among greenery on the television set. There was a candelabra behind the angel, and candles of red and green and white stood singly and in pairs on the coffee table, the end tables, the gateleg table, the smoking stand. Candles were much better for the mood of celebration than electric lights. With candles burning, there was room for darkness, for the emotions that arose only in subdued light, and the flames swayed as though to music she could almost imagine. On Christmas Eve, with all of these lit, the family would be surrounded by shadows that would add to the sense that the past had joined them.

Marie went into the kitchen and four pairs of eyes fixed on her.

"Oh," she said. "Do you want coffee?"

They turned back to their cards and in different tones of voice "Sure, sure, sure" went around the table, as though they were bidding. She filled the percolator with water from the faucet and took down the coffee. In this house, the smell of brewing coffee was more common than perfume; any of the four could empty a coffeepot in a few hours, and there were times when Jerome and Charles took their mugs upstairs and had coffee and cigarettes before bed. What did they talk about?

Marie realized that her father's voice was pitched as it became pitched only when he spoke to her—higher, imperative, and for some reason always impatient. She looked over her shoulder at him. "Yes?"

"I said, 'Don't you think it's about time you took off your coat?' Can't you hear?"

"Oh," Marie said. "I forgot."

She folded it and placed it over the back of a chair and went to the refrigerator. She'd also forgotten the platter of cold cuts she'd prepared. The men in this house were always hungry. They ate hearty meals and ate whenever they had the inclination in between, but none of them put on weight. Why? Though she mostly picked at her food, she was always heavier than she wanted to be; not overweight, really, but not as slim as she'd like.

She removed the waxed paper from the platter and exposed wedges of cheese and slices of ham, corned beef, and liverwurst, rayed around a central arrangement of olives. Charles and Tim loved olives. She popped one in her mouth. She carried the platter across to them and placed it on the table, and her father glanced up at her in an abrupt, annoyed way. Was he losing at cards? He couldn't stand to lose. He'd say, "Oh, well, it's just a game," and go into the living room and slump in his chair, brooding about it, pulling and punishing the hair at the back of his head, and then he'd be at the kitchen table again, riffling the edge of the card deck and saying, "Well, is there anybody in this house brave enough to take a chance?"

Her father didn't seem as restless and displeased with himself since he'd gone back to teaching, five years ago, and in that time he'd worked his way up from coach and P.E. instructor in the junior high to the principalship of the high school. And since the beginning of the summer he'd been seeing Laura, a spirited and youthful widow in Chicago, and had become more demonstrative than Marie had ever seen him. Though he couldn't carry a tune, he'd walk into the kitchen where she was working, throw his arms out wide, and sing in the nasal voice of that old movie star Eddie Nelson, or whoever, "Oh, Marie! Ah, Marie . . ."

Through the fall, he'd been driving to Chicago nearly every weekend, and he planned to spend part of the holidays there. He slammed down a trump to take a trick, spread out his cards on the table, and said, "I've got the rest," and tossed the cards to Jerome. Then he turned his annoyed look on Marie. "I suppose you spent too much again today."

"I think the checking account might be overdrawn."

"Overdrawn?"

"Maybe."

"Maybe? Can't you subtract?"

"Well, you know . . ." Her figures never came out right.

"That money was supposed to last till the middle of January!"

"I know."

"What do you expect to buy groceries with?"

She looked down at the shred of ham she was tearing with her fingers. "I saw some things I had to get."

"Some 'things.' *What* 'things'?"

"You'll see."

"Ach!"

He turned back to the game, shaking his head as he gathered up his dealt cards, and heaved a sigh of exasperation. Laura, who was a private secretary and a bookkeeper, planned everything months in advance, and always carried out her plans to the letter, and from observing how she managed, Marie's father had become more intolerant than ever of the way Marie handled money. Marie realized that it wasn't right to spend so much on everybody at Christmas, when they didn't have that much, but she couldn't help it; and anyway, she knew that her father would forgive her when he saw the gift.

She'd bought him a bedroom valet of solid maple. There was a seat where he could sit as he dressed, with a drawer beneath filled with shoe-care equipment (she'd also bought a shoehorn with a handle of deer antler), and a shelf beneath that for shoes; maple shoe presses came with it, and its back was a hanger for suits. Her father had become more particular about his dress and appearance. He was always going into the bathroom to brush his teeth; he combed his hair in a new way, to conceal his bald spot, his shoes weren't dull and scuffed, as they used to be, his suits were always pressed, and Marie no longer had to tell him when a tie and a suit jacket clashed.

"The coffee will be done in a minute," she said. "Is there anything else I can get?"

"You can get me back that money you just spent," her father said.

Jerome looked up at Marie and smiled a faint smile, so relaxed and easygoing Marie envied him. She smiled back, and then Jerome twisted up his lips as though he'd tasted lemon, shrugged his shoulders, and turned back to his cards.

Marie picked up her coat and went into the bedroom she shared with Susan.

•

It was absolutely quiet on this side of the house. Every time Marie walked through the door of the room, she felt she'd stepped into a sanctum of her own creation. She couldn't hear the television or the sound of voices, and all the clothes seemed to hold silence. They were everywhere. The doors of the closet were thrown back, and it was filled with clothes, and clean clothes and dirty clothes were piled on the dressers, on the chairs and the beds, which were unmade, and all over the floor; undergarments hung from dresser knobs.

Her father complained about the condition of the room, especially in the past months, and last week he had walked in on her when she was half naked and shouted, "Goldammit, get this crap cleaned up or I'm going to throw it out the door!" Which frightened her worse than if he'd actually starting throwing things; it was one of the few times she'd heard him swear. His face was crimson.

She had tried to clean it up then, and she'd made an effort almost every day since, but it seemed impossible. She felt comfortable here. Besides the quiet, it was well heated, always warm, not like some parts of the house, and now the room was filled with a shuddering glow from a candle burning on her mother's vanity.

The candle was supposed to last for the twelve days of Christmas, but she doubted that it would, since it was already half a day ahead. Everything she got for herself was imperfect in some way, it seemed, or destined to break down, like the clock beside the candle. The vanity, though, was still in good shape, and over the summer Jerome and Charles had stained and refinished it for her, and now it was the same shade of maple as the valet she'd got for her father. She sat on the vanity bench and put the tip of her index finger into the pool of wax at the top of the candle, and its flame jumped higher. She held up her finger, turning it to allow the wax to harden, and then held it apart from the others as she pushed back her hair.

Her face bothered her; it always had. Aunts and older women said that she was "adorable" or "pretty," but she thought she looked awful. "Scary-Mare," Tim used to call her, and that seemed a perfect description. Her hairline was uneven, her upper lip looked swollen, her nose was too small, though not as small as Susan's, and her eyes too big. It was mostly the eyes, moon eyes, as she thought of them—large and circular, like half dollars, larger even than her father's, which were enormous behind his glasses.

She looked at the photograph she'd placed, several years ago, under the molding at the bottom of the vanity mirror: her mother, standing in front of a snow-covered lilac bush, dressed in a dark suit, her hands hidden in a muff, was smiling directly into the camera. When was the picture taken? And where? It was Marie's favorite photograph of her mother, and she'd removed it from a family album and put it here to have it close, so she could remember how her mother looked. She had died when Marie was three years old—"passed away," they said, gone. When Marie first put the picture on the mirror, she used to stare at it and whisper, as if she were praying, "Oh,

Mom, come back, come back," until she began to cry. But after a few months she couldn't cry anymore, it was too difficult to keep doing, and she felt unworthy of being her mother's daughter.

Her aunts would say, "Your mother was a wonderful woman—it's a shame you couldn't have known her better," and that made her feel worse. She couldn't really remember her mother, or say what she was actually like. Tim, though he was two years older, had trouble remembering her, too (with him however, it sometimes seemed on purpose), and when they were children they tried to re-create the moods they could recall when she had been there. Tim would pretend he was sick with rheumatic fever, and Marie would minister to him as she felt their mother might. Or Tim would cover Marie with a blanket and pat her back and sing a lullaby their mother used to sing; about waking from sleep and riding a silvery pony. He couldn't remember all of the verses and invented some of his own. Or else he told stories about what he and his mother had done the day before.

One afternoon when Tim and Marie were home alone, they shut themselves in the closet off the living room, and Tim began to talk about their mother as he really remembered her. All Marie could make out in the darkness was the shining wand of the vacuum cleaner, while Tim went on about a picnic, a blanket with pink stripes, pebbles around it, putting the pebbles into their mouths, and then their mother walking up and locking the two of them inside a hot, stuffy car in punishment, and suddenly it seemed the wand brightened and the closet filled with cotton. Tim knocked open the door and ran outside, and never mentioned their mother again.

Marie looked at the photograph. Was that you, she

thought. Did you actually do that? Could you have? Her mother's smile appeared wider, and it seemed she'd shifted her position slightly, as though to remove her hand from the muff and reach out to Marie and say, "Oh, Marie, of *course* not." But how could Marie know? She couldn't even recapture the tone of her mother's voice.

It was as if all of her childhood had passed in darkness; there were no details. Every week she looked through the family albums, all three of them, hoping to find in their pages some clue to the makeup of that time. The photographs were like scraps of sewing material for a large and elaborate project, but the pattern to it had been lost. The photographs were fascinating in themselves—she could look into a pair of eyes and wonder, What are you thinking? Are you happy? Are you sad? How is the day around you, and what happened next? And perhaps sometime in the future, if she kept at it, she could assemble all of the pieces into—into whatever it was they were intended to be.

She picked the wax off her fingertip, putting it back at the top of the candle, around the wick, and then went into the kitchen. Her father and the boys had taken down mugs and poured their own coffee. At her father's elbow was a loaf of white bread, the ketchup, and a jar of mustard with a table knife sticking into it—everything Marie had forgotten to put on the table.

"Would you like some rye bread?" she asked. "I bought some in town this morning."

"No, this is fine," he said.

"Do you want anything else?"

"Not right now."

"Who's winning?" she asked.

"Whom do you presume, Miss Aberdeen-Anguish?"

Tim said, and Marie saw the corners of her father's lips compress with the beginning of a smile. Tim and her father were winning.

"I'll make some popcorn later," Marie said.

"Great," Jerome said.

She went into the living room and found Susan on her knees beneath the Christmas tree, shaking a package close to her ear while she kept her eyes on the television. She turned and said, "Oh, God, you would have to come in just now." She tossed the package under the tree and went back to her chair and slumped down in it, and Marie sat on the couch, behind Susan, and stared at the television screen. She'd developed a habit of watching it out of the corners of her eyes ("Sidewatcher," Tim called her), because she'd sat in front of a television so much when she was a child she'd become skeptical of it. None of the programs were very plausible and she couldn't look at them for long without wondering how people in California or New York could appear inside their living room, engaged in performances she could observe at the second they were taking place, and this caused her to lose the thread of what they were doing.

She glanced around, checking for any detail she might have overlooked. The gateleg table was exactly right with the rest of the furniture. A few months ago, her father had described it, and asked her if she'd seen it anywhere; he said it had been built by a neighbor, a carpenter eighty years old, as a gift for him and Marie's mother when they were married. Marie found it in the upstairs storeroom, underneath an old mattress covered with a tarp. She cleaned it and rubbed it with oil until her reflection appeared over its surface, as though beneath the grain, and then brought it down last week, along with the Christmas decorations, and set it up in the living room as a surprise for her father. "Ach!" Susan said to the television screen. "Baloney on you!"

She got up and stomped through the living room, through the kitchen, and Marie heard the door to their bedroom slam. The program must have been a love story; Susan was in tears. It seemed that one of the two always was, and their tears had become so commonplace that Tim and her father hardly noticed them anymore. And she and Susan didn't pay that much attention to one another's. Susan would say, "Oh, for God's sake, Mare, are you *crying* again?" and then in a while Susan would be in tears.

Marie stared at the table, at the design cut with a coping saw from its side supports, like a pair of hourglasses set end to end, and the gold grain that lifted from the darker wood into another dimension, and then she remembered looking at it like this another time. It was a Christmas from her past. One of the leaves of the table was raised, and a tiny Christmas tree, sprayed with silver paint, was sitting on it. There were strings of cranberries and popcorn on the tree. Had she helped string them? She couldn't remember any lights, and the tree was too small for icicles. Were they poor then? Was that in this house?

She turned to the kitchen, and through its doorway she could see Tim and Charles and Jerome, but not her father. The three of them were talking with expressions on their faces that meant their voices had risen, and were slamming down cards, but her mind was so crowded she couldn't hear a sound. The kitchen was brightly lit, and from the dark of the living room they seemed to be inside a yellow cube, closed off from the rest of the house and her, as if she were seeing them for the first time, as an outsider: they were brothers; it was Christmas, their mother was missing, and would always be.

Then Marie had an image of her mother whipping batter in a bowl held against her side, bending to the oven to check on her baking, carrying a cookie sheet to the kitchen table, where rows of holiday pastries were spread out on cooling racks, slapping her father's behind with a spatula when he tried to snitch one, and then her laughter at his startled expression. The house was filled with the sweetness of baking for days, and while her mother worked she sang Christmas carols and hymns.

There was a cry of triumph from Tim, and then Jerome tossed down his cards, shoved away from the table, and came into the living room and sat at the end of the couch. He'd brought along an ashtray from the kitchen (she'd *have* to remember to put out ashtrays before tomorrow), and he placed it on the couch between them, and then lifted his chin to blow out smoke, and she saw that the cords of his neck were stiff with tension.

"Are you done playing cards already?" she asked.

"They're playing three-handed."

"Oh."

"It's harder to cheat that way."

Marie smiled. Jerome had known about Tim and her father all along. The light from the television gave the side of his face a gray, statuelike cast, and she felt sorry for his lips; they were thick, not very mobile or expressive, and sometimes it seemed he talked so little because of a self-consciousness about them.

"The house really looks nice," he said.

"Oh, thank you."

"I remember how it used to look two or three years ago."

"I know. I'm sorry."

"It wasn't your fault. Nobody picked up after themselves."

"I was the worst."

"Mmmmm." His mind had jumped beyond the conversation and he was considering something else.

"How long has Dad been this way?" he asked.

"How?"

"Angry at you."

"All the time!"

"More, lately?"

"I guess."

"Mmmmm." Jerome put the cigarette to his lips, and his exhaled smoke rolled in overlapping clouds toward the Christmas tree.

"Are you excited about Christmas?" Marie asked.

"Sort of," he said.

"I am."

"You don't seem in a celebrating mood tonight."

"Oh—" Marie stared down and evened her skirt against a knee with her thumbs. "Oh, I've just been thinking."

"What about?"

"Oh, I don't know. A lot of things." She was embarrassed to mention their mother in front of Jerome.

"About Mom?"

Marie looked up. The Christmas-tree lights were reflected in colored dots on Jerome's glasses and she couldn't see his eyes.

"Yes," Marie said.

"What about?"

"Just her. She made times like this so perfect. Even if I knew exactly how you boys and Dad wanted Christmas, I'd probably ruin it."

"That's how you feel?"

"I can't do anything right."

"Everything you've done here looks great to me."

"You're just being nice."

"Nnnn." There were more clouds of smoke, and then he said, "She made mistakes all the time." And after a moment added, "Mom."

"That's not so."

"Sure it is."

"It's not!"

"She made more mistakes than you."

"You're just saying that."

"She had more opportunity to make them."

"What do you mean?"

"Five kids."

No matter how much Marie kept brushing her cheeks with her fingers she couldn't keep them free of tears.

"When do you think it'll happen?" Jerome asked.

"What?"

"Dad get married."

"This summer," Marie said.

"That soon?"

"He's practically said so to Susan and me. A couple of times."

"That's what I was thinking."

"Why?"

"Nobody seems too happy around here."

"*He* does."

"I'm sure he's worried about a lot of things—especially how we'll all take it."

"No, he isn't."

"Sure, Marie. Also, it's his second wife. He's probably wondering if things will work out the same."

"Why does he have to get married at all? After so

many years? Why can't we stay the way we are? We get along just fine."

"I doubt if he wants to spend the rest of his life alone."

"But what about us?"

"I'm sure he's considered our feelings."

"Not Susan's and mine."

"Especially yours."

"But he never really talks to us."

"He will."

Marie wanted to rest her forehead against Jerome. "I was just starting to find out where I belong in this family!"

"You'll keep on finding out."

"I won't have a chance. There'll be too many others!"

"Just Laura. She's nice."

"She has three kids."

"Both her sons are married."

"But her daughter will be here. Her daughter's younger than Susan."

"Mmmm," Jerome said. "Maybe you just don't want to give up the house."

"I don't! I'd never feel right about it! I'd feel like I let somebody else take it from Mom!"

"She's been gone a long time, Marie."

"I know she has, I know that! But I'm still here, aren't I? Can't you see that I am?"

BURIAL

He was awakened from sleep by his head slamming against glass. The train was going into a shuddering turn, and his shoulder was crushed against steel. He pushed himself up in the seat, glimpsing his diminishing reflection in the dim glass, and the act of sitting and the sight of himself, gray and unrelated to who he felt he was, drained away his blood and left him blind for a breath, and he had a hallucination of milkweed pollen floating from a broken pod. Alcohol. The pain above his right eye was like a needle embedded there and pressing upward. What was the form that had been so overarching, so vaulted and protective in his dream, as though he'd been sleeping in a cathedral? He pulled a pocket watch from his overalls; he couldn't have slept more than fifteen minutes. Where was the sun?

The faded velvet of the seat was impregnated with dust, dry and chalklike to his touch, and then his nostrils widened and his brain was blank numb fragments from the bang of a sneeze. He pulled out a handkerchief and wiped the palm of his hand, trying to hold his head steady against the shock and sway of the railroad car, and then took a telegram from his shirt pocket, ironed it smooth over his thigh, and stared at the yellowish strips of paper pasted askew on the telegram blank.

MAHOMET NOR DAK
957 AM SEPT 24 1935
CHARLES NEUMILLER
COURTENAY NOR DAK

DAD PASSED AWAY THIS AM. NEED YOU
FOR BURIAL. GOD SPEED YOU.

AUGUSTINA

He pressed his fingers against his eyelids, as though the message and the mounting pain it brought could be buried in that internal blackness, where shining tangles of vision shook and uncurled, and his cupped hand returned the alcohol on his breath. He'd been drunk three times in his life: in 1913, when his first child, Martin, was born; five years later, when the quartet in which he sang bass received a standing ovation at the state Society for the Preservation and Encouragement of Barber Shop Quartet Singing in America convention (that drunkenness was an accident; it was the first time he'd tried sloe gin); and yesterday afternoon, when he received the telegram. Except for the nap just now, he hadn't slept since he'd received it. He looked up, and the mural at the end of the empty car, bison outlined against a background of tan, lifted toward him away from the wall. He shook his head to clear it, and felt a race of emotion he couldn't name.

At his feet was a faded carpetbag, made a decade ago by his wife, that contained most of his valuable possessions—his suit, a straight razor of German steel, and his portable carpentry tools. A newly set handsaw, wrapped in newspaper, was tied to the carpetbag with twine. He looked out the sooty window and watched the sun, which was still hidden from him, form a hazy arc of light along the horizon, and then light appeared across the plain as if from the earth itself, warming his face, and fall colors became visible everywhere over the flat land.

Now there were familiar landmarks; five elms with a windmill beside them and, beyond the trees, the silvery gray outbuildings of an abandoned farm with a yellow-painted outhouse slanting among them. He leaned his cheek against the window, once again feeling the race of emotion as he followed a green line that wound through the gold stubble and dark squares of summer fallow and then went faint at the horizon. Sand Grass Creek. On the other side of Mahomet, to the east, the creek formed a U around his father's farm. The train started slowing down.

A junkyard flashed past, a patch of sweet corn gone to pale stalks, a vacant lot where implements (hay rake, binder, mower with cutter bar lifted) were lined along a snow fence, a grain elevator, and then, close to the tracks, a long wall of echoing stone—the rear of the old slaughterhouse. He put away the telegram and went onto the rocking platform between railroad cars, a treadle above a cataract, and the shattering noise and cold air, coming in such a rush, flung a constriction around his stomach; he gagged up wine-flavored saliva, closed his eyes; gagged again. There was a shrieking of steel on steel, a scent of rusty steam, and then the train slowed nearly to a stop, and he started down the metal stairs and was thrown off balance as, with a clangor of couplings, it stopped for good.

He stepped onto a platform of railroad ties, down a distance from a green depot, and heard the bell on the engine banging and then a release of steam beside his hand as the train started to move. A sign hanging from the eave of the depot's porch read MAHOMET, which was to him, Charles Neumiller, home. Two men were sitting on a bench beside the open door, beneath the porch, and when they saw him they stood. One of them—Charles thought he recognized the son of the most recent manager of the co-op elevator; he could hardly concentrate for the noise of the train—turned and took off at a trot. The other stood as though waiting, and then moved a few steps toward Charles, and he saw that it was Clarence Popp, tall and shambling and bent-shouldered, with a flat, masklike face and a lantern jaw perpetually covered with copper-colored stubble. Clarence had once worked as a hired man for the Neumillers. He was Charles's age but had always been closer to Charles's father. How did Clarence continue to survive, Charles wondered. He was sacristan and un-retired altar boy at the church, but hadn't had a regular job in years and lived by himself at the edge of town in a wrecked caboose he'd patched up and somehow made habitable; yet he always appeared healthy and always had liquor on hand.

"Chuck," Clarence said, and took his hand, and Charles realized that Clarence was perhaps the only one he knew who would call such a taciturn, solemn, and decorous man "Chuck" and not consider the irony in it. Clarence frowned. One of his eyes was smaller than the other, and gave him a curiously discerning but defenseless look, as though an orphan of five were peering out from inside him. "Or I guess I should call you Charles now," Clarence said. He released Charles's hand. "I heard about the telegram going out and thought you might be on this train. There's not much a person can say at these times except you have my sympathy. You have. I'm terribly sorry. I thought a lot of him."

"Yes," Charles said.

"Was the end difficult, do you know?"

"I haven't talked to Augustina."

"I haven't seen Augustina myself in quite a while."

"Who brought in the telegram?"

"I hear she walked in herself. A crime, a real crime, and now her out there all alone, poor woman. I hadn't seen your dad, either, in—I don't know—three weeks at the least, I guess. He was poorly, and Augustina and I had the agreement that when he was poorly I wouldn't come out—you know, the drinking. Your dad, of course, he wouldn't come to town. He hasn't set foot in this place in a year, and I don't blame him. The way he was being talked about, well, it'd burn your ears off."

"Then I'd rather you let mine be."

"People talking behind his back, blaming him for things he couldn't possibly have a hand in, and the worst going on like he was responsible for even the dust storms. Jesus! Pardon," Clarence added, and colored beneath his stubble; he knew how Charles was about profanity. Then, in a wondering tone, "Lord, how long has it been since I've seen you, Chuck?"

Charles shrugged, conscious that his hair had grayed in the last year and that his face, which was as deeply lined as his father's, was colorless from the alcohol.

"I was out to Dad's this summer but didn't see anybody in town."

"It must be four years."

"It must."

"Will Marie or any of the kids be coming?"

"No."

"No? Why not?"

"Martin, Elaine, and Vince are away at college this year, and it would be too hard on Marie to bring all the little ones. She might be with child again."

"Huh. That will make—how many, then—eight?"

"Nine."

"That's quite a family, Charles."

"It is."

Clarence raised the brim of his engineer's cap and shifted his heavy shoes. His yellow braces, both of which held NRA buttons, were faded and frayed, and his trousers were split over the thighs and showing skin. "Who'll be saying the funeral Mass, I wonder. We haven't had a priest in town for three years, you know."

"I'm sure the missionary from Hankinson will come over."

"He's away to Fargo on a conference, starting today, and won't be back till the end of this week."

"Then a priest from Lidgerwood."

"Charles, they're all gone off to Fargo, too, I'm afraid."

"Then maybe I'll have to bury him without a priest," Charles said, and knew it was wrong to mention so heretical an idea to Clarence, who was a prude himself and a worse gossip than ten women.

Clarence's face took on the blankness of a seasoned magistrate's, and then he winked his small eye and said, "Why not, Charles? And, say, will you need help?"

"If you want, you can come out Thursday afternoon. I should be ready by then."

"But that's tomorrow! That's less than a day and a half!"

"If I could do it today, I would."

"But what about the people that—"

A gray-and-tan nanny goat, a fixture in town for

fifteen years, stepped around the corner of the depot and walked into the shade of the porch, its tapered hooves tapping over the heavy ties, and then the goat drew up and regarded Charles with a coinlike, pragmatic eye, while its tiny jaws moved in a tidy munch. Charles turned and walked past it, toward a road that crossed the rails beyond the station.

"You're not walking?" Clarence called to him.

"Yes."

"Surely somebody will give you a ride out!"

Charles walked on. The road, a dirt road that angled away from this edge of town, was dry and unshaded and soon he was in open countryside. The sun was rising, driving off the morning chill, and occasionally a spout of wind would pick up dust from the road or a field bordering it, and spin itself into oblivion in seconds. Otherwise the day was still. Birdsong, rising from the earth and different levels of the air, swayed and teetered on either side as if from a fixed point at the center of his hearing. The road began to follow Sand Grass Creek, which was lined here with low willows and cattails and dry saxifrage. The cattail heads were swollen and splitting, spilling their silky seeds, and directly in front of Charles, keeping a fixed distance, a red-winged blackbird went dipping from head to head as though stringing between them shining beads of its quicksilvery, reiterated song. The road turned and Charles stopped and shifted the carpetbag to his left hand. He could see, about a mile ahead, the stand of trees that marked his father's farm.

Otto Neumiller emigrated from Germany in 1881, when he was twenty-four. He bought a wagon and a team of oxen in Minneapolis and headed west. In the Old

Country he had read of the virgin Dakota plain, as limitless as the sea to look upon and with resources as infinite, the advertisement said. He entered a homesteading claim in the Dakota Territory in the spring, and sold the wagon and one of the oxen to buy a plow and supplies. Trees were so scarce there was no lumber for building; and what sometimes looked like trees in the distance were the last remnants of the buffalo herds moving off toward the Missouri. He built his homestead shack of sod. The first fall, his garden and twenty acres of wheat, which he'd planted by hand, went up in a prairie fire. His ox and his implements were lost. His shack would have burned, too, if he hadn't situated it in a curve of Sand Grass Creek, where it was nearly encircled by water.

He was penniless, there were no neighbors, and he couldn't withstand the winter alone, so he went to stay with family friends in Chicago and found a job as a drayman. At a neighborhood church he met Mary Reisling, an immigrant girl. He married her in the spring and took her back to his homestead. That year the crops bore, though battered by hail, and he bought a milk cow and improved the shack so it was livable. The following spring his first daughter, Lucy, was born. He planted poplars and maples along the curve of Sand Grass Creek to serve as a windbreak, and when the trees began to grow they were the only ones visible for twenty-five miles.

The railroad extended its line beyond Wahpeton, and it was possible to buy lumber from the East. He built a twelve-stanchion barn and began work on a house. The crops that season were the best they'd been in a decade— a windfall, a bounty, and he opened his first bank account in America. Another daughter, Augustina, was born. He took on a hired man and broke up twice as much acreage, and again there was a windfall. He finished the house, a two-story house with three bedrooms, and bought a dozen head of Hereford cattle and a hundred sheep. That year North Dakota entered the Union and he became a citizen of the United States. He began to acquire bordering farms that had been abandoned by homesteaders, and by the time his son was born, in 1891, he owned two sections of Red River Valley land.

He was a shrewd but simple man, somewhat embarrassed by his German accent, he cared for his adopted country so much, and he mostly wanted to please; he was of the last generation old enough to see, from the vantage of 1900, equally well into either century.

Against the advice of everybody he asked about it, he put in two hundred acres of corn—a crop that had never been raised in the state, except by the Mandan Indians, and it was a phenomenal success. He bought another section of land. A new town, Mahomet, was going up at the junction of the Great Northern and the Minneapolis, St. Paul & Sault Ste. Marie lines, and he made sound investments in the first businesses there. Lucy married and went to live near Fergus Falls. When contributions were being solicited to build a Catholic church, he donated fifteen hundred dollars to the fund. On Charles's twenty-first birthday, he took him aside, handed him a bankbook, and said, "This is one-quarter yours." There was ninety thousand dollars in the account.

In 1915, he built a large house in town, said he was retiring, and gave the farm to Charles. In town he became a public figure; he was elected county commissioner and appointed to the school board. When a group of farmers started a co-op elevator, he invested heavily in it, and persuaded business friends to follow suit. The farmers were uneducated and suspicious of strangers, somewhat naïve about business matters, and the man they hired to manage the co-op, one of their cronies, was mistrustful of Easterners and taken in by buyers from St. Paul, who bought from him below market price, promising bonuses to the co-op at the end of the year for volume, and then reneged. After which the manager became so cautious he failed to sell when he should have, and then had to sell at a loss. The elevator went into debt. Otto Neumiller was elected to the board of directors in 1927, and two years later the Crash came.

He lost thousands of dollars in the grain market, but he was the only member of the board of directors who remained solvent, and all the bill collectors came to him. He felt responsible for the financial state of the co-op and raised enough cash to cover its losses and keep it from closing, but had to sell his house in town and all of his land except the eighty acres he'd originally homesteaded, and would have sold this, too, but the property was in both his and his wife's name, and she refused to sign the papers. Co-ops were closing all over the state, but as long as the one in Mahomet stayed open he never doubted he'd be repaid. When it closed, he and his wife returned to the home place, and Charles moved his family to a farm farther north, near Courtenay-Wimbledon.

Everybody in Mahomet knew that Otto Neumiller's farm wasn't under mortgage, as theirs were, and imagined he had money hidden away while their children went hungry and in rags. He raised a little grain each year, to keep himself and his family in food, and not much more. There was no way of explaining that this was the way it was. People stopped visiting him and inviting him over, and in town they crossed the street to avoid him, or moved out of the vestibule of the church when he approached. He felt guilty about the wealth he'd once had and went to closing auctions and bought articles he didn't need and let them stand on the grounds for others to take.

His wife died. He became dazed and careless about his health, and began to drink too much. His wife had signed her share of the farm over to Augustina, who'd never married, and Augustina stayed on and tried to take care of him. He would go for days without eating and speak only German; he and Clarence brewed beer in the basement and sat up at night drinking and playing cards. He was old, his heart was bad, he'd always been a heavy drinker, and the daily drinking added to his general decline. He let his fields go to pasture, to weeds and pocket gophers, and kept only the garden. And now he was dead.

·

At the head of the lane to the house, Charles stopped at the mailbox. There was nothing inside. Across the box, *Otto Neumiller* was painted, in orange letters, in an ornate Old World script. "If you're going to do a job, do it right" sounded in Charles's ears, as though his father had spoken beside him. His father valued any work brought artfully to completion, to the point of perfection if possible: the care he lavished on the simplest tasks and his involvement in the work—smiling, winking and asking you to come and see, as innocent of his pride as a child. Every spring he retraced his name on the mailbox with new paint. His hand was still steady.

Charles stepped back. The pole of the mailbox had been struck and knocked askew by a piece of pulled machinery or a passing car. Charles put his carpetbag down and shoved and tugged at the box, trying to loosen it, then went down on one knee and drove his shoulder against the pole. It hardly budged. He threw his weight against the pole again and again as he pivoted around it, driving packed earth away from its base in a widening ring, and at last, shaking and lifting at the same time, he pulled it free. He was flushed and fighting for breath. He held the pole at the top, close to the box, picked up his carpetbag, and went down the lane to the house. He propped the mailbox against the chimney, near the porch.

Augustina opened the screen door and came onto the porch. Her gray eyes, magnified by thick glasses, were fearful and apologetic, and she was twisting a handkerchief at her waist. One of her hands lifted, as if she meant to speak, and then she clamped her lips tight and her eyelids closed. Her forehead was higher than his, and her eyebrows thick and mannish. The handkerchief looked ragged, her dark dress was worn and dingy, and her hair, once a reddish aureole around her face, was tan-gray and drawn into a frizzy bun. Charles was hurt by how she'd aged and her apparent lack of concern about her appearance. He stepped onto the porch and took her in his arms.

"Charles. Thank God."

Her body beneath the dress was surprisingly feminine, frail yet full, her large breasts firm against him, and he realized how easily she could have married. Had she remained single out of fear—since adolescence she'd been high-strung and terrified of strangers and subject to "spells"—or was it simple devotion to their father? For her devotion to him was overabundant and colored with awe.

"I thought I wouldn't be able to bear waiting or keep myself sane," she said. "I haven't slept since he died."

"How was the end?"

"It was as if—He'd been feeling all right and I brought him—Come inside. Please."

They went into the parlor, bare except for a faded carpet, a big oak table, and a horsehair sofa, and before

Charles could adjust to the room her arms were around his neck and he felt through his shirt the damp heat of her tears. He eased the carpetbag to the floor and pressed her head to his shoulder. "Here," he said. "Here, now."

"I feel so sick and ashamed!" she cried.

"Why?"

"I helped the doctor lay him out and haven't gone near the room since."

"Why should you?"

"I feel he's still alive."

"That's foolishness."

"I can't help it, I feel it! I can't eat, I can't sleep, I can't eat, I feel sinful and sick and that I'll never be the same from not seeing if he needed me."

"What could you do?"

"Talk to him."

"Ach!" Spiritism annoyed him more than anything he could think of, and he was surprised that Augustina had allowed herself to be taken in by it. "What did the doctor say?" he asked.

"What did he say?"

"What was the cause?"

"His heart, he thinks."

"He wasn't sure?"

"No. He's so restless!"

"Old Doc Jonas?"

"Dad!"

"Augustina, please. Be reasonable. He's at peace now."

"I can't even pray."

"You will."

"I'm too filled with hate."

"Hate?"

"I hate everybody."

"That's no good."

"How can I help it? They've already been out. They heard he died and they've been carting off machinery and grain, and Frank Kubitz even took the team of bays. His only—" She swayed as though off balance and held him tighter.

"That'll stop."

"They tell me it's owed to them and I tell them to wait, at least till you're here, but they won't listen! They walk off with what they want."

"Everybody thinks they're owed something when they're poor."

"We're poor. *He* was."

"I know, I know, but they don't."

"Make them understand!"

"I will."

She drew away and wiped under her glasses with the handkerchief, and then over her high forehead. "I'm sorry," she murmured, her eyes depthless with emotion. "I've never been alone before. I'm so thankful you're here. How are Marie and the children?"

"Fine."

"And you?"

"As well as can be."

"I know," she said.

"How was the end?" he asked.

"I brought him breakfast and he seemed in good spirits, he talked and laughed, and when I looked in to see how he was doing, he had a piece of toast in his hand and he was staring straight ahead—thinking about something, I thought—so I let him be. He's been reliving so much of his life since last spring. But when I went back a while later, he was in the same attitude. He died that way." Charles went across the parlor and opened a door.

The curtains of the room were drawn, the air dim and gold-colored, and on the high bed with its carved-oak headboard he could see the outline of his father's body beneath a sheet. He stepped into the room and closed the door. He dipped his fingers into a font of holy water fastened to the molding of the jamb and made the Sign of the Cross. He turned back the sheet to his father's shoulders. Silver hair was combed up over the pillow, isolating his face, which looked unprotected. His lips were dark and parted, and the white scar across the bridge of his nose was violet. A scar from a fight. When had it happened? The lid of his left eye was halfway open, and a clouded iris showed. Charles closed the lid with his thumb, and it slowly retracted.

In the top drawer of the bedside bureau Charles found a leather change purse, took two silver dollars from it, pressed the eyelid down, and placed the coins over it. He snapped the purse shut, trembling. His father's beard, shorter and thinner than Charles remembered, flared up from his lifted chin like a silken brush. With his fingers Charles stroked the beard smooth, as he'd seen his father stroke it from the time he could remember.

God rest you, Father.

Charles drew the sheet over his face again, crossed himself as he left the room, and sat at the oak table in the parlor. He couldn't look at Augustina. He pressed his fingers against his eyelids, which felt thickened and numb, and the pain in his head brightened and went spiraling deeper. He said, "Did Dad receive extreme unction?"

"Several times."

"Has a priest been out recently?"

"Two days before he passed on."

"Did Dad receive it then?"

"Yes. He asked to."

Charles uncovered his eyes and looked up. "There might not be a priest to say a Requiem."

"I know. There's a conference in Fargo."

"Does it bother you if there isn't a Requiem?"

"I haven't felt we've had a priest in town since Father Meyer left," Augustina said. "And neither did Dad."

Charles took his suit and white shirt from the carpetbag and went to the foot of the stairs, where coat hangers hung from wooden dowels.

"I suppose we'll have to sell out," Augustina said, and he turned. Her look was plaintive, and she was twisting the handkerchief again. "And what will I do then? Could I come live with you and Marie? I could help with the children. I can still do chores."

Charles finished hanging up his clothes. "We'll talk about it later," he said. "I have to rest. You should rest, too, Augustina."

He went over to the horsehair sofa, stretched out on it, and was asleep.

•

In his dream the German word *beste* had a new significance: now it was a homonym of "beast" and a synonym of it, too, and applied to him, because he'd been deformed. He was lying on his back in a meadow smaller than his body when a horse mower came toward the *beste* (beast) part of the meadow and mowed off his hands as easily as hay.

He sat up on the sofa. He'd held his hands, crossed at the wrists, so tight over his chest they were asleep. He rubbed the insides of his wrists with his thumbs, then took out his pocket watch; he'd slept less than an hour. There was a smell of coffee, real or imaginary, in the room.

He went into the kitchen, and Augustina, who was at the stove with her back to him, swung around and put a hand to her throat. "Oh," she said. "I didn't know you were up."

She'd set a place for him at the table—a china plate with the silver next to it resting on a white napkin—and he sat with his back to the window, as he'd sat in this kitchen most of his life. Augustina set out sliced roast beef, a plate of homemade bread, a dish of honey, hard-boiled eggs, corn relish, sour cream, and sliced turnips; a butter dish with a butter knife in it. She took a long-handled spoon and fished an eggshell out of the coffeepot, and poured Charles a cup, then herself, and sat down across from him.

Charles took a swallow of coffee, lukewarm, as he liked it, and said, "I think you should ask Lucy and her husband to come live with you."

"Oh?"

"He's been laid off by the railroad, and they're having trouble keeping up with their rent. They don't have children and they'd be good company."

"Oh." Augustina looked reflective and less anxious; Charles knew that children confused her and got on her nerves. "But I thought Marie might like help with the kids."

"It would be nice. But unless things change for the better we'll be moving on from this country soon."

"Where to?"

"Illinois."

"To Chicago?"

"Further south."

"If you need money, Charles, sell this place. It's actually yours, I've always thought of it so; Dad gave it to you."

"No, the place is free and clear, and it's best now to keep whatever you have."

"Why Illinois?"

"J. D. Prell is there. He used to be with the Hankinson bank, and I brought him out once to try and talk sense to Dad about that co-op. Now Prell is working for a land bank around Havana, Illinois, that's buying up farm properties."

"And you'd do that?"

"It wouldn't be to my taste. A lot of the farms are bought by paying off a mortgage or back taxes. Prell says that the barns and outbuildings on most places have been let go and the land bank, or Prell's development company, or whatever, wants them repaired before they sell. He's asked me to come down and start a carpentry crew. I'd work for him but more or less be my own boss to hire and fire and fix things up as I saw fit."

"It seems a good opportunity."

"It does."

"Could the boys work with you?"

"The oldest ones, I suppose. If they want."

Fall sunlight coming through the window lay in a broad band across Charles's back and around his sides, embracing him with warmth. He thought of his sons with affection, and of his hopes for them, and realized he no longer had a father. He lifted up a spoon of honey and tipped it and let the honey spill in a strand into the dish.

"Do we still have bees?" he asked.

"One hive. Dad kept them up until spring and then Clarence took over."

"How is the garden?"

"In good shape."

"Are the strawberry plants covered with straw?"

"Clarence did that."

"Clarence will be out tomorrow to help me."

"Poor man, I don't know what he'll do without Dad."

"Yes, they were close. Clarence doesn't have any real friends."

"That, too, but Dad's kept Clarence in money for the last few years, you know."

"I should have," Charles said. "Well, you could take Clarence on as a tenant farmer. He certainly knows the land, and then you'd have a little income."

"Oh!" she said, and then looked down.

Charles sighed. "I won't move from where I am unless I have to. I love this country, and a farm is the only place to raise children."

He felt sententious and as if he'd spoken more in the last five minutes than the past year. He finished his coffee and pushed back from the table. "I have to be busy."

"But you haven't eaten, Charles."

"I'm not hungry."

He got his carpetbag in the parlor, went outside and got the mailbox, and walked down to the barn. He unlatched the side door, a Dutch door whose halves were hooked together, and propped it open with the mailbox. The barn hadn't been used for years and smelled of musty hay and old oats going bad in bins. His vision hadn't adjusted enough to see them, but he could hear the scrabbling and the thumps of rats as they scrambled for cover, and there was a flapping of wings in the loft overhead as a bird left by an opening. Lumber was stored on brackets suspended from the joists above him. In a horse stall were two wood-burning stoves, two washing machines, a half-dozen horse collars and some hames, fence posts, a dynamite crate filled with a tangle of fence staples and nails,

Burial / 159

and stacks of old catalogues. There was a pair of sawhorses. He pulled them out and sat on one and sketched a coffin, with measurements, on the back of the telegram.

He stood on the horse and sorted through the lumber and located several long pieces of one-by-eight shiplap and pulled them down. He took out his folding rule and found that they made up enough board feet. In the horse stall he picked up a scrap of hardwood, sawed two pieces of pine to its length, a foot and a half, and nailed the pine to the hardwood in a channel shape. He took out his protractor and in the bottom of the channel drew a pair of opposed forty-five-degree angles, and then sawed edgeways through the pine boards to his pencil marks. A miter box. He glanced toward the house, and the sunlight—so brilliant from the interior of the barn it revived his headache—caused the trees and grass of the barnyard to seem bleached.

He began to saw the boards for the base of the coffin to length. The sound of the saw—the *rarp! tssss rarp! tssss*—echoed in the empty barn in a rhythm as regular as his breath and matched the pattern of sunlight and shadow on the dirt floor, where sawdust went snowing down. The smell of pine pitch cleared his mind of death, and the air of the barn seemed to brighten around him. Drops of sweat started falling from his face onto the boards and were soaked up in a second, the wood was so dry. He slipped his overall suspenders off his shoulders, removed his shirt, hung it on a harness peg, and slipped the suspenders onto his shoulders again, his bare back sensitive to the building's dimness.

He cut three cleats to go across the boards of the coffin's base, beveled their edges with a block plane, nailed them in place—moistening the nails with saliva to prevent the dry wood from splitting—and then turned the base over and clinched the nail ends that were pointing through and polished bright. He turned it back and nailed pieces of one-by-three hardwood over the two end cleats, letting the hardwood project six inches on either side, and had handles for carrying and spacers so the ropes used to lower the coffin could be pulled free. He began to miter one-by-eights for the coffin's sides and ends, and felt eyes on him and turned.

"Charles," a figure silhouetted in the open door said.

"Clarence?" Charles couldn't make out his features, and the voice reverberated beyond recognition in the barn.

"Yes, Clarence." He shambled up to Charles as though gliding, his face a dim mask. "I noticed the door open and heard the saw. I got to thinking after you left. I thought you might like a hand today, you know, with——" Clarence gestured with his jutting jaw toward the coffin base.

"It's really a job for just one person. Thank you."

"Well, then, I thought you might like some of this." Clarence pulled a partly full pint of whiskey from his hip pocket. Charles removed the cap, poured a dash of whiskey in it, and tossed the whiskey down. "Thank you," he said, and handed the bottle back to Clarence.

"I know you don't drink, Charles, but, goodness, you can sure have more than that and not get stumbly."

"That's just enough to remind me of yesterday, which was enough for the rest of my life, I believe."

"Oh-ho," Clarence said. "Yeah, I thought there was a kind of cloud hanging about you. Well, here's to the good days that are gone."

Clarence put the bottle to his lips and tipped it, and the whiskey appeared to percolate as his Adam's apple rose to the top of his throat and throbbed several times. He recapped the bottle and became contemplative. "Well, I was also wondering if you didn't want me to get started in at town, at the cemetery, you know, on the grave there. I'm the one who usually does that." The whiskey was working in him; half-moon-shaped creases appeared in his stubbled cheeks with his smile, and his eyes turned lustrous.

"I'm going to bury him here," Charles said.

"What do you mean?"

"I'm going to bury him on the farm."

"Here?"

"That's what I said."

"But your mother's buried in the cemetery at church! The gravestone there has your dad's name on it!"

"I'm aware of that."

"This isn't consecrated ground!"

"To him it was."

"What will the priest say?"

"I have no idea."

"Charles!"

"I believe a priest can bless the area of a gravesite, if he'd like."

"But this is against all your beliefs!"

"If it was, I wouldn't do it."

"What will people say? You know, your mother buried where she is, in the cemetery there, and your dad way out here?"

"People always say what they want, no matter what. I've decided."

"It's heathen," Clarence said. He uncapped the bottle and sat on the dynamite crate. He shook his head, as though to shake free his daze of disbelief, and finished the whiskey. Finally he said, "Well, Charles, if that's your decision, then how about me starting the grave here?"

"It would make things easier, but I'd best do it myself."

"You don't have to pay me."

"I'd rather, because I would. I want you to help

tomorrow, though, as I said this morning, and I can pay you four dollars."

"I don't want money, Charles. You have a wife and kids, you—"

"I can pay you four dollars."

"Whatever you say."

"I want to bury him at noon. I'd like you to be here an hour earlier."

"I will. Absolutely."

"It was thoughtful of you to come out. I want you to stay for lunch"—Charles pulled out his pocket watch—"and I think Augustina would like you to stay, too. We have something to ask you. And it's lunchtime right now."

Charles got his shirt from the harness peg, and Clarence brushed off his clothes, lifted his cap and smoothed back his hair, tucked his shirt tighter into his pants, and dropped the whiskey bottle inside one of the wood-burning stoves. When they were both at the open door, Charles turned to him and said, "But after lunch, Clarence, I want to be alone."

Charles finished the coffin at two o'clock. He sealed the cracks and seams in it with wood putty. He found a binder canvas with most of the slats missing or removed and cut it in lengths to fit the sides and base of the coffin, then painted the interior of the coffin with tar, and pressed the lengths of canvas in place. The lid was identical to the base, but with a flat strip around its edges that he hoped would form a seal, and the cleats on it faced inward. He painted the top of the lid with tar, laid canvas over it, nailed over the canvas another thickness of one-by-eights, rasped their outer edges round, and sanded them smooth.

He wanted to trim the base of the coffin to match the

lid, but there was no more one-by-three material. He began ripping a one-by-eight in strips. The rasp and sob of the crosscut saw going with the grain. A sharper smell of pine pitch as the saw blade heated, and a sense of rising with it, incorporeal as the aroma and omniscient, observing nicotine-stained fingers and calloused hands perform work in a world below, where light and shadow clashed. He cut his thumb and blood soaked into the board in a spreading stain. He raised up and spatters of blood appeared over the board as if springing through its surface from beneath. There was no pain. He pinched the thumb at its base, took out his handkerchief, tore a strip from it, wrapped it around the thumb, and pulled the knot tight with his teeth. He finished ripping the board and trimmed the coffin's base.

He brought the mailbox into the barn and removed it from its pole. He cut into the domed top with a hacksaw, the parted metal shrieking against the hacksaw's blade, and sawed off the side of the box that held his father's name. He drew marks radiating from the center of the name, used the marks as a guide to sketch an oval around it, and cut the oval out with tin snips. He placed the oval on a piece of wood beam and, with a nail set as a stylus, hammered into the orange paint of each letter, counter-sinking *Otto Neumiller*, as his father had printed it, into the metal. Then he punched holes through the sides of the oval and nailed it at the head of the coffin lid. Darkness spread over his back, and the barn door slammed.

He picked up an iron bar leaning against a feedbox and propped open the door with it. He'd brought out the crucifix from his father's room after lunch, and now he fastened it to the center of the coffin lid. He tarred the inner edge of the lid, tarred the top edge of the coffin walls, and then started nails at two-inch-intervals along the lid for securing it down. From the stall he took a fence post, nailed the channel-shaped miter box to one end, filled the saw cuts in its pine sides with putty, fitted a block into one end, and then roofed the box with a wider board. He put the post over his shoulder, grabbed the iron bar propping the door, and went out to the road. He set the post in the old mailbox hole and tamped rocks and dirt around it with the bar. He stepped back; it was standing true. There, Augustina, he thought. There, Augustina, or whoever else lives here.

He went behind the house, past the woodshed and the garden, to the flat where Sand Grass Creek formed a U, and searched around in the weeds until he found a shallow depression. The depression was nearly square, and there was a ridge around it that had been formed when the walls of his father's homesteading shack deteriorated and sank back to the ground.

One of Charles's memories was of his father pointing out the depression and saying, in German, "You see that, Charles? That's where my real home is." When Charles was older, he remembered walking behind his father through the depression while his father said, "Dis is where da stove was. Here da table. Food in a wall here. Here we slept." And as his father grew older, every time he passed the place he'd say, "There's where I want to be buried, Charles." The last time Charles came to see his father, his father said from his sickbed, "Where do I want to be buried?"

"You shouldn't be thinking such things. You're a strong man. You have years ahead of you."

"Naw, I'm done. I feel done. I'm past the Bible age. I want to be buried." He winked. "Why not? Everybody has to. I'm tired of the days, the days, the days. I want to die and sleep forever. Now. Where do I—"

"Dad, this sort of attitude—"

"*Ach!* Attitude! Do you hear what I'm saying, boy? Now. Where do I want to be buried!"

"You used to say where your shack was."

"Good! You're right! I *do*. And if you got anyting to say about it, you'll see it's there, *ja?*"

"Mother's not buried there."

"Ah, well, your ma wanted better tings, she always did, God bless her. I don't. I want what I want. If there's a Heaven, I'll meet her in Heaven, and if not—" He threw up his hands. "Our bones ain't going to do nothing in the ground together, locked up in steel boxes."

Charles was about to say that these weren't light matters.

"Shush!" his father commanded, and lay back and closed his eyes and said in a weak voice, "I've spoke my piece."

Charles had started out of the room, when his father added, "And I don't want to be buried in no steel box. I want a wood one."

.

From the low ground of the homesteading shack, looking across the creek to the north and the east, the plain stretched off in golds and lavenders and grays to the line of the horizon; to the west, Charles could see the buildings of Mahomet and the road to the farm. A prairie willow grew a ways downstream, and standing closer was an oak his father had planted, nearly bare now, with large mismatched limbs bent by prevailing winds, and a brown-gold layer of shed leaves at its base.

Charles walked into the depression, to the place where his father had said, "Here we slept," and lifted the iron bar with one hand and drove it into the ground.

God forgive me if I'm doing the wrong thing, he thought.

He went to the barn, picked up an armful of feed sacks, his metal tape, a tiling spade and a shovel, and returned to the gravesite. Using the bar as a center point, he measured the grave's dimensions, cut its outline into the sod with the tiling spade, moved the bar, which he'd need for rocks, and spread feed sacks over the weeds to receive the spaded earth. He began to dig the grave. When he reached a depth of three feet, the sun started to set. There was an aroma of a storm in the air, and the temperature had dropped ten degrees; he could see the gray vapor of his breath as he worked. He looked up at the sky—greenish blue, banded with yellow ribs of cirro-cumulus that were tinged pink and bending toward the horizon as though being bent by the sun—and thought, Surely it will snow tomorrow.

He stepped the spade into the bottom of the grave and got up onto ground level, went to the creek, lay in the grass at its edge, leaned and drank his fill, then removed his cap and plunged his head in up to his shoulders, blowing air out his nose, came up for a breath, plunged his head in again, and shook it and scratched at his scalp to get it clean.

He came up and pressed the water from his hair and wiped his face with the scrap of handkerchief, and as he stood there, with his shirt soaked to below his shoulder blades, the atmosphere darkened and a wind tore most of the remaining leaves from the oak and carried them across the creek. A sheet of blowing dust filmed his eyes. He turned his back to the wind and blinked his eyes clear.

Why did he care for this godforsaken country so much? He turned again, and though he felt like running as he had when he was a boy, he walked up to the house at his usual pace, jumped up on the porch, and stepped into the parlor's warmth.

Supper was cooking. It was mutton stew—one of the dinners his mother prepared with such regularity when he was a boy he could tell a mile from home what day of the week it was.

"Charles?" Augustina's voice came from the kitchen.

"Me."

She walked into the parlor, her face flushed from the stove, and he saw that she'd tidied her hair and changed into a different dress.

"Will there be a storm?" she asked.

"It feels it."

"A freeze?"

"Perhaps."

"You aren't sweating in this weather."

"I washed."

"Your eyes look bad."

"The dust."

"You're worn out. Why don't you rest before supper? I've made up the bed in your room."

"I believe I will rest," he said, and started up the stairs. "Oh. I'll need a basket of clean rags, a sponge if we have one, some clean sheets, towels, the rose water, and a needle and thread, probably. Why don't you just leave out your sewing basket. Also, lay out Dad's best suit."

She nodded, and then bowed her head, as if she'd forgotten why he was here.

His room was nearly bare. There was a bed, a dresser, and a straight-backed chair shoved against the wall beside the bed. A picture of the Sacred Heart (with palm leaves plaited into the shape of pine cones dangling over its frame) was suspended on wire from an eightpenny nail above the bed. He went to the window and listened for a sound he'd heard. A pane of the window was loose, and the high, shifting wind was causing the pane to hum in nearly perfect fourths: F sharp, B, F sharp, B, baaaa, beee, baaaa, beee, it kept repeating an octave above C, in the tenor range. He hummed a low D and held it while the pane passed through its pair of notes several times. How he'd love to be able to afford a pipe organ for the Mahomet church!

It was nearly dark, but when he lifted the curtain he could see the gravesite, the mound of dirt, the upright iron bar, the blue of the grass and the outbuildings, the blue-black of Sand Grass Creek. This room had been his father's favorite, and when Charles was young his father invented any excuse in order to come upstairs and talk to him here; and from the time Charles's mother died until a few months ago, when his father's final illness confined him downstairs, his father had slept here. Charles let the curtain fall.

He went to the closet, opened the door, and was surrounded by a smell of cedar and camphor balls. Who'd put the camphor balls in a cedar-lined closet? The unnatural odor and the needlessness of it here returned a wash of the nausea he'd felt on the train. When he was a child, he used to sit in the closet with the door closed and pretend he was on needle-blanketed ground with boughs above him, in the green center of a forest—or a forest as he imagined one; he'd never seen a real forest in his life, not to this day. Sitting in the closet, he visualized the walls of his bedroom around him, and around his bedroom the house, and around that the farmyard, the shape of the creek around the fields, the shape of the county around the creek, and around that the rectangle of North Dakota, at the center of North America, and he felt enclosed in layers of protection, invulnerable.

Why was it that he so seldom thought of his past?

He never thought of it. And why, when he thought of himself in this room as a child or a young man, could he picture himself only from the chest down, as though he'd had no face? Because there was never a mirror in the room? He sometimes fell asleep in the closet and slept through the night, and it was here he'd first committed that boyhood sin he was so ashamed of, God forgive.

Clothes covers made of chintz, like old cloaks, were draped over garments hanging from the closet rod. He opened one out. Inside were dresses—his mother's, from the dark colors and the cut of them—and behind the dresses he saw the shoulders of a man's suit jacket. He unhooked the hanger, pulled the jacket out, and lifted it open by a lapel. There were trousers with it. The label over the breast pocket read *L. J. Frantz, Fargo*.

It was his high-school-graduation suit. His father had taken him on the train to Fargo to buy the suit, making an occasion of the day, had embarrassed Charles by telling the clerks and old man Frantz that his son was a high-school graduate, and had picked out the suit himself. It was black, of a heavy hopsack weave, and its cut, Charles had thought then, was old-mannish and European. He'd hated it. Had he worn it a dozen times? A half dozen, perhaps.

He removed the jacket from the hanger and tried it on. It fit so perfectly it could have been tailored. He took it off, hung it over the chair back, took off his overalls, and pulled on the trousers. They fit nearly as well, but were big at the waist. The suit he'd brought, his only suit, was tan-colored and baggy on him, and he decided to wear this for the burial. He lifted the upper mattress, held it aloft with his head, smoothed the trousers over the bottom mattress, and lowered the upper mattress down on them.

He went across the room in his undershorts and closed the closet door.

He pulled open the top drawer of the dresser. Inside were mismatched stockings heavily darned; a bronze bust of the Virgin; a white statuette of an elephant that tasted, he knew, like alum; a sachet; a slide rule; a screwdriver; and a clump of tangled rosaries. He took out a wallet-size notebook with a cover of stiff brown paperboard and thumbed through it. Poems, mostly of the self-improvement sort, were copied on the pages in Augustina's correct and girlish hand—"The Psalm of Life," "Aim High," "Daughter, Don't Let Mother Do It!"—along with inspirational quotes from Abraham Lincoln.

Following the quotes and poems were several pages, which must have been dictated, and were entitled "Edicot":

Stopping to look in shop windows is against the rule of street edicot.

To eat anything on the street is a sign of bad breeding.

A lady must recognize a gentleman by bowing before he can acknowledge any acquaintance with her.

And farther on:

In entering a carriage be careful that your back is toward the seat you are to occupy.

If there be a step for entering the carriage land on it with your left foot, or there are two steps put right foot on the first and left foot on the next in order that you may enter the carriage with right foot.

Sink easily into the seat and if you are to sit on the other side reverse the action.

The seat facing the horses is the seat of honor and should be given to the eldest lady.

What was this from?

Charles flipped the pages backward and saw, on the inside of the front cover, Augustina's signature, and after it an address in Chicago. Their father had sent Augustina to an academy and finishing school when she was sixteen, but Charles couldn't remember, now, a time before he got married when Augustina was away from the farm. He did remember stories about her and her difficulties in the city; how she was terrified of the crowds, the forward men, the trolley cars and the noise, and especially the big lake she couldn't see the other side of. She kept to her room, and took sick often, and didn't finish out the year.

He dropped the notebook into the drawer and closed it. What was he doing while Augustina was away? If she was sixteen, he would be what? Eleven? Twelve? All he could remember from most of his boyhood was working here in the fields, and the changes of season—as though his past were composed of only four memories: the work in the spring, the work in the summer, the work in the fall, and in the winter little work, except tending the stock and digging out after blizzards. Details were heaped within those divisions, and he'd never bothered to sort through the details again.

He realized he couldn't remember when Augustina was away because he was away then, too. His father sent him to a Benedictine abbey west of Bismarck for the seventh and eighth grades; he wanted him to have a better education than the country school could provide before he entered high school—because he was determined that Charles finish high school—and he also hoped that the life of the abbey might appeal to Charles enough to interest him in the priesthood. Was his father hurt that Charles had asked to leave the abbey after his second year?

Of course.

He'd learned his Latin fairly well. All of the teachers were Benedictine priests, and his Latin teacher, the only teacher he really remembered, a flashy Irishman who knew seven languages, referred to him as *Der Alte*, because he was so formal and solemn-faced even then. It wasn't that he disliked the abbey, he simply knew from the beginning that he'd never become a priest.

He went to the bed and lay down on top of the covers, drew the comforter at the footboard up to his chin, willed himself to be awake in one hour, and fell asleep.

•

When he woke he rolled in bed and reached for his wife and then realized where he was. He took his pocket watch from his overalls on the chair; it was eight o'clock. He dressed and went downstairs. Augustina had laid out the articles he'd asked for on the parlor table.

After supper he said to her, "You'd best go to your room now."

She took a kerosene lamp in both hands and went to the foot of the stairs. "I'm going to write Lucy and her husband," she said. "I think they might like living here."

"I'm sure they would."

"And it was good of you to think of Clarence. I won't worry about him now. I won't worry about the farm. I feel I've been delivered from worry."

"I'm glad."

"God bless you, Charles. I'm so grateful to you, I—"

She turned away and went up the stairs. He followed her footsteps after she was out of sight and realized as she passed his room that he could hear, from where he stood, the two notes of the windowpane, and he wondered if she would marry Clarence. He turned up the lamp on the table, went into the kitchen to the sink pump, pumped a basinful of water, and brought the basin in to the table. He pushed everything aside and laid down a thickness of sheets, then turned to his father's room and put his hand on the doorknob. He'd never prepared a corpse.

He opened the door. The room had a warm, rank, sweetish-foul gastric smell, and he waited inside the doorway until he became acclimated to it. He drew the sheet away from his father's face and was startled to see the silver dollars. As he moved around the bed, the floorboards groaning under his shoes, he pulled the lower sheet loose from the mattress, folded it over the sheet already covering his father's body, and worked his arms under his father's back and thighs. He lifted and went backward, off balance, the silver dollars crashing on the floor, and struck the bureau with his rear and caused its legs to grate. A silver dollar circling on its rim chattered to a noisy stop. He'd braced himself for a hundred and fifty pounds, his father's weight, but his father couldn't weigh more than eighty. His body was as stony, dehumanized, and rigid as bone. Charles carried him to the table and laid him on the thickness of sheets there.

He sloshed a bar of soap in the basin of water and washed his father's hair and beard with the sponge. He held a cloth over his index finger, dampened it, and wiped over the features of his father's face, where light from the lamp lay yellow-gold, and remembered his father saying, "I'm not pretty, but it's me, so I guess I've got to like it, and I do." He went to the stairs where he'd hung his suit, took the straight razor from the breast pocket of the coat, hearing F sharp, B, F sharp, B, and placed his foot on the second tread of the stairs and stropped the razor across his overall thigh.

He rubbed his fingers over the cake of soap and moved them ahead of the razor as he shaved the stubble grown in around his father's beard. Sweat was falling from his face in gray splashes on the sheet, and his intestines tumbled and gave out a groan. He was grateful for the notes of the windowpane and concentrated on them until he became abstracted from this task.

He emptied the washbasin in the kitchen and refilled it. He drew the sheet away from his father's chest, matted with straight gray hair, and washed it with the sponge. He drew the sheet down farther, below his father's stomach, which was swollen and discolored, and swabbed it gingerly to the line of metallic-gray pubic hair. The yellow-gold light on his father's face trembled and faded, his features went brown and orange, and then the wick recovered and the lamp burned evenly over a face no longer a face. Charles laid a towel across his father's chest and stomach to absorb the moisture of washing, and removed the sheet completely.

It was the first time he'd seen his father's genitals.

He washed his father's arms and hands, his legs and feet, then cleaned his nails with his pocketknife. He rubbed rose water over the length of his father's body. He folded a clean towel, placed it beside his father's head, his mind moving from F sharp to B to D, and turned his father face down. The backs of his father's arms and thighs, his shoulders and buttocks were flattened and plum-colored, and his rectum was plugged with a cloth. Charles washed his father's back, rubbed it with rose water, and turned him again.

He got the clothes Augustina had laid out and worked
the trousers up his father's legs to his waist and then put
on his stockings and shoes. His father's arms, bony and
blue, were so rigid against his sides Charles knew that he
couldn't put on the shirt and coat without help. It might
be possible to pull them up his father's arms, but his
father's skin, which was parchment-like to the touch, slid
so easily over his flesh Charles was sure it would tear. He
took a pair of scissors from Augustina's sewing basket and
cut off the sleeves of the shirt, cut through the back of the
collar and along the side and shoulder seams, and removed
the back panel. He tied the tie around his own neck,
loosened the knot and removed it, and then laid the
shirtfront over his father's chest and slipped the tie underneath his father's head, around his head and down to
his throat, tucked the tie under the shirt collar, and used
the tie to draw the collar tight.

Then he took the coat and began to rip it up the back,
at the center seam, but the sound was so amplified in the
silent house that he murmured a prayer and used the
scissors to cut the seam up to the collar. He stopped there.
From the center seam, at shoulderblade level, he cut across
the back of the coat to the right sleeve and down the seam
of the sleeve through the cuff; he did the same with the
other sleeve and opened the coat out. He slipped the collar
under his father's head and buttoned the front of the coat.
He had to remove, at the side seams, the two panels of
the back, which made too much material to work with. He
tucked the sleeve edges between his father's arms and his
body, tucked the top of the coat under his shoulders,
folded the towel beside his father's head so that a clean
side was out, and turned him face down again. He drew
the sleeve edges and coat sides through, up to each armpit,

laid the panels he'd removed in place, and then took needle and thread and sewed up the whole coat.

He turned his father, unbuttoned the coat, sewed the sides of the shirt to its lining, and buttoned it up again. He put the razor back in his suit near the stairs, removed a comb from the breast pocket, and combed his father's hair and beard. He took the best sheet Augustina had left out and went into his father's room and spread it over the bed. He raised the window shade. The woodshed and the weeds beyond were silver-blue, the weeds swaying with the wind in the moonlight, and from the window he could see, far off to the left, the mound of dirt and the upright bar. He drew the shade. He carried his father into the room, laid him down, and folded the clean sheet over him. He found the silver dollars—one beside a chair leg, one under the bed—and put them in the change purse in the bureau. He crossed himself at the font and closed the door.

He washed the table, gathered up the sheets and towels, took them into the kitchen and washed them in the sink, then went into a utility porch off the kitchen and hung them on a clothesline. He returned to the parlor, turned the lamp low, and took it with him up the stairs. There was a line of light under Augustina's door, and he remembered that she read at night, sometimes all through the night, until exhaustion overtook her. Something was wrong in his own room. The bedcovers had been straightened, and the jacket was missing from the chair. He opened the closet door; Augustina had hung it up. He set the lamp down on the dresser, glanced behind him, and then drew open the dresser drawer and took out the notebook again. What was there about this that unsettled him?

Never open your napkin entirely but let it lay on your lap partway folded.

To blow soup to cool it or pouring out tea or coffee for same purpose shows ill-breeding and is never seen in society.

Many of the entries weren't in Augustina's usual hand, were ragged or wholly illegible, as though she'd been forced to take dictation too fast, or was under nervous strain, and he wondered what she'd been put through over that year. He felt eyes on him from the doorway and turned. Nobody was there. Augustina must have seen him with the notebook and stepped back in the hall, out of sight, to keep from embarrassing them both. He dropped the notebook into the drawer, closed it with his hip, and cleared his throat. He could feel a presence outside the door and turned, waiting for Augustina.

The presence moved into the room.

Charles stepped back and struck the dresser, and lamplight rocked in wobbling lines over the walls. The atmosphere of the room had changed as suddenly as the weather. It was cooler and less claustrophobic, and then the presence moved past him to the window. Had he summoned his boyhood self to this room by remembering, earlier, so much of his past here? The presence was so tangible he could gauge its height at the window, just above the second mullion, and it was not his height as a young man. It was the height of his father. The presence turned a new side in Charles's direction.

"Ah!" Charles cried. He grabbed the lamp and hurried into the hall and saw Augustina in her doorway in a nightgown, silhouetted by the light in her room, her hair undone and down to her waist.

"Charles?"

He couldn't speak.

"Charles?" she said again.

"Water," he said, and it sounded as if not he but somebody else, a fugitive inside him with a hand at his throat, had spoken.

"What is it, Charles?"

"Overtired. Need some water."

"Are you all right?"

"Yes."

"You're sure?"

"Yes."

He started down the stairs, and her door closed. At the foot of the stairs he stopped, realizing how he'd react if any of his children came to him in the night and told him they'd felt a similar presence; he'd say it was foolishness, their imagination, and tell them to go back to bed. He climbed the stairs, entered his room, and went to the window. There was no presence now, and the air was as mellow and cleansed as summer air after rain. It was the alcohol, the sleeplessness, his nerves, and handling his father's body that had affected his mind to such a point. How many times had he traced the shape of his father's body while he washed him and rubbed him with rose water? Charles hummed the D to harmonize with the pane, nearly noiselessly this time, slipped a suspender off his shoulder, and turned to the chair.

The presence was now lying on his bed. He went to the bed and lifted the lamp high. There was no indentation in the covers. He passed his hand over the mattress and felt nothing but bedcovers and mattress, but when he drew back he could sense the presence lying concentrated there. He'd heard that the spirits of certain people, troubled or restless people, sometimes wandered searching until the detail troubling them was resolved, or their restlessness met with affection and prayer. Was it right to bury his father so far from his mother? Should he wait for a priest?

He took a rosary from the dresser drawer and went down the stairs to his father's room. He put the lamp on the bureau, closed the door, and went to the window and opened it. The outbuildings and the weeds beyond were the same shade of blue, but it was colder now, and he could feel dew falling through the night air. He set a chair beside the bed, turned to blow out the lamp, and noticed his father's missal on the bureau. He picked it up, and a square of paper adhering to its back cover dropped onto the bureau top. The paper was folded several times and had been handled so much it was oil-saturated and had the feel of cloth. Charles unfolded it with care, seeing that most of the creases were worn through and parting, and opened it to the dim light. It was dated three years ago and it was written in German, in laboriously formed old-fashioned script. Charles saw that it was from his son.

Greetings, Dearest Grandfather!
I send you this on the occasion of your 75th birthday to let you know you have my admiration and fondest wishes. A 75th birthday is a great event and needs a grand celebration. Please enjoy the day! You are many times in my thoughts here at the University, where I'm working my hardest to get an education as fine as I can, and I hope this letter will let you see that I've learned more than a little! God bless you, dearest Grandfather, and once again my greetings, my love, and my warm thoughts are sent to you.

Your Grandson,
Martin

Charles slipped the letter into the missal. He felt chastened by his son, ashamed that he himself had never been as affectionate to his father. He blew out the lamp. He sat in the chair and drew it closer to the bed, and when his eyes became accustomed to the dark he realized he could see, visible through the sheet against the moonlight, the shape of his father's body. He thought, *Have I displeased you, Dad? Should I have shown more filial love? Am I wrong to bury you here? Would you like a priest and a Requiem? Is there a way you can let me know what you want? Should I pray now or just sit beside you? Do you want me to sit with you here until morning?*

He tried to say the Rosary but couldn't and put it aside. He began his boyhood bedtime prayers, which he hadn't said since he left this house and which once had a soporific effect on him equal to ether, and before he was halfway through them he woke to see sunlight shining in the open window.

There was a sound of metal wheels spanging over gravel, and a horizontal pole passed the window, and then the implement to which the pole was attached, a hay rake, rolled into view. Charles got up and ran out on the porch. A man in gray coveralls, Sy Rolfe, a young fellow Martin's age, the son of the neighboring farmer, was pulling the hay rake through the yard by hand. Charles ran out and took hold of a wheel. Sy pulled hard on the pole, swayed the pole from side to side, jerked it, and then said, "Now what the——" and turned. His eyes were the luminous, unsuspecting blue of youth.

"Oh. Mr. Neumiller," he said. "I wasn't sure you'd got in. Hi. I'm sorry about your dad."

"What are you doing?"

"Pa told me to come and get this."

"Is it yours?"

"No."

"Then, why?"

"Pa said your pa owes us for seed oats from five years back that Clarence got, or something; Pa figured they was worth about this much, er—" Sy raised and lowered the pole of the rake as though measuring its weight in money.

"Take it back where you got it," Charles said.

"But Pa said I was to come home with it."

"Tell your father he can make claims on the estate, if he has any, through the lawyer in town when the estate's being settled. Now, take it back."

Charles released his grip on the wheel and Sy rolled the rake backward, close to the woodshed, let its pole drop, and went up the lane toward the road, glancing around at Charles as if his back felt vulnerable. Charles went out to the curve in Sand Grass Creek, where the weeds were silvered and dripping with dew, and began digging again. He finished the grave at nine o'clock. He brought ropes, a hammer, and the coffin lid from the barn, laid the lid over feed sacks on top of the mound of dirt, concealed the ropes under it, and then got the coffin (the smell of tar was hardly noticeable in it) and carried it to the front porch. He went over to the river beside the oak, pulled off his shirt and washed himself, and then removed his shoes and let his feet soak in the icy water as he took out a sack of tobacco and a package of papers and had a cigarette for the first time in two days. He went to the house and washed again at the kitchen sink, a more thorough washing with soap, and then he shaved, told Augustina he wouldn't have breakfast, and went upstairs and changed into the black suit. He knelt at the bed and prayed for the repose of his father's soul, and asked forgiveness for himself if he'd done anything amiss.

Clarence arrived from town at ten-thirty, wearing a jacket and bow tie with his worn trousers, and he and Charles carried the coffin into the parlor and placed it on the table. Charles went into his father's room and folded back the sheet and saw that both of his father's eyes were open and bulging in their sockets. Clarence came into the room and stared down at the body, frowning and shaking his head. Then he sighed and his small eye wobbled with emotion. He looked at Charles, glanced over his shoulder to the parlor, where Augustina was waiting, and eased the door shut with his hip. "Charles," he said, and pulled a pint of unopened whiskey from his pocket. "Do you mind?" He gestured toward the body with his chin. "You know, if I sort of give him this?"

"No."

Clarence slipped the bottle into a pocket of the sewn-together suit coat, folded the flap closed, and patted the pocket. "Who knows, Charles?" he said. "Who really knows? The Indians used to do it."

"It might have pleased him."

Clarence opened the door. Charles rolled the sheet into a tight roll on one side of his father, Clarence rolled it on the other, and then they lifted. "He's so light!" Clarence whispered. And Charles was astonished to see that his father's limbs were now as limp and slack as if he were sleeping. They carried the body to the parlor and lowered it into the coffin, and Charles unrolled the sheet, drawing it into gathers, and arranged the gathers along the base of the coffin and around his father's sides and head. Charles had built the coffin small, only two feet wide by five feet eight inches long, and still his father looked dwarfed by it, so diminished that Charles had the sensation he was retreating from the three of them as they watched.

Charles went into his father's room, took the missal from the bureau, and handed it to Augustina. Her face was ashen, blotched with red, and she'd removed her thick glasses to dry her eyes or keep from seeing clearly this representation, this husk of their father.

"Clarence," Charles said, and went to the head of the coffin, facing down its length, and nodded for Clarence to go to the foot.

"Didn't you tell me it was to be at noon?"

"We're ready. I'd rather it was done." They were both whispering.

"Whatever you say."

Clarence took the foot of the coffin by the hardwood handles, Charles the head; they lifted. Augustina opened the screen door, and their heavy shoes scraped over the boards of the porch as the weight of the coffin swayed between them. Clarence held the foot higher as Charles came down the steps, and Charles saw a line running from Clarence's miniature eye down his shaved cheek. Clarence took another hold and turned, facing forward, and they went around the house, past the woodshed and the garden, and through thick weeds—the brush and lateral sweep of their polleny heads across their trousers and the coffin— and Charles sensed a sudden race of hope, that nameless emotion he'd felt on the train, and then looked down at his father.

They set the coffin beside the open grave. Charles took the missal from Augustina, unable to meet her eyes, and read the last rites at the grave in Latin. He sang "Requiem aeternam dona ei Domine . . ." and Augustina and Clarence gave the responses. He placed the missal beside his father's right hand and saw that his father's forehead and nose and beard were dusted with gold pollen. The shadow of Charles's head across his father's body looked deformed, and he reached up and discovered he was wearing a cap. He removed it and was amazed; had he actually been wearing this striped work cap with his suit? And the shredded strip of handkerchief was still around his thumb.

He stood, his thigh and chest muscles trembling, and began to sing, from the Benediction after Mass, *"Tantum ergo, sacramentum . . ."* His voice found its natural placement and began to open in deep tones, his breath appearing in columns of different lengths in front of his lips, and after *"Tantum ergo"* he started without a pause his favorite song from Benediction, the slower, more sedate and minor *"O Salutarus hostia, quae coeli pandis ostium . . ."* And he could see the censer at Benediction swinging from its chains, myrrh burning on charcoal, the ciborium beside the tabernacle, beside that the sunburst of the monstrance, which suddenly sent its rays through the walls and ceiling as his voice rose, and then there were arched windows letting in light, then arches of pure light, and he was lifted into the center of his voice, bodiless, and went gliding down the arches and emerged over a field of ripe wheat, limitlessly gold under the sun, until the sun became an entrance his voice passed through.

"Amen."

Charles stared at the coffin lid, the crucifix, the oval with his father's name countersunk into it, at the nails along the lid, each with its black shadow, at the hammer beside the lid, and was overcome by such uncharacteristic and malevolent bitterness he had to lock his knees to feel his legs beneath him. He wanted to see lightning across the entire sky, a violent storm, falling snow, or a dove burst from his father's breast and fly off from the coffin—

some sign that his father's life and good deeds had not gone unnoticed on earth, not for his father's sake or his own sake, but so his sons and daughters would understand that he believed in a just and a reasonable God. He replaced his cap, got the lid and laid it over the coffin, picked up the hammer, went down on one knee, and drove the first nail home with a single blow. Augustina touched his shoulder, and Clarence said, "Wait." Charles looked up, and then to where Clarence and Augustina were looking, and saw, in the direction of the farms to the north and the east, and in a ragged procession along the road from town, dark shapes, mourners in black clothes, grownups and children moving over the plain, coming to pay their last respects to his father.

1982–1989

FIRSTBORN

Charles tried to settle himself where he sat on the edge of the bed. It was a bed they had bought from the couple who had lived in the apartment before them, and consisted of a mattress on a metal frame equipped with casters (concealed by a dust ruffle Katherine had sewn), with a loose headboard that had to be wedged against one wall in order to stand upright, and a footboard that kept falling off—too capricious an affair to sit comfortably on. But comfort had never been an asset to him in any crisis, he thought. Actually, the opposite. Lack of it kept you alert.

He looked up from the book between his knees, keeping his place in it with his index finger, to the clock on the top of her oak secretary. 5:15.

The clock was rectangular, white plastic, a revenant of Katherine's single life, with a crack down its face and her maiden name written across its back in slanting exuberance, with a marking pen, as if the hand that didn't bear his ring would always dash away on its own under that other name, denying that marriage had made them one, proving her to be as divided on this as he was. He looked over his shoulder at her. She was still on her side, turned away, the covers over her hair, her knees drawn up; one arm flung over the other edge of the bed, her hand hanging limp from its swollen wrist. As far as they were able to tell, she was in labor. Their first child.

Faint beginnings of morning light appeared as milky blueness at the windows in the turret off their bedroom—one window oblong, one circular, one square, with a balanced shapeliness to them he hadn't noticed until now. He was seldom up at this hour. Drapes that matched the mahogany of the dust ruffle, drawn back in eloquent swags from the ceiling, framed the alcove of the turret, where an ivory telephone sat on a steamer trunk below the windows. It was September. The crown of the pin oak outside, which he could begin to see in outline, was straggly and insubstantial from shedding its leaves.

He'd been reading to her from *War and Peace*, a last straw in the whorl, or a raft in it, and she'd fallen asleep. That quick. But he'd gone on to the end of the section, after Andrei has learned of Natasha's attempt to elope with Anatole Kuragin and, like anybody afraid of his anger, has sent a go-between, Pierre, to return to Natasha her portrait and her letters, signifying the end of their betrothal, and Pierre, who can't think that this is final, plans to lecture her for falling prey to his frivolous brother-in-law, but finds himself so moved by her and her state that he says if he were not Pierre but the handsomest, dearest, best man in the world, and free, then he'd be down on his knees asking her to marry him (the first intimation of what is to come), and then goes out in "twenty-two degrees of frost" and sees from his sledge the comet of 1812 arrayed among the stars above Moscow—a comet that is supposed to portend a multitude of disasters but for him speaks to "his own softened and uplifted soul, now blossoming into a new life."

A residue of the moment and Pierre's emotion still troubled the room; the shapes of the three windows sparkled as if out of that night's moment of change. Which came at the middle of the book, indicating the swing the story would take in the opposite direction from that point, as if pulled by celestial powers, and now Charles looked down at the parted pages, as if to measure their ability to affect him in this way. He'd begun the book the month they were married, when they first moved into the apartment, and she had picked it up; she'd completed a major in Russian but had never read War and Peace.

They dropped everything and let the apartment lie in disorder around them during three days of immersion in this Russia that bore the dimensional stability of Tolstoy's moral stamp. And just as they looked up from the end of the book, blinking still, or so it seemed now, the Soviet film of it appeared, and they sat through the eight-hour extravaganza of that. (Just as when they'd met, two years ago, he'd finished Doctor Zhivago to appease her, and then the movie of that appeared.) He was appalled at the paucity of his imagination within Tolstoy's world, or at the timidity of it, so far as it went, since it was leagues removed from the actual opulence of that life as it was lived on the grand scale, according to the movie's depiction of it—or was this Soviet propaganda?—and she was furious that it was dubbed. She kept shifting in her seat, as fitful as the images reflected over her, he noticed, uneasy, and when they went out for dinner during the break that was provided, to an expensive restaurant he'd chosen with her in mind, she said, "I wish this place were old-style Roman, so we could lie down and eat, I'm so sick of sitting through those ugly Britishy accents. Ugh!"

"Vomitorium?" he asked. It was at about this time that they'd become a kind of comedy team, with him responding to her puzzling pronouncements in these quirky, semi-sequitur twitches.

His reading was meant to recall those days to her—a form of reconciliation, and the closest he could come to being straightforward with her, now. She was pregnant when they were married, four months ago. He assumed the child was his, since they'd been planning to "legalize their status" whenever circumstances were right for them both, and she assured him it was. And then recently, in the center of this same bed, hysterical, her hair down over her newly ample nakedness, she had confessed to another liaison while "finishing" the relationship she was involved in when he met her, meanwhile insisting that the child had to be his, or she wouldn't have married him. As if she'd reached the ultimate in logic at last.

He had started for the telephone, to call a lawyer about a divorce, but since he hadn't carried through on the impulse, he could never mention the possibility to her, though he still considered it. Then, as they were leaving a neighborhood party a couple of weeks ago, and he was stepping down the stairs with that practiced carefulness that too many drinks can bring on, her provocative backside suddenly seemed packed with such shifting and separated willfulness he kicked at it, and when he could next see, he saw her thumping like a child down the bottom stairs of the flight. He'd been in a remorse that gripped under his ribs like talons ever since: for the danger to the child, the bruises she still bore, and his lengthening vision of the sick fits that any marriage, even theirs, which he'd presumed to be one of the best, could find itself thrashing within as if for life.

They'd had arguments, loud shouting ones that had

caused the neighbors below to pound on the ceiling with the handle of a mop or a broom—and these got worse, until his senses felt worn raw with an endless colloquy of his rights and wrongs, as if even the halves of his brain were in conflict. He'd always thought that one of the most fatuous statements he used to hear was "I don't see how she puts up with it," meaning injustice in a marriage, since it never considered a woman's ability to turn around and walk off, but now he saw how it applied to them, and he was grateful that she hadn't left yet.

He stared at the clock and then through it, in the outpouring of his impulse still to crush and break, and was retrieved by the thought that it was up to him to time the intervals. 5:17. She'd seen the secretary in an antique shop on Montague, the Madison or Third Avenue of Brooklyn Heights, depending upon which side of the street you were on, and he'd walked over one Saturday afternoon and talked to the dealer until they'd arrived at a price he considered bearable; and then, after he'd paid, in cash (the only medium that satisfied his sense of anonymity in the city), the dealer said that the price of course didn't include delivery. So he came back the five blocks to their apartment, got one of the burlap carrying straps the movers had left behind when they'd brought up the heaviest pieces, returned to the shop, and carried the secretary all the way home on his back, in the bent-over shuffle he'd watched the black movers adopt, and had been so invigorated by the look on the dealer's face, and the flex of strength returning to muscles he'd hardly used for years, he hadn't once set it down. He'd been a high-school athlete, a quarterback of the sort who would spend so much time trying to outthink the opposition, from the coach on the sidelines to the tackle hurtling toward him, that he'd have insights he never should have had in the middle of a pass, or become impulsive, led by his imagination, "like a *girl*," his coach would growl—unpredictable.

The secretary was solid oak. He had scraped and sanded and worked it, from its squat turned legs to the fragile basswood of its pigeonholes, and now yellow-gold striations rose in relief from the broad hashmarks of black grain in the growing light. It had become her niche, or nest. Her nature was to be in control, to the penny, to the framing of the proper response in writing at the proper moment, and she worked on their accounts here, running down his cash outlays; and sometimes sat for hours composing letters to her family or to friends, many of which she never sent. Or, when she did send them, most remained unanswered. None of her family knew that she was pregnant. Nobody in his family did.

They had both come to the city separately, far from those connections, largely to sever them, for their own complicated reasons and to their own satisfaction. He was from the Western Upper Plains, she was from the Northwest (two unrelated regions that in New York came under the category of "the Midwest")—Wests they wanted for the moment to be free of, and here be *Eastern*, as was true of most of the disenfranchised people their age that they met in the city. He had worked before as a performer and an announcer—"live talent," in the creeping jargon of the medium—and could do that again, but for now preferred a shadowy role. He sold time for an FM station, his hours his own.

.

"Katherine," he said, sure that she'd moved, and turned and put a hand on the covers, over the thigh he'd bruised, he realized, and drew it away. He thought he'd felt a revelatory swelling, but there were so many unpredictable areas to her now, extra padding in unexpected spots and new curves over the familiar ones, it was as if the body he'd charted so many times were being withdrawn inside this other. "Katherine, did you fall asleep?"

There was no answer; then a wash of the covers as she moved. A contraction, as she and her OB, Harner, called it? He'd begun to shy from their technical vocabulary at about the time she came home from a visit to Harner and stripped and lay down on the bed to demonstrate her "Braxton-Hicks contractions." 5:22.

He turned. "Are you awake?"

No answer.

"Are you"—he couldn't quite get out "contraction" but didn't want to say "labor pain"—"feeling another—?"

Nothing.

"Would you like something to eat?"

"No! I'd puke it all up!"

"Do you want me to go on with the chapter?"

"No!"

It was as well. Her attitude had eroded any equilibrium left in him, and the events of the last day had worn his nerves to visionary frailty. She'd hear that in his reading voice. She was stronger than he would have suspected—it was all he could do to keep her nails from his face during some of their arguments, as they rolled over the bed or the floor—and stoic, usually, shifting without a hitch into the next situation and moving through it at her own speed, her eyes ahead, as if she'd been raised in the absence of any expectations and whatever arrived, no matter how troublesome or perverse, was a gift to get open and onto her desk and put into place. She was able to shake off circumstances the way she shook off her umbrella, entirely, so that she didn't have to leave it open in the apartment to dry, and after she'd recovered at the bottom of those stairs, wiping a hand under her eyes, smearing her running mascara, she looked up at him and said, "I deserved that."

But through yesterday and the night, into this morning, she'd been absent from the level of the commerce of life, as if the child in her had taken hold and was drawing her under. He'd never pretended to be able to enter her inner state, but he was usually able to reach her. Or she was able to reach to him out of her concentration that became so pure she could take on the aspect of stone. Artists and photographers came up to her and asked her to pose. She gathered her intellect like an essence in her, unreachable, and its concentrated power drew your eye over a harmony of lines of resolved womanhood, or that was her impact, at any rate, and she'd begun to get work as a model, which was her work now. In the last months she'd withdrawn to even deeper recesses of solitary silence, into an intensity of beauty that left its mark on every eye (or negative; she continued to work), until he feared she'd be refined away into oblivion. As now. As it seemed to him.

They had gone to the city the day before to look at a lamp she liked, which might well have been a chromium sculpture, it was so expensive, and on the way back, on the subway, as he rocked in a semi-trance on the seat beside her, as content as he'd been, in spite of her recent revelation, she took his hand and said into his ear in a breathy moistness, "You'll never believe this. I think I've lost control of an essential function."

"Faction?"

He tried to study her, as full of interior upheaval as the car shaking over its rails; lately, any reference to her body took on this evasive, almost clinical cast. There was a sunken expression of fear in her eyes, which had widened so much over the last few weeks he felt he was looking into a diminished face overtaken by their enlarging, liquid presence. But her face was broader, too, and her nose and nostrils were, as if every cell in her were making accommodation for the child; the arch, even, of each nostril had heightened, along with an accompanying looseness he could feel in her limbs (present now in her hand), which made him wonder with uneasiness whether the cartilaginous parts of her weren't being consumed.

She drew him closer, so he couldn't stare, and, in the pretext of putting her head on his shoulder, whispered, "It seems to have really given out this time—ah, I mean, you know, my bladder."

"You're joking."

"You know how improvident I've become."

"Incontinent?" he asked, somehow in time and tune to the train, so that the syllables seemed shaken from him, not voiced, and once out of him not spoken.

"Well, neither, literally," she said, and settled against him as if to sleep. "Neither, but both. Sometimes it's an affront to reason to be at the mercy of a body you don't know." Then it was their stop. "Get up before I do," she whispered. "Walk one step behind."

He obeyed and noticed only what might be a spot of rain at the back of her trench coat. He maintained his position across the platform and up the ramp to the elevators. Outside the hotel, in the September sun extending a rich spill of copper over car tops and bricks, he felt a rush of renewed hope for their marriage, as if it had just begun. He looked across the street and up the block to their corner, at the ornamental iron fence whose scrolled yet jagged lines were like his impatience for this newly perceived future, and was about to say, *Let's get home.*

"How do I look?" she asked.

"Great!"

"No, I mean"—she tipped her head as if glancing into a mirror, and her hair swung wide in a whitish shine—"there."

"Oh, fine. Wonderful. Nothing."

"Good, then let's go to the store." She took his arm. "We haven't shopped for days. It's time to. What a weakling I've become!"

"And me?" he said, and saw that she didn't catch this, and was relieved. When she planned to do anything, she carried it through, shifting the expected order of things into an altered state resonant of her, until the doing itself took on her distinctiveness—a new aspect he kept trying to compare with what once had been, but never could, since it was gone. That quick. It was a pleasure for him merely to witness her effects.

But at the supermarket, as she lingered over every item in her new, slow, considering inwardness, which he'd forgotten about, as if she were agonizing over the details on each label, he wandered off. His impulses had become as unpredictable as hers, and when the fatherly internist who saw them both suggested that this younger crop of American husbands had a tendency to enter into couvade at the onset of pregnancy, long before birth, and they'd returned home holding the word like a sweet on their tongues, and had looked it up in the dictionary, and then looked at one another, they both had to nod.

The man's name was Weston, and he was a forensic expert and a collector of first editions of nineteenth-century philosophy, and a dispenser of it—one of their few real friends in the city, in their consideration, even though they had to pay to see him. He was a willing participant in the tragedy (as they saw it) of their daily, domestic unease within the dedicated depths of their love. As they saw it. How were they to go on, given that imbalance?

There were some good discussions, they felt, or dialogues, as Weston called them; he was well enough read in current literature so that his apparent mintings of this month were next season's jargon.

He kept careful records, and whenever they stepped into his inner office after an exam, into the sunlight from French windows that looked out on a balcony with a stone balustrade, and found Weston at his desk in a suit jacket already exchanged for his smock, every hair in place, jotting down notes, they couldn't help smiling. The thickness of his file folders on each of them was that reassuring. *Home*, Charles almost sighed, feeling as particular as family under the care of this scrupulous man, who knew absolutely what he was up to, and who, with his Century Club manner and Manhattan dapperness, was valued highly, Charles realized, among people in the places that matter most.

When they had got their apartment decorated to the degree that suggested a newly married couple on their own in the city and making it, they had a party, and the first person they invited was Weston, who of course didn't come. They invited all the tenants in their building, but only the couple from the apartment below showed up, as if to observe first hand what sort of degenerates were able to cause such resounding bedlam. On their way out, after a quick drink, the husband of this couple suggested putting padding and carpet down in all of the rooms. "Bathroom?" Charles asked, as they started down the hall. "Let me know with a bang of the mop if the thickness isn't suitable to you, okay?"

"Yardstick," the man said, and turned on him in a sudden, reddening fury. "I use a yardstick!"

A can of imported corned beef caught at an urge, and Charles looked around to ask her about it. She was at a freezer case with her back to him, her head held as if listening, and he saw her, with a shock, as separate from him, an abstract, pregnant woman, and then felt a chill as if from the case where she stood. A clear liquid, like the pure line of a song, was pulsing in a threadlike stream down her inner calf. The top of her tennis shoe was wet. He hurried over and saw a wet track on the floor behind her, where she'd taken a step. He put a hand on her shoulder.

"We better go," she said, without looking at him. "Get what you want."

•

At the apartment she dropped her coat and pulled off her dress—a lime-colored shift imprinted with miniature flowers, which she'd removed the belt loops from and wore wherever they went, drawing the line at maternity outfits, or "advertising costumes," as she called them—and got into the shower. He picked up her coat and hung it in their closet and paced around as if pursued and then went into the bathroom and drew the shower curtain aside. She was soaped, soaping, and when she shifted her weight he could see the liquid dart in a pulse down her leg through the suds. "Kath!" he cried. "That's not—" And didn't know whether to use "urine" or a commoner term.

"What are you doing in here!" she cried, the sunken fear again in her face, and covered her stomach with her hands.

They called Harner, her obstetrician. He'd been recommended by Weston, who said that a woman's response to her obstetrician was apt to be "chemical." So Katherine might like this man, he said, and might not. If she didn't, she was to ask him to recommend another. Harner was his wife's OB, Weston said, but his daughter couldn't stand him. "He's fairly brilliant, I believe, but a bit impulsive." Katherine was vague about Harner, as she recently was about so much, and seemed to stay on with him mostly to keep from calling the taste of Weston's wife into question.

Charles had met Harner at her first interview, and he had appeared to Charles too ready to pass off their questions with a humor that didn't seem natural, as if he'd learned it from somebody else, or with his authority, which didn't rest lightly on him. He was young, portly, going bald on top, and his remaining hair looked combed back in haste with heavy oil, which offended Katherine; she'd mentioned that much. He promised them that Charles could be with her all the way through labor, right up to delivery, which was what they wanted, and then he went off with Katherine to perform an examination.

Over the phone, as Charles sat on the steamer trunk and stared at her on the bed, with a towel around her after her shower, Harner said, "Well, we'll soon know whether it's the amniotic fluid or not."

"How's that?" *Herr Harner*, as Charles thought of him, because of his smiling Germanic demeanor, which Charles could picture over the phone.

"She'll go into labor. If she does, call me right back."

"But this is only her seventh month."

"I'm quite aware of that, you can rest assured. We'll have to handle the situation as it develops."

"Isn't there anything I can do? I mean, wouldn't it be better if we went to the hospital now, and—"

"Oh, no, I don't think that will be necessary—not till we see where this is headed. Unless you're afraid. Give her some hard liquor, if you like—it's marvelous for premature or false labor—and keep her in bed, on her back. If things stabilize, I'll have her in in a day or two for a checkup. These things happen. Give me a call otherwise, okay?"

He hung up.

She'd been in bed ever since, and when it seemed to them that labor had begun, in the middle of the night, Harner said, "You might be getting a reaction to losing some of the fluid. Don't call me again unless the contractions get real hard—it's unmistakable—and about ten minutes or less apart, okay? Time them." He hung up.

Charles had gone over to the St. George and persuaded a bartender to sell him a bottle of Old Bushmills, her favorite whiskey, but after a couple of sips she set it aside, as if it were a placebo she wasn't about to be taken in by. He had poured it straight over ice cubes, and its pale remains now sat on a wooden chair beside the bed where her arm was outstretched. He hesitated to touch her, and then did.

"Kath, do you want to leave for the hospital now?"

"I can't believe this is happening to me! I'm worn out just from the movement inside! My stomach's like a rock!"

He tried to modulate calm into his voice. "Well, Harner said if—"

An arm struck him as she rolled and drew up with the force of another struggle, starting to pant. He knew why this was called labor—for the effort it was—and why travail; he was sure he'd never be the same as he watched her features flatten as if by extra-gravitational force into a face that wasn't hers. Then she began going "*Gur, gur, gurr,*" as every shade of color emptied from her.

"Katherine! We have to go!"

"Ah! All right!" she got out, and her tight-shut eyes fluttered open on unfocused depths. "Just—*stay* with me *through this!*"

He took her hand, icy, its veins going vivid in wheyey paleness, and held on tight. Her fine blond hair was whitened from bleach and afternoons spent sunbathing on their roof (*ghostly* came to him, as he stared down on its snowy disarray), except for an area over her crown in the shape of a skullcap, coming in in her natural blond shade—an effect he'd noticed from their windows one day when she'd gone shopping. Now it seemed the place where the power of her will was concentrated, vulnerable. He placed his other hand over it, wondering how he'd let her go off on her own that day, and she said, "Thanks. Thanks. Oh, thank you a lot."

All he wanted was to have this over, so she would be herself again. But it was clear she couldn't admit that it was already beyond her control. He didn't even care about the child anymore, for her sake. The child seemed the cause, and he was well aware that women died in childbirth.

"Put your hand here!" she said, still fighting for air, and pulled it with both of hers over her stomach. Her skin was extraordinarily sensitive, delicate as a baby's neck over her entire body, but here so much more so it was nearly a profanation to touch, and now it rose tented over a hump like a stone. An elbowish bulge revolved under his palm from beneath, and he started to pull his hand away, then felt a sensation spread from there and concentrate in an unsettling tickling under his chin.

"Must be his *head*," she got out. "Currents from it."

What? He didn't dare ask. They were so convinced it was a boy they'd named it Nathaniel.

Then her eyelids, shiny and purplish, closed down, and her lashes went flickering over crescents of white. And then it was over, as if a wave had passed.

"All right," he said. "That's it. Get ready. We're going."

Once something like this gets off the tracks, he thought as he ran down the street, his throat still ticking, it keeps plowing into places that get worse. There wasn't a cab in sight in the early-morning quiet of the streets. There weren't any at any of the hotels he ran to. He took off for Fulton Street, and the rattle of being winded brought up a picture of her alone and fighting for breath, which sent a shock through him he couldn't contain, and then he was on the curb at Fulton, beside a chain-link fence clogged along its weedy bottom with paper and wrappings like leavings of the bulldozed lot it enclosed. He was aware now of the cold and of being in shirt-sleeves, probably the picture of a burnt-out derelict suffering his ultimate vision of absolute destruction—the worst sort of prospect to pull over a cab at this hour—and he couldn't keep from jumping off the curb, and then wading out into the street, as if to bodily stop one. Finally, an old Checker swerved over, and he was in the back, spilling his situation to the driver, who seemed incredulous, already enmeshed in it all.

He was an older man, with twists of gray in his tangled curls, which he pulled at, wide-eyed, as if to pull them out, and his rumpled clothes were aromatic of the nervous hours, or days, spent in them. Charles directed him down the narrow streets to theirs, lined with cars on both sides under the slim oaks and maples (too early for the alternate-side-of-the-street parkers to have started their morning shuffle) and barely wide enough for the bulky Checker cab to squeeze its way down. Charles had hoped she would be outside their building, waiting, but she wasn't. "Here," he said, and hopped out before they were stopped. "I'll just be a second."

"Hey, you haven't paid—"

Which the door clopped off. But he was reminded to get money as he went up the steps to the vestibule in two bounds, and was inside. He'd forgotten his keys. He rang the buzzer. No response. Then he remembered their signal and repeated it several times. There was another mind-dimming shock he couldn't contain, and then the lock went into its rattly vibrations, and he took the steps in leaps and bounds around on their landing to see the door ajar. He hit it with his shoulder and felt it thud against something inside. Her tennis shoes. Their soles were facing him, their laces loose, and she was on her elbows and knees, her head down, hair splashed over the carpet, her spilled makeup and compact beside her, its mirror shining up at him, rocking on her haunches and crying, "*Ahh!* Oh, ggaaah!"

He tried to lift her up.

"No!" she screamed, then got control of her voice. "No, wait—*till* this is over. Can't *talk* when—"

He hurdled her and was in the spare room, which was to be the child's but wasn't fixed up yet—dammit!—and where a plain door was laid across stacked milk cases filled with ring binders and station logs. His desk. Under this he jerked open the drawer of a file and fumbled out his manila folder of cash, and noticed at a glance, as he stuffed the bills into his pocket, over two hundred dollars. He sprang into the bedroom to their closet and jerked on a suit jacket, coat hangers clashing, and with an emerging hand swept up the watery whiskey from the chair and knocked it back (seeing an image from somewhere of a well-dressed man down on his knees, head thrown back, draining a bubbling bottle)—a mistake. He would need every ounce of clearheadedness and nerve he could summon, the convulsion of his stomach suggested. And from the altered angle it took to drain the dregs his eyes rolled toward the bed: it was disordered, gray with damp over one half, and across its center were streaks of blood.

She was at the table, her hands pressed on its top, leaning so far forward her hair hid her face in a whitish cloud. Her lime dress looked stained. He put his hands around her from behind.

"Do you think you should wear this?"

"It was all I could do to get it on and it's all I've got on and I mean *all!*"

He went down on his knees and started tying her shoes from behind and realized what a blur his haste had built to, and forced himself to slow down by watching his trembling hands attempt this simple task, with its folding intricacy and—

"Oh, this is absurd!" she cried, identifying for him the feathery ascension troubling his throat, and then they were gripping one another for support at the laughter that broke from them in diabolical barks.

•

The cab was gone. No. The man had parked at the hydrant a few buildings down. Charles helped her into the back with the premonition that they'd never make it, and felt this undercut by the realization that the cab needed new shocks. They pulled away, and she closed her eyes against the lurching and uncushioned impacts. Her mouth drew down at its corners. He put an arm around her but felt at such a distance he wanted to lift her into his lap.

"Move over," she said, and as he slid to the other side she lay down, dropping her head into his lap so hard it hurt, as though she'd read his thought at least in part. He drew away filaments of hair caught in her eyelashes and stuck to her lips, and smoothed them back. Her forehead, with bits of perspiration glittering in its pores, was as icy as her hands, and as the cab yawed around a corner and she groaned, he yelled, "Can't you speed it up?"

"Who'll pay the tickets?"

"I will."

There was a surge of acceleration, and then the purling of the bridge's grid beneath their adhering tires, and he experienced their rising suspension over water as a chasm opening under him, seeing the idiot uprights of gray-black stone ahead, with their paired, churchlike arches, apparently in the process of sinking, both still to be passed through, while the swoop and stutterings of the cables out the windows were like projections of his nerves in strumming onslaughts across the city below. Then he pictured his keys on the grain of the table, next to her outspread hands, forgotten again, and felt his focus narrow in on them as on a vision: he had held the keys that would have opened up an easy passage for her through this, and had let them slip. Every lie he'd told and every person he'd hurt had led to this, he saw, and started pulling at his hair, like the driver, as if to tear his thoughts loose from the tangle this implied.

"Take it easy," she said, and smiled crosswise below. "It'll be all right. Can you move over more?"

"I'm against the side."

This time she chewed at her lips in her attempt not to cry out, as her body went into its arch, sending her darkening crown in a crush against his privates, like an assault on the cause. Then she raised her knees, gripped them, and pressed down on him with her entire force. "Ow!" he cried as they slid underneath a red light somewhere and he had to grapple with her and an armrest to keep them from striking the seat ahead. There were cars with people in them on all sides and horns were going off.

A man at a wheel an arm's length away, out her window, looked over and did a take, eyes widening, and Charles wished he had a pistol to blow the pervert away, for taking advantage of her in her helplessness. He gave the fellow the finger as they squalled off, and then reached up and dropped a twenty-dollar bill on the driver's seat.

•

Inside the emergency entrance, he was told he'd have to check her in before they could go up to the maternity ward. "But she's fainting!" he said, because she appeared to be. He had to support her; her legs were giving way. The nurse was young, with blond hair up in a French roll—exactly as Katherine wore hers whenever they went out, to look older—and now she touched an arranging hand to some wisps at her neck at his attention. She'd been summoned by phone and had appeared pushing a wheel-chair. "I'm sorry," she said, and looked appealing and flustered. "It's procedure here." But Katherine grew worse, so that he had to lock his arms above her breasts to hold her up, and the nurse said, "All right, I'll take her up and go ahead and prep her, if you'll admit her right away. Then come right up with her papers. Okay?"

The procedure took a half hour, carrying him to the opposite end of the building, where he had to fill in a four-page form in the forgotten cramp of a student's writing chair. A woman behind a counter, at a teller's window he was directed to, wondered if it could be true that they actually didn't have hospitalization insurance. "We pay for everything by bank draft or cash," he said, and pulled out what he had in his pocket.

"Oh," she said, and stared at the bills as if in distaste, while covertly trying to tally them, it seemed. Then she paged through a floppy book of computer printouts, turned her back and made a phone call, and finally said, "We require a three-hundred-dollar deposit for maternity."

He counted out a hundred and fifty and said he'd bring the rest later.

"We'll have to have it before three this afternoon."

"What will you do if you don't?" he asked. "Kick her out?"

It took him some time to get to the seventh floor and find the correct "suite." A graying nurse in half-glasses, at a desk inside the swinging doors, accepted the papers and said he'd have to wait. Katherine was being prepped, she said—whatever that was. He felt a cold caul of air-conditioning over his scalp; a fluorescent-lit anteroom swung off behind the nurse in lines that verged on circularity, with doors leading off it all around, as in a maze. A huge column at its center was encircled by a desk partitioned into pie shapes with slabs of glass. Nobody was at the desk. Heads of bolts showed in uprights and ceiling beams and in the metal panels of the walls, as if he were in the interior of a ship, and horizontal strips of chromium reflected the unsettling curves of the place upon itself.

A stretcher banged through a pair of metal doors and went wheeling along the opposite wall, the young blond nurse pushing, and he saw by the swinging drape of hair and profile that the sheet-covered figure on it was Katherine. The nurse at the desk cried "Sir, *sir*," as he took off, but the blond one beckoned. An overweight Latin attendant in a white suit who had come through the doors behind the nurse and was forced by her pace into a tripping step that had him out of breath, while a stethoscope jogged in wild loops from one ear, gave Charles an okay sign, so he joined the entourage as it went banging through a single door.

Into a tiny room, a cubicle really, hardly large enough

for them all and the stretcher, on the other side of an elevated bed, which had bars up on both sides—the whole place also fashioned of metal, trimmed with the same chromium, like a miniature hold within the ship; or, worse, like a quadrant at the outer perimeter of a centrifuge just starting to spin. Because now Katherine rose as if in protest, white as the smock she had on, like a quadrant at the outer perimeter of a centrifuge just the sheet flying up. Bars on her side of the bed banged down, and he reached across as if to pull her up from drowning but missed her grasping hand. She was reaching back at the attendant, who now had her under the arms, so that his big belly pressed her head forward, forcing a cry from her cramped throat.

"Hey!" Charles yelled. "What the hell—"

"*Please*, sir," the blonde said. "Or you'll have to leave. You may help with her feet, if you would."

He leaped around and took Katherine's ankles while the nurse, placing a hand below his shoulder blade, passed with a taut swish across his backside, and eased away the attendant, who acted so inept he must have been new. The fellow gestured apologetically at Charles and gave a dog's overacted gape of shame. Then sudden sweat seemed to strip his face to its essence, grainy fat, and ran in streaks around his eyebrows, dripping from them and the manicured band of his mustache. They got Katherine on the bed and Charles saw indentations left by his grip in her ankles. He hurried around to the other side, to be out of the way of the attendant, and reached over the bars and took Katherine's hand, and in the light from a window above he saw her closed eyes pouring tears.

"Where's Harner?" he asked, with a fear that collapsed his voice into breathlessness.

"He should be here any minute." The blonde. "He was almost in from the Hamptons when he responded to his beeper. They're vacationing there." An intimacy had been touched on; her eyes widened, then she blinked this away.

"We're paging him right now. Dr. Ramirez is our resident on duty. He'll fill in till then." She wheeled the stretcher out.

P. Ramirez, M.D., Charles saw on the plastic clip above the stethoscope pocket of the "attendant." The man now drew the sheet down from Katherine and then pulled up her smock, jerking at it, and Charles was shocked to see the clenched bulge slide across her shining abdomen. Then he realized she was shaved clean. He draped her there with the sheet and discovered himself caught in a kind of contest with the resident, who was trying with his stethoscope to keep up with the strumming sidewise roll of the bulge. The man's eyes bugged. He pressed his hearing piece so hard it became buried and left little red hoops, and Charles, as if from a deafening distance, watched her arch against it and cry out and saw the exposed swath of her as this man must, as meat.

The bulge revolved in reverse, and now a three-way struggle began as she pushed at the resident's hands, one of which Charles was trying to restrain while the other dug into the scoop of her hip as the man leaned close to listen. She cried and coughed to get her breath, and her lips, usually so blood-infused they didn't need makeup, blued, and then she went limp and her eyes rolled up.

"Holy God, she's passed out!" Charles cried. "Watch it!"

The man swung to the head of the bed and fumbled at the wall with equipment there, his hands shaking, got loose an oxygen mask and set it over her face, the strap awry and in the way, and then swung back and fiddled with some knobs. There was a hiss and he picked up the mask and listened to it, shook it, and then sniffed it. "Hole dis," he said, setting it over her face in the same way, and Charles lifted the strap free, onto her hair, and pressed the mask in place. "Say 'Breeze deep,'" Ramirez said.

"Kath, please, breathe."

An outside force seemed to seize her ribs and pull them up in shuddering bands, and he saw water pool over her lashes as her eyes squeezed. "Ahhhh!" she cried, so loud he had to gasp at the noise. "Hurts me!"

"Breeze deep," the man commanded, and then, beginning to pant himself, pointed and said to Charles, "You. Tell hor." And in quick squeaking strides he was out the door. In a frantic scrambling to reconstruct the moment, in order to make sense of it, Charles realized the man had pointed not at him but at a sign before he'd left: NO SMOKING. Did the fellow think they would here? Now? With what was in the balance?

She was awake and trying to focus on him. She shook her head and flung the water in her eye sockets free. "Oh, hurts," she said, under the mask, and her voice came to him as over the telephone, distantly metallic, with most of its overtones abstracted into a nasal, girlish version of her—a child with a cold. She took his hand that held the mask.

"Don't leave me," she said, in the same tinny girlishness, which he heard as through a disk at his ear.

"Don't worry, I won't."

"What happened?"

"You needed air."

"Am I in delivery now?"

"No."

"Everything exploded in slow motion, all blue. The Battle of Borodino."

The window above, oblong and blank, appeared to

pulse, and he saw through to the moment she meant: choreographed columns of uniformed men going down to death through billowing smoke. Then Ramirez walked in with a thing like a trike horn strapped to his forehead, with the blond nurse at his back, her face set, carrying something like ice tongs, as if to protect him. On their side of the bed they lifted the smock Charles had drawn back down, the nurse more sensitive in her attuning to abasement, and used the tongs, or calipers, to take a measurement, then covered Katherine except for the active bulge. Ramirez inserted listening tubes into his ears and bent down to force the trike horn into the now relaxing mass. Katherine pushed the thing away. "Not that," she said under the mask in her tiny voice. "Hurts!"

The man's shoulders went up and his hands out as if to say, "What can you do?" to the nurse, whose face had turned the naked red of a blonde. She slipped on her own stethoscope and moved it over the area of the bulge with a cold agility. "Try here," she said, and placed two fingers flat. Then she gripped the horn and guided it as the resident hunched over with his eyes rolled up in the swarthy polish of his face. He listened, and when she let go he shoved the thing so deep that Katherine began to kick and arch, the sheet flapping, and again was unconscious, in spite of the mask.

"Dammit!" Charles said, grabbing the horn and lifting the man upright with it. "Stop that crap!"

All three of them stilled, frozen in confrontation, and then as Charles bent to get the mask back in place he heard in his ears what he thought was his heartbeat, but it was footsteps, and Harner came through the door. "What?" he said, and stopped, startled, studying them with birdlike concern, in a trim tan summer suit, with a blush reddening his wrinkled head, as if locked in a conflict to establish his control. "What the—" This came out half-cocked. "What's going on here? Answer me at once."

"She's ten *sahn*-timeters dilated, Doctor," the nurse said, all professional, as if to obscure some complication with jargon.

"What!" he said. "Good God, why didn't somebody give me an idea of the problem?"

The blonde let this pass and in a swoop got the mask from Charles and over Katherine's blue-spotted face. Harner pointed a finger, surprisingly small and delicate, at Charles's forehead, only inches away in the cramped room, and said, "What the hell is *he* doing here?"

"But you said I—"

"And where's his sterile gown and cap, for God's sake?" Harner asked the nurse, ignoring Charles, so that the *he* stung worse.

"Katherine specifically asked me—"

"This is an emergency. Get out!"

"But my wife asked me not to—"

"Get out! Do you understand English? Get the hell out!"

Charles turned, nearly colliding in the doorway with the resident, who apparently felt Harner meant him. In the anteroom Charles found himself fighting an anger so fierce it seemed brighter than the fluorescent tubes flashing overhead as he walked, as in the aftermath of a stunning concussion in football, when criticism from a coach, as much as the injury, could throw his body off balance. The nurse at the desk smiled as if she'd overheard the scene, and said, "Why don't you wait in the lounge, down the hall to your left?" And then plucked at his coat sleeve as he passed, so he had to turn to her. "I could never see the sense of those gowns in the labor rooms anyway," she confided. "Since we go in in what we've been wearing all day. But that's what I was trying to tell you when you ran off. And then Dr. Harner—well, he can be so touchy."

She wrinkled her nose at him.

•

The lounge was lined with chairs upholstered in primary colors, stilled in a compression of sunlight. Windows went from ceiling to knee-level along the length of one wall. It was empty. To sit, to him, was to concede to the hierarchical unreality closing around Katherine, like the structure of the hospital itself, until it seemed she would disappear. So he went to the wall of plate glass and stood like a sentinel for her on the real world. His knees, at the level of the ledge below, had been magically unlocked, he felt, and would suddenly bend in the reverse direction. He was staring down at the river they'd crossed, in a muddied surge at this point against the city's sculpted edge, cut as fine as if by a razor. A growing sound like voices at the fringe of understanding was, he realized, from the traffic building into its morning patterns over the streets below—a tentative stir that reached him like the first billow of an unexpected, unpredictable wind.

The grayish cavern of a basement under construction—a further addition to the building—opened into the ground directly below, and he could make out reinforcing rods, like wires bent awry, rising out of the lines of future walls, until his exact place in relationship to them was brought home with such an impact everything in him blanked out except a central sexual core, growing in magnitude, so that he had to battle the perverse pull to throw himself down.

It was this silence. The still sheen of the glass with bands of gold sun resting in its thickness— He felt a spraylike dispersion within him, which seemed to spill outside his boundaries through the window, hesitating in the air beyond, and then he was blinking back tears as he tried to remember how it was that Pierre had—

He couldn't get his breath and felt afloat as he watched his own unfeeling hands slapping over his front for cigarettes. He finally got them out and lit one as if to anchor himself. Then he had to fight visions of the glitter and gore of an operating room where he had Harner strapped down and was hacking at him with every instrument he could get his hands on.

He had to talk to somebody.

He'd cut off his family, since none of them appeared to approve of Katherine to the degree he believed they ought to. What could his father or a brother say anyway if he called, not even knowing that she was pregnant? He'd talked to Katherine's father so little the man could hardly be considered an acquaintance. Maybe he could talk to Weston. Sure he could, certainly he could. He might even meet Weston in the halls; Weston taught here.

He caught a reflection coming toward him and turned. It was Harner, who halted at his look, taking on an air of also being afloat, in a ballooning green gown and a cap like a housepainter's cap but without the bill, which gave the grin he put on a sillier aspect. Harner came up and put a hand on his shoulder, and Charles felt a response there like the sparking at a battery's terminal; he didn't like to be touched.

"Say, I'm sorry," Harner said. "I guess I blew my top back there. Nobody likes to walk in on a situation like that."

Charles looked into his eyes and encountered only an evasive fear—as if Harner had had glimpses of his operating-room assault—and managed to say only "How is she?"

"Well, it was a precipitate delivery, a classic case of it."

"Is that bad?"

"It's not so common that it didn't have us thrown a bit, you'll have to admit that." He tried to smile, and Charles felt that they were high-school enemies who'd met on a street corner and decided to be civil, and with that illumination Harner's smile came clear; it was the slack-lipped grin that cowards get, of having secretly eaten something tasty, just before they're socked. "It's not from anything either of you might have done, but unfortunate coming this early in her final trimester. Also, she's pretty badly edematous."

"What's that?"

"Gathered fluid. The swelling you see in her extremities. I wish you had told me about that."

"I did, over the phone."

"Oh, I guess you did, yes," he said, and looked down to recover himself, then up with a professional stare. "I want to reassure you that as far as we can tell it's doubtful that anything you or she might have done yesterday or the day before could have caused this. Certainly nothing that happened a week or more ago. Rest your mind on that. These things happen."

He'd seen the bruises.

That wiggly smile appeared again, and he said, "We'll want to keep a close eye on her, though, after this, and next time I might recommend some conjugal restraint over her last trimester." His eyebrows bobbed. "In certain cases, that seems to trigger the contractions."

"Precipitate delivery?"

"Yes, it's precipitated by God knows what and comes

on like gangbusters. It takes a fraction of the time of usual labor and delivery, once it gets started, and there's no way of knowing what to expect. We'll have to watch that, too, the next time around."

"You mean Katherine—"

"Oh, she's great, you have a wonderful wife there! You're a lucky guy! She came through it like a pro, wide awake all the way. The sedative didn't even have time to take effect before it was over."

"It's over?"

"Well, yes—that is, the birth is, yes."

And now Charles had to wait while the enemy, who seemed to have been priming for this, underwent an alteration that appeared in his eyes, like awe, before disclosing his dirty secret. "You had a boy. We have one of our best pediatricians with him right now. There's no use falsely getting your hopes up. He's very small and weak, almost two months early, and this has been a terribly severe trauma for him. His respiratory system isn't responding as it should be. He's fighting for his life right now."

"What about an incubator, for God's sake!"

They both flinched at the tone.

"We're giving him oxygen. We've done all we can, actually, medically."

"I want to see my wife." Needlelike intrusions started stitching at the corners of his eyes.

"She'll be in the recovery room soon. There are a few more things we'd like to check out, and then I have to tidy her up a bit."

He put a hand on Charles again, this time over his flexed arm muscle, as if to intercept any violence, and wrinkled his nose (had the nurse talked to him?) and said, "There are some restaurants and some little"—he waved his hand at the window—"some little *places* across the street. Why don't you make it an hour, say."

This seemed a command.

"I'll wait right here."

But a few minutes later, when Harner came back and told him the child had died, he walked out.

•

The bartender was scattering violet sweeping compound over the floor of one of the little places that had recently opened. Charles took his bottle of beer to a table, to be alone, although nobody was present but the bartender. Low morning light came through the open door at an angle that didn't quite reach to his shoes. The sprinkled boards beneath gave off cold and damp. The door faced the river, with the ascending stories of the hospital between, and half of the pedestrians wore white, as if to claim their affinity with the constant newness of the business they hurried toward.

He was too terrified to feel remorse. He had sensed that this would happen and was sure that when it did he would be off at a distance, apart from her, the expendable party. No recourse. No help. He'd had complete freedom most of his life, he realized now, or he'd taken it, even after they were married, but this he wouldn't be free of. This was on him, and he didn't know how he'd ever get out from under it. He would take the responsibility for it upon himself. He'd tell her that.

There was no possibility of divorce now, not for him. He couldn't live with this if he didn't have her side of it, or her portion of the experience, under him in support. She'd done all she could, given the circumstances. He was lucky to have her, as Harner said, and lucky she was alive. From this moment, their relationship would have to be as open as that door. He'd tell her that, and how the thought had come to him, like further sunlight through the door, but first he had to ask her forgiveness. The way had to be cleared with that, or they couldn't take the first step to begin anew. He'd do what he could to exist from day to day after that, for her sake. No promises. No—

A raying silence, like the silence that invades a house in a driving rain, spread through his consciousness. He would not sit and imagine what it would have been like to have had a son.

The door darkened, and an elderly woman with a stocking cap pulled over her ears came rocking into the place, carrying a shopping bag in each hand. She sat at the table next to his, talking to herself as she sorted through her bags and smoothed scraps of paper from them on the table as if they were dollar bills. Under a sweater, under a number of open coats, she appeared flat-chested above her pot belly, and her wide face was kept active by her licking at and worrying a single lower tooth. He thought with an impact that set him back in his chair how his mother would be this age if she were living.

He'd had enough; this was over; he wanted off; and he was about to move from the pall of irritation the woman spread, when he heard "Could you get me one of those, sonny?"

He set his face toward the light, in case she was referring to him.

"Hey! Sonny, could you—"

"Aggie," the bartender said from behind. "Leave the kid alone."

Charles put down a dollar. "It's all right," he said.

"You know the house rules," the voice said. "Not unless she walks in with you. You know, Aggie."

"Get her one."

There was a silence of restructuring accommodation, as if they were contemplating the movielike beams within the broader band of light, with only the sound of traffic in its breezes of accompaniment outside and, as if in answer to that, the broom sweeping the floor behind. Then the woman's talk seemed to stir in a different direction. "You hurt?" she said. "It's my fault, it's all my fault. You think you're the only one who suffers? One-crack mind, one-crack mind. One of these days you're going to wake up with your voice changed and realize you was always queer."

Sensation gave like snowslides in him, and his joints ached from dread. There was something terribly wrong with him, he was convinced, that he kept attracting these grotesques. He must be more than monstrous himself (he had to fend off textbook images of abnormalities at birth), if he was already acclimated to this death, or acting as if he were. Because what had been disturbing him under everything else these past months was that he'd had an affair at the same time Katherine had had hers, as if they'd been signaling one another of their need to break free at the thought of being bound, and he felt he got what he deserved when she confessed. But then he'd feared, first, that the child wasn't his and, next, that it wouldn't live.

"Like you lost your best friend," the woman said, and he turned and found her eyes on him, gray-gold in the light. She sucked at the tooth awhile as if to extract its essence. "Don't let it get you down. They're always at you. They never let up. You got an ounce of sympathy your-self? You got sympathy with me?"

"Yes."

"Yeah, you say you do, but they all do." Customers had come in, and she threw her head back as if to indicate them, then called in a loud voice, "Ain't that right, Jack?"

"Sure, Aggie," the bartender said.

"'Sure, Aggie,' he says, like he's my echo. They don't let up no matter what. I said to him, 'You want a mother, a wife and kids, you want a young girlie type, or you want a queer?'"

"What are you after?" Charles asked.

She leaned toward him and smiled a sweet-old-lady's smile, pegged at its corner by the tooth, and said, "A nice big jug of rosé wine. Maybe a hunk of you, Butch."

He took two dollars and dropped them and the other over the papers in front of her on his way out, feeling mistily benevolent; she'd never know the state in him this had risen from. Then out in the sunlight, blinking as if stunned, he felt he'd been lanced through the place near his ribs where the talons curled. He couldn't tell Katherine he'd come here. Not while she'd lain over there alone. How could he have listened to Harner? And then he sensed something further hurrying close and heard in a whisper at his ear, *Murderer. You'll never quit paying for this.*

•

The gray-haired nurse stood up from her desk as he stepped through the swinging doors; she, too, had her duty to see to now. He'd decided to talk to Katherine, and let everything take its turn from her. The nurse gripped him by his coat sleeve and said, "This time we won't forget," and led him to a line of lockers behind a wall of the curving anteroom—dim atmosphere of high school and the stripped-down purity of physical sports, with their innocence of the actual world, he now knew, in their unvarying perimeters and established rules, not to mention the false assumption that they were training grounds for life. From a shelf over the lockers she got a gown and shook it so it unrolled, unraveling its billowy length, and then held it out for him, and he stepped into it, over his jacket and all. With a hand on him as if to hold him there, exhaling something minty, she came around and started tying it at his back, and in the starchy chill of its cloth drawing close he felt he'd entered the hospital at last, and the hospital held Katherine and their dead son.

He gulped at the grief that went down his throat like brine and saw sudden dark spots traveling over the front of the gown as though its substance were eroding. "I understand," the nurse said, and set one of the caps on his head, then rested her hands on his shoulders. "It's terrible to lose the first. God comfort you." She shook him.

He recovered, but in the anteroom, seeing Harner at the column encircled by the desk, in his suit and tie once more, motioning him over, he felt his anger and grief collide. "We have some forms we'd like you to sign," Harner said, and put on his slack-lipped grin. Two minutes alone with him, Charles thought, just two minutes.

"It's merely a formality," Harner said, and his eyes swerved at the freezing cry of a newborn. "Then you can see your wife."

In heavy type on the top sheet on the desk Charles saw *Death Certificate*. Farther down, written in: *respiratory failure*.

"Why should I sign it?" he asked. "I haven't seen him."

"Oh, not that," Harner said, and shuffled the papers until he came up with two others, one of which read *Waiver*.

Again Charles said, "I haven't seen him."

"Well, in effect what these say is there's been a birth, and then that you'll be making a gift of the case to the hospital. Our research is acknowledged across the United States, and this might be a way of helping out somebody in a similar situation. We would take care of all matters of disposal, so you wouldn't have to worry about that."

"It's no worry. I want to see him."

"I think perhaps it might be better if you didn't." That smile once more, which quivered now at its corners with Harner's authority.

And cut into Charles's own fears, so that he couldn't ask why it would be better if he didn't, while "disposal" brought to mind the whirring mechanism that can shake a whole sink. He pictured a miniature casket at the edge of an open grave, with Katherine down beside it, the air black around her, and wasn't sure he could take that. He was trapped. "I want to talk to Katherine first."

"I don't know if it's something she should have to handle now, seriously. Do you? I know it might feel like a tough decision, but it's pretty much routine, or procedure here, because of our research."

And then Charles saw, as down a corridor darker than the one where the lockers stood, a flaking fetus in a jar, on a set of shelves among hundreds of others, and heard the refrain from a folksinger's ballad, that for every child born another man must die. He felt an exchange of that sort, with deeper implications, taking place right now, while the tick and cluck and shuffle of doors and footsteps and equipment seemed to be those actual lives and deaths moving in and out in an endless passage. The only light of exit at the other end came shining from the promise of seeing Katherine.

He signed the papers.

Harner gave a nod, as if to confirm Charles in his manliness, and then led the way to one of the branches off the anteroom, down a hall, to a door. "She might be resting," he said in a rasping whisper, as if he'd injured his voice. "If she is, maybe you should let her. Just take a peek so you can say you were in. She's been terribly excited about this—maybe overly so. We'll give you five minutes, and then in a while get her to a room—you'll want a private one for her, I know—and you can spend as much time there with her as you like."

This place was still smaller, with monitoring equipment against one wall and only enough space to pass by the stretcher where it was parked. The blond nurse stood facing him, at its foot.

"Done," she whispered, her eyes enlarging on him, and then there was only the door at her back flapping in its frame at her retreat. A hypodermic syringe, with a final crystalline drop depending from its needle, lay on a stainless-steel tray on the stainless-steel counter supporting the equipment.

Katherine's hair, curled from exertion or moisture, hung less low from the stretcher, and she was moving a hand under the smock, testing her stomach. He stepped around to where she could see him, taking her free hand, and was confronted by a glossy incandescence in her eyes.

"It's so flat!" she exclaimed. "It's hard to believe it's so flat! That's me! I wish you could have been with me through it all. I was totally engulfed by it, by the birth—by him, I mean. I'm sorry I was so out of touch before. I got afraid. Once things were going all right, I kept saying, 'Nathaniel! Nathaniel! I'm here, I'm with you all the way!' I felt his head come out—it was wonderful!—and then I knew something was wrong. The rest was hardly there."

She looked away, toward the monitoring machines, and he knew he couldn't tell her what he had to until this, which must be the ecstasy of birth, had subsided. She turned back with the incandescence in her eyes at a further level. "Suddenly he was entirely himself and left such feeling with me. I'm the only one who understands it right now, but you will, you will! My only regret is how I failed you."

"You came through it like a pro, I heard."

"No, no, he's gone. I know. I lost him. They told me. He died."

"You haven't failed me, I'm the—"

"I've failed you. You wanted him so badly."

He realized now that he had. "You haven't failed me. It's my fault."

"I was afraid you'd say that. I knew you would. Don't, please, for me. Please. I wanted to see him, but Harner wouldn't let me. 'I guess he just couldn't wait,' he said. All I wanted to do was see him. It wouldn't have bothered me. If I could only have seen just his hands. But maybe it's better. Maybe I'd have nightmares. They rushed him away, and then I saw Harner and another doctor, across the room by the windows, working with him. Their backs were to me. I couldn't see him. The nurse was so great. She—"

"The blond one?" He wanted to get this all straight, as if for the terrible recompense to come.

"Yes, she was great! Back in the recovery room, well, here, I said, 'I just wanted to see him. I don't care how ugly he was.' And she said, 'There wasn't a thing wrong with him. He wasn't ugly. He was a beautiful baby. He was simply too tiny.' Can you imagine how intelligent he must have been to have done this?"

"What?" The talons in him flexed.

"He wanted to bring us closer together, and this was the only way. He knew that. He was so much like you, really—ready to give up everything to make things right."

"Kath."

"I'm in a different perspective. It's from the feeling he left. I know that time and events can't really destroy love. It's something you can't understand by reading about it. I had to learn that, and he knew it. We both had so much to learn from him!"

She laughed with an openness he seldom heard in her, and he began to shrink from this and her growing vision of the event. He was diminishing by degrees, he felt, until he had to take hold of the stretcher at her head to keep himself from being drawn into her, consumed. Then she pulled him down to her and kissed him on the mouth, and whispered with the intimacy of their bed, "No doubt about it. We've had our first child."

⋅

Then the perineal bottle in the bathroom of their apartment, in the stilled and grayish light through frosted glass; the green dress she never wore again, in shadow at the back of their closet; the barrenness of her secretary, as if she'd cleared it of even the essentials; the crescent-shaped planter of flowers he'd brought to her room in the hospital, with an eighteenth-century figurine in brown knee breeches and a long yellow coat with lace cuffs and lace froth at the collar, fixed in a contemplative pose, standing among the blossoms, which the florist at the last moment had set in place, and which Charles was unable to look at from the first without *Nathaniel* registering in him, followed by a tickling trill down his throat; the few articles they'd got for the child, chiefly a red-and-blue banner imprinted with stylized Buckingham Palace Guards, which followed them through every move (like the figurine he kept gluing and regluing until one day it was gone, with no explanation from her) and would suddenly appear out of a box, like another presence, striking them speechless; her feeling of betrayal that he'd signed the body away without telling her, and her depression that remained so long it seemed it would never leave, and when it did it would reappear without warning and set up further silences within her, making her mistrust her ability to work as she once had; his anger at Harner and the hospital, which kept revolving in him and reached its peak in the fall, so that more than once he started toward a lawyer to sue, but found himself foiled each time as if by the season, his favorite, in a release of grief and melancholy—for he was never able to bear the loss with equanimity, or with her wholly physical sense of loss.

It wasn't until after they'd had not only a second child but a third, and then a fourth, graced by this heritage, and he was leaning under the hood of a pickup on a fall afternoon with gold-red trees around awash in a wind and a son underfoot, running off with his tools, that he finally coughed out, "Good God, forgive me." And felt freed into forgiveness, for himself, first, then for her, the rest falling into place—for her because she'd never explained her experience during the birth and what she'd learned from it, as she'd said she would. But he knew now that the child had always been with him, at the edges of his mind and in his thoughts, as much as any of their living children (more, he thought, as he set aside the wrench in his hand and watched the tops of the trees above him springing in the wind), and he began then to look out on those children, on this boy with his hair going back in the wind, and on Katherine and on others, with less darkness in his eyes: that is, he began at last to be able to begin again to see.

A BRIEF FALL

One world that's mine alone to live with is this one, Katherine thought, and stepped into the alcove off the bedroom, where loose parquets clattered underfoot with a sound like dinner plates—this otherworld of waiting, this *time*. She sat on the curved-leg settee that had replaced the steamer trunk and heard the wiry activity of springs in the settee's seat with the consolation of overhearing a familiar voice. The settee was covered with an antique Turkish rug, worn to the texture of twine at its center, and by rubbing her fingers over the worst of the wear in it and thinking of the evening when Charles had finagled for the rug for her in a shop whose whole front opened onto the sidewalk like a warehouse, she kept from reaching for the phone. She would give him another hour (she glanced at the clock on her secretary without taking in the time) and then begin again her round of calls to their psychiatrist, the police stations, the— She didn't want to think about it.

She turned to the window. It was almost dark. The branches of the tree outside, next to the streetlamp which had begun its twilight blinking, were still orangy in the light, and across the street the line of sun was moving up the breast of the concrete unicorn, rampant, with a foreleg hooked over a coat of arms that rose above the cornice on the building opposite. When the last of the sun lifted from the unicorn's spiraled horn, it would be six. Forty-some hours since she had seen Charles, or heard from him. On the windowsill were names and telephone numbers he had printed in his geometrical backslant, and at the edge of them she saw "1965, 66, 67"—the years of their marriage. There was a tumbling sensation under her heart, followed by a sharp knock near her pelvis, and she put a hand there.

Could you feel a child move in the fourth month?

When Charles didn't return after the first night, she felt it would be perilous to hope to hear from him, because of how it would affect her if she didn't, but decided to hope for twenty-four hours. She had extended that.

The tree had shed its leaves almost overnight, from the way they lay in a heaped circle on the sidewalk beneath it. The day was that windless. A Japanese painter, in his ground-level studio apartment below the unicorn, seated a woman at a white table behind his windows and poured two glasses of wine, laughing. On the table-desk at the side of his studio, where he usually sat under a blaze of adjustable drafting lamps and worked at one of the butterflies that were his specialty, pots and vessels of food stood ready.

There was nobody on the street, although it was Saturday night. Everybody must have entertained on Thanksgiving, two days ago, as she had—except for those two. Bowls of food were steaming on the white table between them, and Katherine felt hunger as she hadn't since she was a child—a compact pain closing inside a larger pain as diffuse as loss. You should blend up some tiger's milk, she said to herself—a terrible mixture of brewer's yeast and milk and molasses she'd begun to drink. At first she couldn't keep it down, and in the morning it brought on morning sickness, which she hadn't been bothered by until this regimen: tiger's milk five times a day. It rested in her stomach like a solid, as if reassuming the shape of the drinking glass, abrading her insides. If she weren't considering the health of the child, she couldn't take it. Already, it was necessary to regulate her weight; she felt blimplike, overflowing her outlines, a mushy lay.

She'd last seen Charles in the East Village. Two friends from school had called the week before, to let her know they were in the city, and she had invited them over for Thanksgiving, then was afraid Charles wouldn't approve; he avoided company, lately. But he seemed to enjoy the evening, and then insisted they take her friends home in a cab, mumbling in the nearly incoherent manner he'd adopted the past month. He'd been too precise for her taste in almost everything before, as in the case of the neighbors overhead, two middle-aged women he called the Gay Divers, a pair so well matched you thought of fate, seeing them together—one demure and airily femi-nine, the other hefty and squarish, with dark hair cut in a DA, outfitted in black slacks and a leather jacket. She wore a pair of clogs that Charles claimed she weighted like the boots of a sea diver. If he brought work back to the apartment, it seemed the woman began to pace at about the moment he opened his briefcase, until one night he shouted at the ceiling, "I wouldn't mind her wearing brick sandals! Or whatever those are! If she didn't have to march around in them for an hour to turn Cutie on!"

There was sudden silence; they hadn't heard the pacing since. But whenever Katherine encountered the women in the vestibule, the fey one blushed and glanced down and the other huffed at her in haughty admonition, and then stomped and scraped her feet, as if to say the clogs still worked, and she'd like to have Katherine under them.

Katherine and her classmates, Gail and Joyce, had attended a finishing school that was church-affiliated and Pollyannaic, though slyly socially attuned, and Gail and Joyce seemed so far behind even the school's nineteenth-century atmosphere that they had paired up to help each other through. They and Katherine were always reading and discussing books on art, which was their bond. Gail and Joyce were younger than she was, in their early twenties now, and when Charles heard about their unworldliness, and understood that they were living in the area of the Village where he'd once lived, he looked concerned. "The worst street," he said. "Speed alley."

"He hasn't been revealing his feelings," their psychiatrist, Stevens, recently said. "Or anyway, not after the initial excitement at your pregnancy." They had started seeing Stevens a year ago, singly and together, after Charles became so despondent he spent days in silence, and one night said from the edge of their bed, where he sat with his head in his hands, "Any couple that has to contemplate its own sanity isn't fit to live with."

Last week, when she saw Stevens alone, he had said, "He's kept the channels of communication closed, I feel, because of the child. Look at his history, even previous to you; I mean, his mother. If you don't lose this child, like your first, he'll lose you—or so part of him probably goes. He might be afraid it's some sort of monster that will expose him." She understood that Stevens was suggesting this, perhaps, for her sake, since it was her own worst fear, although she'd never mentioned it. Stevens believed that most psychiatrists squandered too much time listening, and so was confrontational. He was slight, like Charles, with a blurry mustache that concealed his mouth, and he kept swiveling in his chair as if inching closer to the area in you he was after, then leaped: "For the last couple of years, Charles has been running on guilt. Both of you have to come to grips with that. Everything in his life—you, your place, his pay—is predicated on a kind of joke, in his eyes. The child will expose that."

But she knew that something other was troubling Charles—from the way he carried himself, as if unwell. With a problem that didn't take on such physical characteristics, she might question her ability to gauge the depth and reality of it, but with this she knew. He acted afraid of her, and since of course she couldn't ask if he was, his fear seemed to spread in him like a form of the flu. From the time they'd started seeing Stevens, Charles had been voluble about his feelings and so inquisitive about hers—"To keep in touch," he would say—that he could be a pest if they spent the day together, and for a while she had dreaded weekends. But at the same time he became outgoing, though sometimes in an antic way, and they were seldom home three nights a week.

The McCarthys, the couple upstairs (down the hall from the women), were the closest to friends of any couple they knew. McCarthy and Charles now worked at the same advertising agency, due to McCarthy's deflected intentions, and McCarthy had recently unearthed a retiring colleague who had been a Whiz Kid on one of those radio shows that Katherine had never been much interested in but that her father had; the fellow was now a feuilletonist for a fashionable city magazine, while managing to hold down his copywriting job. He had sold a collection of pieces to a publisher, and now McCarthy and others at the agency believed they could be "writers"—the secret wish of every copywriter, Charles claimed. "They read their copy to one another, and their wives, too, I'm sure, as if they've just received the Yale Younger Poets award." Charles had once believed that he would receive a Tony for his work on Broadway, but so far had only had comic bit parts at La Mama.

Lately, he would bury himself in a book, usually with a drink at hand, and resented being interrupted, even to eat. If she asked if he minded going for a walk, simply to the promenade, a put-upon look would appear on his face until she mentioned exercise; that usually reached him—his vanity. He would push up from his chair, and out in the street would stride at her side in a dutiful way, sometimes moving off ahead, unconscious of her, his hands in his pockets, and then back here would drop into his chair and pick up the book again. He even lost interest in the child; at first, he'd followed its development in a photographic book called *The First Nine Months of Life*, which she'd bought. She was obsessive about keeping up on every detail of what was taking place inside her, and Charles encouraged this.

"Sure, get it," he would say about a book she might mention. "It sounds right for you." He bought them a membership in the local health club, so she could get the exercise she had to have to remain healthy through this pregnancy, but he went only once. "Who wants to sit in steam and cough their lungs out?" he said. She went swimming every afternoon for two hours, or a hundred laps, besides twenty minutes of treading water, until this holiday. One night when his despondency seemed to have returned, as he was paging through *The First Nine Months of Life*, he pointed to the umbilical cord in the final picture, and said, "This looks big enough to skip rope with, right?"

That was his last on the child.

"I'm going out to get the *Times*," he would say now, in a kind of absentminded commentary on the mundane. Or, "I'm going to bed." Or, "I broke this glass. I didn't throw it. It fell out of my hands—shaking from Stevens's drugs. I'm sweeping it up." Or, "I just finished this book."

"Did you like it?"

"Sort of."

"What was it about?"

"A triangle."

"You mean, three people?" She had recently been wondering how they could ever handle another person in the apartment. "You mean, some sort of sexual involvement? What happened?"

"You read it. I have to go to bed."

She preferred his silence, or even the talkative phase of his "keeping in touch," to this recent monosyllabic commentary, as if he were intending to reduce their life—which before, for all its twists and unhappy contours, had at least been full—to a single flat surface. He had been getting away by using the McCarthys' apartment, while the McCarthys were in New Hampshire, where McCarthy had gone to write a book. Charles was supposedly sitting their apartment, and he had intended to use it for work, but mostly went there to be alone.

On Friday she checked the apartment twice, and then again today, even though Charles didn't have his keys, and she might go up now if it weren't for the look of it. McCarthy's wife was waiflike, thin and anxious, with eyes so dark she appeared to be drawing everything into their depths—her entire being bent on McCarthy's success—and with her away the apartment felt stripped. There was a typewriter and a punched-open can of Bloody Mary mix on McCarthy's empty desk. The mix was a product Charles was writing copy for, and there were attempts to describe it on a sheet of paper, splattered with the mix, wound tight around the typewriter platen. She'd pulled open a drawer of the desk on a sloshing half bottle of gin, and that was enough for her.

But on Thanksgiving Charles surfaced as if from sleep, engaged. Her friends had changed. Gail, who once had short dark hair and used to hide behind horn-rimmed glasses, a recluse who sucked on a blanket or sat with her nose in a book, was now a long-haired blonde. She kept blinking against a pair of contacts that produced a startled expression, while she gave an ecstatic but disjointed account of her first trip on acid, a week before. "The walls were this needlework I'd seen my grandma doing when I was about eight, see . . ."

And Joyce, who'd been as willowy as Gail now was, and for all her provincialisms had had the blustery vivacity of a cheerleader—indeed, she'd been a cheerleader one season at school—and had served as the captain of their field-hockey team the last year Katherine was on it, had gained thirty pounds. She was glum and blasé but full of a restless momentum, and became so openly bored with Gail's recounting of her "trip" that she got up from the table and started pacing around the room with her shirttails hanging out of shorts that looked like boxing trunks (at this season, for dinner!), poking into things and carrying around a half-quart can of beer from the six-pack she'd brought to keep herself supplied.

It was inconceivable to Katherine that the three of them had attended the same school, and she was sure that Gail and Joyce (who wouldn't accept the glass offered for her beer) were trying to provoke her. When Joyce tasted the espresso Katherine had brewed to cap the meal, she cried, "Hey, what are you trying to do, Petey,"—this was her school name—"*asphyxiate* us with this stuff!" Then Joyce added, out of nowhere, "We've kicked the parents. Working for Welfare"—they both had jobs with the Welfare Department—"is a crap job in this crap city, but it pays the rent."

Joyce's pacing kept returning her to their Victorian sideboard of oak, which she examined with her back to them. Its drawer pulls were carved gargoyles, each with a separate expression, and its upper shelf was supported by a pair of griffins two feet tall, apocalyptically equipped with lions' paws and heads, dragons' tails (curled thickly under them), and raised wings with feathers carved in detail. It seemed to interest Joyce as much as it did Phil, the owner of the building, who occupied the first floor and was in the fabric end of interior decorating; Phil brought over a friend who dealt in antiques, and on sight the man had offered them three times the price Charles had paid for the piece merely for the griffins and their shelf—for a client, the man had said, for a bar. Charles had closed his eyes and smiled, as he did when he was particularly pleased, and had shaken his head; he'd found this for her.

Below the shelf he'd fixed a rod and hung velvet curtains, rigged with a miniature pull, which opened onto patterned glass he'd fitted in place—so wonderful with his hands, always busy fixing, adding, repairing. He planned to remake their apartment into the perfect frame for their lives, he had said, a variation on the maxim of Erikson, Charles's mentor since college, who had written in one of his essays on the theory of scene design, "How can you ever hope to even suggest reality unless you incorporate a frame?" Charles had always pictured Erikson as manager of his career.

Joyce began looking through the liquor bottles and glasses on the sideboard (or bar, as they called it, after the dealer's visit), her back to them, and then lifted up a hank of her chopped-off hair and said, as if addressing a griffin, "I'm my own barber now. Nice, huh?" It was so short you could see her neck, and her neck was no longer attractive, with her added weight—no more than the rest of her, from the rear, in her boxing shorts and sweat socks. Then she turned and said, "Hey, Petey, do you or your beau here know where we can pick up some of that good old speed?"

She was purposely speaking like a hick, and they ignored her question, although Charles still had contacts in the Village he would visit when there was a deadline for copy he couldn't otherwise face.

"Then what's this?" Joyce said, coming down on the last word with a false awed gaucherie, her eyes wide. She was pointing. "Anything for a buzz."

"Aquavit," Charles said, and was at her side with one of their expensive Finnish glasses out, as if by prestidigitation, and already half filled. He'd always handled these matters with the offhand ease of a butler more aristocratic than those he served. Erikson called him "Mr. Easy Street," after this trait that seemed inborn in him but certainly wasn't in his upbringing; his people were teachers and laborers and farmers, which had set up affinities between her and Charles when they met; her father and uncle were dairy farmers, although her father had later gone into industrial manufacturing—a *nouveau riche* entrepreneur. Charles then poured himself some aquavit, clinked glasses with Joyce, and said, "Skoal!"

Oh, no! Katherine nearly cried aloud, and when she saw him spin toward their small marble fireplace, which he'd got going tonight for the first time this year, she closed her eyes. She heard the glass shatter and pieces fall in a delicate splash to the hearth.

"Hey, Jeez," Gail said.

"What the hell," Joyce said, and knocked back her drink and then, with the mannish overhand swing that had gotten her into trouble with her hockey stick, she sent the glass bouncing off the fire screen to shatter on the hearth. "What the hell," she said again, softly, as if taking in their place for the first time. "Rome."

Katherine had heard the first glass go months back and had run from the bedroom to find Charles sitting in front of the dead fireplace, in darkness (except for the purple-green highlights from the streetlamp), in the high-backed Spanish chair whose seat he had upholstered in orange leather; its back, a plank with geometrics carved into it, rose above his head, while his shoulders on either side appeared to form the surface that he leaned against, because they didn't seem his shoulders. It was his shoulders she'd loved from the first—substantial, with his arm muscles rolling out from them, and set toward the world with that ease of a self-assured servant. They were off kilter now, and she saw that his head, at the center of the chair's back, was bowed to his chest. She was afraid to go a step farther.

·

The settee springs did a reversal of their wiry agitation as she went to the bed and lay down on her side, her hands between her legs, and closed her eyes, in order to picture Charles beside her. His shoulders were what marked him as Mr. Easy Street. He could wend his way through a cocktail party or crowded gallery with mere inclinations of them, and they would swing in the direction of any appeal (difficult to keep up with, unless she had a hand on him) with the frontal attention he gave everyone. What a gift to have had those shoulders here in bed!

The force of them was an affront to her when they met, and for months she hadn't spoken to him, though he wasn't offended by this. He was known at their university for his theater roles, as if he were a Broadway star, and she was having trouble then with her painting; she wondered if she should view each canvas not only as it occupied the present, from every perspective, but as future eyes might see it, too, and was afraid to ask her classmates if they looked on their own work in this way, when they stepped back from it, since none of them mentioned such a thing. She felt a dislocation, with the future dropped between her and the canvas, that brought the immediacy of its lines to a full stop, and this was probably what inhibited her painting.

It was inhibited, or tended to be, with an amateurish taint at the edges that revealed her lack of will to push the composition entirely open, finally, or seal it off for good. She was a skilled draftsman, and liked the correct heft and shine she was able to bring to appliances and tools; she'd managed to avoid the hugeness and showy splash of the mathematical shapes and neo-cartooning that were the vogue, and she might be a reasonably good graphic designer, she thought, but Charles encouraged her to fight her inhibition and continue painting. "It's in you," he said. "You have to believe that. If you don't, nobody will. Please keep at it."

He'd been hired for his present job by an executive filling in for a friend on the day when Charles stopped by the agency, at McCarthy's urging. "We need a good voice for a spot I've done," he said. Charles had been getting regular work as a voice-over, while he looked for acting jobs, and he had along his portfolio and a folder of letters of recommendation. The man looked only at the letters, which spoke in general terms of Charles's "gifts," and apparently assumed he was interested in a copywriting job the agency was trying to fill. He hired Charles on the spot. It was Erikson's letter that had done it; he had recently published a book, the Museum of Modern Art was doing a retrospective of his scene designs that spring, and his name or pictures of him seemed to be in every publication in the city you picked up.

Erikson was the new Granville-Barker, it was said—that multi-talented—with a string of classical productions reaching back to the thirties, his books on scene design, plus a set of commentaries he'd started to issue on the "realism" of Shakespeare. These were as remarked upon for their literary touch as their erudition, although it was the elegance of his simple stage sets that had done the most to earn him his name. He'd started as a commercial artist, and thought it wouldn't hurt Charles to try his hand at copywriting; the job was a sure means of support, as acting was not, Erikson said. He was sure that Charles's time would come, and meanwhile it wasn't shameful to take a job, which didn't have to be viewed as a compromise, he said, as long as Charles kept his humor about it.

Was Charles hurt by all this? Surely. He had met Erikson when he was eighteen, new at the university, and Erikson had arrived to give a lecture for the Theater Department. Erikson had walked through the theater classrooms and studios on a hurried tour, and hadn't taken in much, it was felt, but a few weeks later Charles received a long cardboard tube in the mail, and inside was a rolled sheet of rice paper on which Erikson, in his distinctive style, had sketched Charles as he had sat in a chair doing a reading from *Henry V*, and in the corner where you might expect the artist's signature, Erikson had written, "Charles, regal even in repose." On the back was Erikson's telephone number, and below, "When you come to the city, give me a call."

"I can't explain how much that meant to me," Charles told her when they met. "I'd vaguely thought of maybe ending up in New York someday, *maybe*, but with that my fate was sealed." Charles had had the sketch framed and now it hung on the wall at the foot of their bed, the first thing he saw when he woke. She took a quick look over her shoulder, to reassure herself; it was there.

Erikson had never found the right role for Charles in any of the productions he'd staged since—actually only two; Charles was too young or too short or not a recognizable enough entity to risk with a lead, so he'd earned his way as a voice-over, and with her work, as a photographer's model, it was enough. When the executive hired him, Charles was pleased to have his real talent, as he saw it, untouched, and they were able to keep the apartment, which had become a problem. Charles didn't want her to work once she was pregnant; she was sure that was why he kept insisting that she paint.

If she could have let those glasses, which seemed the beginning of their grief, go! After Charles broke the first one (absently, she believed), he and McCarthy saw a movie together that featured those toasts, and when Charles and McCarthy returned, half tipsy, they went up on the roof and fought violently with Charles's fencing foils—did McCarthy see Charles as a usurper?—and on their way down, the upper-floor tenant stepped into the hall in his bathrobe, and said, "I know you guys might be troubled, but just knock on my door, come on in, I'll try to help you settle your dispute." Then the two of them stumbled back down here, where she was trying to sleep, and shattered a pair of the glasses.

They were part of Charles's wedding gift to her, meant to set off the sideboard, and he had let her pick them out. Each had its distinctive shape and was tinted a subtle color: smoky-gray champagne glasses on short, sturdy stems, with bases nearly as broad as their rims; wineglasses, old-fashioned glasses—six sets of six, including straw-tinted drinking goblets. When McCarthy had left that night, she jerked open the bedroom door, and cried, "That hurts me! It hurts me terribly when one of those breaks. You got them for me!"

"Yes." Barely a whisper. He was staring into the dead fireplace, in darkness again, in the same chair.

"All right, forget about me!" she said, and wished even then she hadn't said it. "Those were forty to fifty dollars a set. That's about seven dollars a glass. Does it give you a kick to destroy something like that in one—one—"

"One fell swoop?" he said, as if asking himself the question.

"Do you get your gun doing it?"

He stood and the narrow-backed chair hit the floor with a wallop; but she couldn't stop herself. "Does it make you feel like a he-man? Rich, hot stuff, for McCarthy? How do you expect to get ahead?"

"Ahead?" he asked, and his voice began to give. "That's what my mother wanted. *Get ahead.* I'd as soon get behind."

"When you talk through the bottle, all you say gets blurred."

"When things get off the track . . ." he began, as if they were speaking from separate worlds; then stopped.

A few weeks before, he had ordered a tape recorder, voice-actuated, so he could rehearse speeches in bed, but by the time it was delivered he seemed to have forgotten about it; their buzzer sounded and he rose from his deacon's bench, excusing himself to their guests, and went in an absentminded way to the intercom. "Oh, yes," he said, to the person waiting in the vestibule. "That's right."

They had invited the couple who had moved into the building that week down for tea. They were from Georgia, and the husband had the groomed gentility of one who would appreciate tea done right. The two looked quaint and at home here, Katherine thought, on the couch with its nappy fabric the color of monk's cloth, with the cobbler's bench of maple, used as a coffee table and refurbished by Charles, in front of them. The husband looked thirty years older than his wife, but was, as it turned out, prematurely gray. He handled even his pipe with a fussy, pastoral skepticism; he was enrolled at Union Theological Seminary.

"We found the Heights more congenial to our perhaps lackadaisical tempo," he was saying. "And surely more soothing than the city for Pal dear." His wife's name was Pal; Charles had had to have it repeated three times ("Payel," the man pronounced it) but hadn't registered anything when he realized he had finally got it right. Pal was hugely pregnant, the real reason they'd asked the couple in; it was rumored that Phil wouldn't allow children in his building, although he'd never said so, nor did his leases, but he signed only two-year leases, as if to retain the upper hand. But Phil might have made an exception with this couple, they had just learned, because the Southerners planned to be in the building only a year, while the husband completed his dissertation.

Then the gong on their door sounded and Charles let in a black man, with a good-sized box under an arm, who was dressed in jeans and a sleeveless T-shirt and one of those tweedy Irish caps—a pencil under its brim at a jaunty angle. She felt a proprietary joy that their new neighbors were getting an inside glimpse of the actual workings of the city in this apartment, under her eyes; Charles handled situations so well. He wrote out a check on the table in the entry, to put the man at ease in the midst of their prissy tea scene, and then hit all of his pockets, looking for cash, for a tip, she knew, and then went slack as if he'd been shot: being reminded again of all the economic and other responsibilities to a child? She knew he didn't want to give up this apartment any more than she did.

He checked coat pockets in the closet off the entry and then hopped out to the kitchen and came back with the pint of Jack Daniel's he'd been sipping while he prepared himself some coffee, saying he had to work later, and held the bottle out to the man. She'd never seen such a color change come over black skin. The man glanced on every side, shaken, and then looked into the room to where she and the couple sat, as if to gauge how far he could get before he was stopped, and then he placed the box on the table as if it contained explosives, and said to Charles, under icy control, "Son"—and she saw the word go like a jolt through Charles—"Son, I'm a man with work to do." And walked out.

The couple sat blanching, wide-eyed, as if they'd bitten through their teacups. And then the recorder didn't work well, as if a hex had been put on it, Charles said, and after a while it moved into the room off the kitchen used mostly to store her paintings, soon to be their child's. It sometimes took her entire imagination to place a child here—like the wailing infant daughter they'd been hearing from the Georgia couple's apartment. They would stand unmoving at the sound of her voice, their faces lifted, as if re-hearing the judgment passed down on them. The couple had never invited them up.

•

While Charles and Gail and Joyce drank too much on Thanksgiving, she sat sipping Postum alone, at the tilt-top table Charles had bought her for the holiday. And then Charles broke out his canister labeled TEA and rolled a half dozen clublike joints. She passed, because of the child, and Charles hadn't been smoking lately, either, since they'd begun their sessions with Stevens. She could feel the animality of the attraction between Charles and Gail, who, with her ironed blond hair and newly acquired repose, now bore a youthful resemblance to *her*, Katherine realized. But Charles focused on Joyce, which might have been a ploy; he was crafty with women when she was present. Her friends were suddenly laughing as if she'd revealed her fears, and she glanced down at her hands in her lap; they looked like a man's. How had she expected to pour tea with those?

Then Charles insisted that he take them home in a cab, mumbling something as he pulled out their coats, then hers, and slipped it on her. He put his arm around her waist in the cab, as he did when they were happily affectionate, so she couldn't judge where his thoughts were. But she was sure it was youth other than hers that had put his arm there, and was aware now of her weight, the new layerings of fat, of the receptacle she'd become ("One in the oven," in that awful expression men used), and of the way in which she was leadenly attached to an existence unacknowledged by anyone else in the cab.

She shoved Charles's arm away.

Even he couldn't conceal his surprise at their apartment. It was a one-room walk-up, with a double bed, unmade, jammed into a corner, past droppings left by a whining dog. Joyce's restlessness went into a higher level and she started circling the confines of the place (there was a kitchenette opposite the bed) with her former athletic grace, so that Katherine could understand what Charles had seen in her, since he would have observed this beneath her weight to begin with. And then it seemed to Katherine that Joyce was a herald from another time, hurrying down circling flights of stairs to reach their level, in order to deliver a message of warning. Suddenly she started stomping, on purpose—which startled Katherine—and flickering in and out of a resemblance to the mannish woman above their apartment, and then she was kicking at unpacked boxes and clutter, crying, "Dammit! Damn this stuff and the damn acid dirties!"

There was one wobbly wooden chair which the three of them grabbed at the same time and shoved under her for her to enthrone herself—the Pregnant Queen—and there she sat, wondering which of the walls had reminded Gail of her grandmother's embroidery. They were all soiled or water-stained. Besides the boxes, some of which were broken open and spilling clothes, and the general clutter on the floor, there were mounds and pools from the dog, a huge Saint Bernard—a "puppy" that Joyce said they were trying to train.

"Housebreak," Gail said. "Apartment-wire." She was giddy. She lay down on the bed, and the dog leaped up and lay beside her, setting mattresses aquiver, panting, one big paw on her back, then rooted through the rumpled covers and came up with a bra in his mouth.

Katherine was so affected she had a lopsided headache. Charles stared at the dirty dishes heaped in the sink and piled across a streaked stove as if ill himself. "I've been thinking I should just pitch *them there* dishes out the window," Joyce said, apparently sensitive to where eyes were. "Sort of like some dudes across the river fireplace their glasses." The dishes had the appearance of being bound by brown ribbons with the ability to shift position yet maintain stability within their wavering loops and ties. Roaches. Charles hated roaches; either his mind was set on leaving, the way he stood there, or he'd set it against letting the place offend him.

He finally turned to Gail in his frontal way, as if he'd put her off long enough for her to appreciate this, and Gail became as giving as cream. She'd brought a gallon of wine to the bed, and he sat beside her and sipped from it while Gail eyed him as if she were keeping him alive with her sexual energy. She might as well be as direct about it as she was in the attention she began to give to the relit joint Charles set between her lips. He'd switched to his talkative phase, whacking one knee with a hand as he laughed—she couldn't take in what he was saying for the commotion that the clutter and roaches set off in her— and she remembered how, at school, she had quoted to these two from a story about everybody needing squalor in their lives. Now she felt they were paying her back for that. A clap of laughter came from them, as if at how they'd paid her back, or the phony pretentiousness of her altruism to begin with. Gail went into the bathroom, whose wall formed the rear of the kitchenette, and then Joyce joined her there, and it became clear that the two were arguing.

Katherine turned to Charles and said, "Let's get home."

"It's not even eleven. It's Thanksgiving!"

This from one who sometimes criticized her logic. She placed a hand over her stomach, and said, "We have to."

After a polite glass of wine, he said, as if he had to mollify her friends for judging them by their place—his worst flaw; and once Gail and Joyce emerged from the bathroom, subdued (were they fighting over him?), and they had their polite glass of wine, and then another, they left. A silver drizzle was falling, and Charles shook off the British coat she'd got him for his birthday, with its attached rain cape, and draped it over her shoulders. This unthinking inclination in him, even in his state, caused her to examine her fingernails, turned into her palm, with smiling satisfaction. She told him to detach the rain cape and put it over his own shoulders, so he did.

They found a cab off Tompkins Square and he helped her in, and as she was settling herself, pushing damp hair back from her face, the door slammed. He had rolled down the window and was leaning in at it, his head nodding and unsteady from the mixture of all he'd had.

"What is it?" she asked, and slid over on the seat to him.

"I'm staying awhile."

"With them?" She was barely able to ask this, out of fear.

"Just in the neighborhood."

"Why don't you come home." It wasn't a question.

"Not quite yet, okay? I'll get a nightcap. These are my stomping grounds." His voice, close and muffled in the cab, sounded as if it came from under a hat brim, and she realized that her perceptions had become abnormal. Then, from the sensation expanding inside her she realized she was suffering the effects of a contact high. His face against the drizzle was molecular.

"Oh, please," she pleaded. "Have a nightcap at home."

"Let me walk around a bit. This is like home base."

She felt a warm line extending from her right eye to

her chin—the involuntary tears that began before she knew she would cry.

"I'll be right there," he said, and his head shifted so quickly she thought the cab had jerked. "I'll be back in an hour."

"At least take your raincoat."

"You need it."

"You'll be out in this. You'll get sick."

"It's hardly sprinkling."

"It's cold, it's awful! What are you planning to *do!*"

He withdrew from the window and said "Walk" with a sound that reached her like the quack of a duck, and then he glanced birdlike around at the drizzle, as if he'd only then noticed it.

"Please," she insisted.

"All right." He reached in and lifted the raincoat free as she shifted her weight, then leaned farther in and kissed her cheek. "Soon," he said, and walked off, and as the cab pulled away and she looked out the open window to see him striding in the opposite direction under a streetlamp that formed a frazzling fan of the drizzle, with the coat draped over his shoulders and the cape like a sunbonnet around his head, she started sobbing. She was sobbing so badly she couldn't stop even when the cabbie parked outside their building.

"Lady," the man finally said, after several sympathetic sighs. "Lady, take my advice. Drop the guy. Go get laid."

•

In the apartment, she turned on every light, then lay down on the bed with her clothes on. How completely she'd adapted to sleeping with him—merely his body being there! The lights pressed a ghostly flatness into the walls, revealing new planes in corners and around objects—all of which stood at a remove, remote. She walked quickly through the place, glancing away from the gargoyles and griffins on the bar, and shut off the lights. She sat on the settee, in the alcove, surprised to be in her coat, since she was also wrapped in a quilt she'd grabbed from the bed. She stared down at the street corner where Charles would have to appear if he took the subway; then at the tree, lit from beneath by the streetlamp, as if to memorize the novelty of its silver-purple branches, now that they were bare. There had hardly been a fall; the heat of summer had persisted through September, and now the weather seemed at winter's edge.

She must have fallen asleep. She woke on the bed, startled by a sound she thought was Charles arriving. Then she was sure she heard footsteps going from room to room—a second-story man. Or a rapist who would sock and grind away any remaining self-esteem and destroy the child. She gripped her hands between her thighs and felt a presence of faces about to break through the darkness into visibility. She couldn't make them out, but they seemed to have the blocky symmetry of the heads that overtook the painting of hers that was Charles's favorite. She passed into another state and saw a miniature of herself, numb and naked, go swimming down a crystalline shaft of water of the sort she once dove down in a quarry mine, distantly making it to the boulders at the bottom, executing kicking movements in the depths to hold herself down, until her senses gave out.

•

She was conscious of colder morning air on her face and the presence of a body bending close. She opened her eyes on something that retreated so fast she couldn't take it in, then she heard a *woof!* as she wakened entirely. There was a bang as if the closet door she was studying had been kicked. Or was it the man from Georgia, who leaped down to the landings every morning in his happiness to be off to the seminary? She was still in her clothes and coat, wound in the quilt, sweating mink oil, from the waxy scent of herself.

She took a quick look over the roll of covers. Erikson's sketch was still there, as if proclaiming Charles's existence, and she recalled how, these last months, Charles would stand at the round window for hours, observing the Japanese painter work at his commercially tainted butterflies—the man's source of income. Charles would say, when a delivery boy arrived for another batch, "They pick them up and take them to a framer. Or a dealer. Is there a magazine that features butterflies? No, these are a bit beyond a magazine." One day he lowered the binoculars he'd begun to use. "Though they're artsy and slick, there's an almost-redeeming feature to each one. The way he'll do the veining in a wing, for instance, so it resembles leading for stained glass. Or use an overlay of color over one wing as shadow. Well, he ought to be pretty good at it; he's done enough of them."

Why didn't you leave him alone? she thought, staring at Erikson's sketch as if the force of her thought could break the glass and frame.

She decided to assume that Charles had let himself in and made it to the couch, and the sounds she had heard were from him. She got up, dropping the quilt on the floor, and walked into the living room. Charles wasn't there. She started toward the kitchen and felt a tugging at the pocket of her coat, still on, then reached in and pulled out a clump of keys. Charles's set. She threw them at the table and with their impact half expected to see a note that began "I'm sorry, but . . ."

She ran back to the bedroom and dialed Gail and Joyce's number and sat through minutes of ringing, out of breath, and then had an image of Charles rising from the covers of their bed and holding up a hand to discourage them from answering. Bitches.

She called Stevens, who sounded sympathetic, and promised to call back if he heard anything, or if Charles called him.

She went out to the kitchen, into a silence like a thicker wrap than her coat, and sent the hanging palette of her Le Creuset pans banging with a swing of her arm. Another of his damn gifts! Gail and Joyce had at least helped her clear things, so now she had her own stacks of plates. She slammed these around, to create the noise of life, and felt an urge to jerk open the bottom drawer, where Charles kept his tools, and take a hammer to them over the wastebasket. She piled everything into the sink and turned the water on. No roaches. Finicky Phil the faggot had the bug men visit their building every month. She reached under the upper cupboards and slid her blender out across the counter—or the base of it that contained the motor—and plugged it in. She shut off the water and put her hand on the formed allure of the base, one of those designs that MOMA kept on a spotlit pedestal so far removed from its place of actual use the incongruity of it could make you weep.

Her right eye gave its leaking warning at the thought of him setting her up like this in order to run off! She was afraid to go downstairs and get their milk from the locker on the stoop, so she slopped the milk from two cartons in the refrigerator into the bell of the blender, locked it into the base, and turned it on that way, with nothing else inside, for the relief of the noise, then was blinking against white spatters covering the cupboards, unable to get her breath. She hadn't put on the top.

If she could turn out meals that others admired—former classmate Joyce, you slob—she could still be all thumbs in the kitchen. Clean, however. She wiped everything up, then washed under the faucet, cupping enough water so that when she lowered her face into her palms she was reminded of last night's sensation, or whatever, of the miniature swimmer.

She added her tiger's-milk ingredients and got the cover on and the blender going at top speed, and then dropped a peeled banana through the hole in the center of the cover, which was fitted with a little cap. There, she thought. Ground to a mush. Every last bit of you. She grabbed a glass from a shelf of the oak hutch against the wall and poured the foamy mixture into it with a flopping noise. Its taste was like the air in her uncle's dairy barn after he'd sawed off a cow's horns and cauterized the stumps with a red-hot iron. Her hands were shaking so badly she felt she'd been drunk for a week, and she decided she couldn't allow herself even one drink until Charles returned. She sipped. And shoved her tongue against her teeth to keep from gagging. There was a taste of the rest of the barn in it, too. She tried dainty sips, but then the solid shape of it was in her stomach and she ran into the bathroom and went down on her knees at the toilet, the cold comfort of porcelain against her cheek—usually a preventative, as it was now.

Call Erikson? He seemed the sort of person who was unimpressed by what he saw in the mirror, as she was, and so was able to turn on from that elegant image with ease. He had kept up an interest in them; every few weeks he'd be in touch. "If you feel you can't bear the job," he'd said to Charles, after Charles had taken it, "try and see it as bankrolling your future. Most of the younger folks I know have done something of the sort, early on. The point is to keep working." Charles wouldn't admit that he hadn't opened a script since they'd moved to the apartment, and they were already living at the limits of his income, if not beyond. "It isn't enough!" she almost shouted once, when she was balancing the checkbook. "Not with me not working!"

She grabbed his keys off the table, went out the door and up the stairs to the McCarthys'—the prisonlike look of which sent her up the last flight to the roof. In the brilliance of the smoky autumn light she felt she'd emerged from that quarry pool into correspondence with the sea. There it was. Two deck chairs sat on a surface of white gravel, like a Dali couple, overlooking buildings to a patch of the bay. The roof sloped slightly in that direction and she stepped onto the gravel that gave grit and solidity to the view—like a vision; as if she'd always known the city from this spot.

A brick wall at the edge of the roof, capped with concrete, rose to her breasts. She rested her elbows on it and felt the concurrence of brightness and noise go widening into the stepped-up tempo the city maintained twenty hours a day. A helicopter was landing at the Wall Street pier and an orange-and-blue ferry started pulling out of its slip for Staten Island, putting out so much black smoke from its center spout that it curled down and hid its hull at the waterline. From Columbia Heights, or the chasm that was Columbia Heights, the only street before the bay, she heard the *"Vo-tee-ho-ho!"* of the vegetable man. Friday. In the courtyard to her left, a pair of workmen stood at the base of a partly dismantled chimney, foreshortened in a scattering of bricks. A girl in purple tights on the lawn next to them was lifting a white puppy above her head, and now the helicopter rose from the Wall Street pier and swung in her direction, hacking the air into flat echoes she could feel all through the concrete.

The stepped ranks of buildings along the prow of Manhattan were like a mirage, and a cream-colored ferry nosed out from them for the Statue of Liberty, whose torch she could see above a hotel of peeling brick. The back of this hotel and—farther to the right—a high mansard roof, with a pair of dormers set into its slate shingling, formed a U that was the center of her vision. At the base of the U she could see the adjoining roofs, like folds in a fan, of the blue warehouses along the dock below the promenade; beside it, white spars and landing cranes of a ship. Jets kept coming over, and gulls in the distance often seemed a jet she was hearing. And then a real plane, a seaplane, entered the U at a steep angle, droning like an ache through the sky, and skimmed to a landing on the bay, leaving a pair of silver wakes in which a sailboat, suddenly tacking into view, was set rocking. "How can you even suggest reality unless you incorporate a frame?"

One of the workmen began striking a chisel held to the chimney in gentle taps, as if the brick overlaid the nerves in a tooth. Fix it! The vegetable man's "*Vo-tee-ho-ho!*" now rose from Willow, behind her, and she could hear the metal wheels of his pushcart on the street, and then a moth came at her, so close compared to the other wings that she went back, a hand up, aware that her appetite for Charles was as encompassing as this view—monstrous.

•

She hurried back down the stairs, down dark halls, as if she'd just returned from seeing him walk off under the lamp, and then pictured Joyce striding down those endless stairs to give the warning she must have given to Gail in the bathroom. Katherine had run past their door. She went back to it, trembling so badly she didn't think she could get the lock undone before somebody came, and then stood inside with her forehead against it, caught in a pant that brought the tiger's milk rocking up her throat. She swallowed and swallowed.

She went to their bedroom closet, shoved back its sliding doors, and felt the appalling attraction of letting herself go entirely. She pulled a pair of Charles's corduroys off a hanger and pulled them on under her skirt—they fit exactly—and felt as a widow must about clothes: the cold absence of what they once enclosed. She threw off her coat and undid the skirt and let it drop and kicked it onto the bed. She'd got a chill on the roof and she shoved through their clothes, a mix of his and hers, toward the rear of the closet, and encountered something like skin. She pulled out the jacket and it wobbled on its hanger—a rust jacket of suede with a worn and frail feel that people who describe skin as velvety probably mean to describe: the texture of a young man's cheek. It was torn at the shoulder, its cuffs frayed, with dark stains down its front, and a ripped pocket.

It had been given to her by the first boy in college she'd cared for; he'd taken it off and slipped it on her. A month later, he was injured so badly in an accident on his motorcycle he never fully recovered, or not for the year she tried to keep in touch, and he wouldn't speak to her. The accident had happened the same day they'd had their first argument. Finally, she'd mailed him the jacket, along with a letter in which she tried to explain her side of the affair, and he'd mailed the jacket back. Their relationship was only a few years in the past, but it already appeared so distant they seemed adolescents hurrying down streets done in the gaudy purity of primitive paintings, and what she remembered most was how she set herself on his motorcycle, her feet outside his on the pegs, her arms around his chest, the side of her face pressed against this jacket. He had been the first but hadn't been attentive enough to draw her out of herself, as Charles had been and then had held out for more of her.

She jerked on a sweater, pulled the jacket over that, and went out the building to the promenade. She walked to the railing at its edge and heard the whining hurry and wallops of air from traffic on the Beltway below. In front of her was the ship whose spars she'd seen from the roof, the *Ciudad de Cádiz;* Charles had promised her a trip to Spain: the light. She turned and saw a single man, on the park bench behind her, staring at her with a hungry join-me-in-my-stylish-exile look, and knew from his expression that he would want her to talk first, and within minutes would ask her up to his apartment.

There was a bustle over the brick walkway farther down, in the direction of Brooklyn Bridge, followed by a beep of sound from a bullhorn, and a half dozen men in suits started in her direction. A slight man out front walked with Charles's air to a park bench, where a woman was rocking a baby in a stroller, and went down on a knee on the bricks in front of her. He placed a hand on the stroller's tray, and talked with what seemed complicity, then twiddled his fingers for the baby to play with.

The other men maneuvered and backpedaled and formed a weaving crescent around him, as if to memorize every angle of this self-effacing chivalry. Some were taking pictures. A movie? They weren't the right cameras, she was sure, but was partially blinded by the thought that Charles had found a job he hadn't told her about, or was involved in something unimaginable. The man rose and started for the fellow who'd been trying to stare her down, but suddenly swung away, with a curious jerking nod, as if recognizing something common, and came at her with such directness she could only take in the tailored cut of his suit at first. It was Robert Kennedy.

"Miss," he said, and the photographed smile looked rough-edged, with an apologetic tuck that exposed the uneven weaving of his lip line with his skin. The smile wavered and he took her hand in both of his and mentioned something about taking these walks, now that he was her senator, and then said, "Miss, er, *Ma'am*"—as if he could tell at a touch that she was pregnant. "Ma'am, is there anything you'd like me to do, as your senator?" This seemed at least partially sincere, and an interest began to move in his eyes until he was staring directly at her. There was a reddish, scaling spot beside his nose, abraded from rubbing, and his neck looked thin behind the tailored collar and perfectly crimped Windsor knot of his tie. Suddenly he pivoted toward Battery Park, releasing her hand as if he'd just seen the place, and then with a nod of surprise noticed the Statue of Liberty.

"Goodness," he said, and one hand covered the tie. "It's a beautiful view. Beautiful. Aren't you enjoying it?" He seemed about to ask something personal—they were on familiar ground now—but the pressure from the men in the background distracted him, and finally he was forced to move on. He glanced over his shoulder at her, unsmiling, and the fellow who had propositioned her in silence and the woman with the stroller and a dozen others started following in the wake of the men at his back.

She was about to ask him to do everything he could to find Charles, and he would try, she was sure. It was a life. Three, now. His presence was so similar to Charles's, the sight of him moving off set her eye running, and then she suffered a picture of the shattering end of his brother, the President, which seemed the end of youth, and of Charles.

She ran back to their building and found Phil in the vestibule, with the cover on the mailboxes folded down but pulling letters only out of his box. He reached into theirs and handed her an addressographed letter and a flyer from Bohack's.

"Is Charles around?" he asked.

What? Phil was fiftyish, and his mourning face, with its shadow of beard and bushy nostrils, had an incongruous force; such a fruity voice came from it. "What do you mean?" she asked.

Phil cocked his head at her; did she look that bad? "No, nothing shocking," he said. "I was merely wondering about the rent."

"He hasn't paid it?"

"Not since last month, he hasn't." A sudden smile tugged up the corners of his mouth, but was gone so quick it was as if he'd committed an indiscretion; the McCarthys claimed he cruised the promenade, with his mourning look of shame, for young men.

"He's usually so prompt," she said.

"That's why I was wondering. Maybe you could light a match under him, huh? I got bills." He shook a fistful of them close to her face.

"I'll tell him," she said, and started up the stairs, sure that Phil knew something; that he'd seen Charles, or let him in, or was aware that she was pregnant. Charles believed that the "client" Phil's antique-dealer friend had mentioned was Phil, and Charles had said he was sure they could stay in the building, even with a child, if he offered Phil the griffins from the bar at a reasonable price, and she'd said, "Don't you dare! That's mine!"

She was in the apartment, out of breath, staring at the kitchen, which looked reduced, a shed skin. She threw the letter and flyer on the table and glanced into the living room, then slid open the door of the entry closet. His coat wasn't there. She underwent a graphic display of him entangled with Gail, while Joyce revolved her hefty body around them in some further manipulation—roommates from a religious school!—and ran into the bedroom and dialed their number. It kept on ringing until it seemed the trilling of an internal scream, and then her mind dimmed and she saw Charles lying alone, naked and bleeding, on the filth of their floor.

She called Stevens and at the sound of his agreeable "Hello?" she said, "I don't think I can make it."

"Ohhh," he said, in his tone of commiseration. "I'm sorry you're feeling so bad you have to say that. So you haven't heard from him, then?"

"No," she said, and her eye began running. She grabbed the receiver with both hands as if to hold herself in place. "You?"

"I said I would call if I did, Katherine."

"I feel I have to have some kind of confirmation that he's okay. This is unreal!"

"That's perfectly normal—I mean, moments of seeming unreality in this kind of situation. How long has it been now?"

"Eighteen hours? I don't know."

"I'll tell you what. Let's wait until we get into Saturday, or better Sunday, and then if he isn't back, let's get concerned. He's bright and resourceful and this type of thing isn't uncommon, for a man who's looking at thirty coming up. When it happens, it usually spins itself out in a few days. Did he have his medication along?"

She was crying, but didn't want him to know; she wiped at her face and the slippery receiver with both hands. "Does he need it?"

"I'm thinking of his possible anxiety, *Please let me take care of this call*," she heard in a semi-muffled voice; she'd called him at the hospital, where he worked half days as director. "Of course the drinking will ease that somewhat; you said he was drinking. I'm sure this is a further development, ah, the change in him we've talked about. But I'm pretty confident it won't prove to be the kind of change medication is needed for, as in psychosis."

"Please!"

"You'll be able to help yourself out a lot if you can keep calm. I feel— You develop a sense about these things. I feel, I guess, not entirely surprised that he's gone."

This damaged her in a way she was sure Stevens could never fix.

"Why didn't I say something? Why open up another worry, or hand him a direction to head for, if it's not going to happen? Once he's back, I'm sure things will settle down to near-normal."

"Once!"

"I can't make any guarantees, you know. This is the city. You have to be willing to give up your anger at him, Katherine."

"I have to do something before I go insane! If I'm not already!"

"You sound fine. The anger has you pushing hysteria, and you're crying, but that's normal. I suppose there is something else you could do, if you want, if you've already called the hospitals I mentioned."

"Yes."

"Call a precinct station or two in the last neighborhood you saw him in. Ask them to check around. If you want to be sure about what I feel you're not quite saying, call the city morgue."

"Good God."

"If you're up to it, it might help you. Do you want to see me?"

"No!" What occurred to her, as never before, was the money.

"All right, then. Call if you do. Let's keep in touch. Right now I'm afraid I'm with another patient. Could I call you back?"

"No." She hung up. That he would say what he had with another patient there! Then she remembered calls he'd received while she was present—from a young wife who had reinstituted an abusive affair she'd had with her boss before she was married; from a suicide's husband— and the artful way in which Stevens had leaked details of the other half of the conversation, as if to summon gratitude from her for the order of her life, in spite of its setbacks. Now he was talking about her.

The phone at her former friends' kept ringing. She could take a cab over, she thought, and imagined herself in their stinky vestibule, with her finger on the buzzer. They wouldn't answer. Maybe they were actually at work; maybe they had to work today. Finally she called Erikson, who was in. After she explained the situation (hoping Erikson would interrupt with news of Charles), he said in his whispery voice, "There's only one thing I can think for you to do, Katherine."

"Yes?"

"Trust that he's all right. People like Charles, who by nature are vulnerable, seem to have angels or other creatures of benevolence attending to them. We'll trust in that. His gift is too valuable to be lost. There. I've said it. Tell him so the minute you see him."

"I will."

"I wish I could convince you this is a temporary aberration. Would you like to come over and spend the night with us?"

"Oh, no." *Please*, she almost added.

"We have plenty of extra room. You wouldn't be a bit of bother. You could leave Charles a message that you're here."

"What if he calls?"

"I see you're much closer to this than I am. When I was his age I once walked the city for a day and a night. If that's what he's up to, maybe he'll decide to give up that godawful job. How is your own work?"

"Nonexistent."

"I can understand that at this point. I'd like to see some of it soon."

"Yes." Erikson mentioned her work every time they talked but had never pursued her enough for her to take his interest seriously; he'd never seen a stroke of it.

"I've been meaning to suggest to Charles that he ought to leave that job, but I feel I've put him on the spot enough as it is with my meddling. You may also tell him that. This might be an opportunity for you, too, to resolve that it's high time for him to quit."

All right, then, she thought, when she hung up. She walked through all of the rooms, except the one off the kitchen, trying to take in everything, and stopped at the far end of the living room, in front of the deacon's bench where Charles installed himself when there was company. The bench was of oak, with a globe segmented like an orange at the center of its back, and carved leaves extending from either side of the globe, so that from a distance the decorations looked like an eagle with outstretched wings.

Charles had built their stereo into a compartment below the seat, which swung up on hinges, and directly above its back, at eye level, was his favorite painting of hers, which he always kept hung: a central blocky head with variations on it, viewed from different angles, radiating into the background—heads she had done over and over, in a fury, when the boy on the motorcycle wouldn't speak to her. It was of him, but she'd been too ashamed to admit that to Charles. He called the painting *The Actor*.

The person in it had finally written to her, after all those years of silence, through her father, and they'd met in the city one afternoon when Charles was at his job. A brief fall.

She ran to the phone, her eye running, and a man at the city morgue, after checking records, said, "No, ma'am. No one of that description in the last twenty-four hours. There's one the right weight and the rest, but he's Puerto Rican—Latin, I should say."

She dropped on her knees beside the bed and put her head on the quilt, pulling it around her face, and saw herself as she'd walked through the rooms. All right, she thought. All right, Lord. I'll give it all up. Every bit of it. I'll live in a place like Joyce and Gail's. I'll try not to hate them so much. Charles, either. She paused. I'll move out of the city with him, if I have to.

She went out to the bar and grabbed a bottle of vodka from beside a griffin and poured some into a champagne glass, spilling a bit, and at the first sip felt a convulsion inside: betrayal. She spun around and there was a fragrance of scattering vodka as the glass glanced off the wall above the fireplace and went through the air and struck a side of the deacon's bench, exploding over its cushion. There, she thought, taking hold of the bar and sinking with a weakness so complete she couldn't stand. She stretched out on the carpet in front of the bar. There, she thought. I've killed him.

•

She'd slept on the floor most of the night. She managed to endure today by going to a movie, a foreign comedy she wasn't sure she could sit through, thinking that Charles might call (although this hope was diminishing), and then she stayed to see it again, because the first time around she'd fallen asleep. Then she fell asleep at the same point. Back here, between naps, she took calls from Erikson, Stevens, Erikson again, who reminded her of his message. The man at the morgue could identify her now by voice, and would say when she called, "No, ma'am, no news."

She took a bath, finally, feeling she was washing the last of Charles from her, and afterward fell asleep. Every time she woke she felt she'd awakened not only to a later hour but to further maturity, as though there were a deeper passage of time now in her life. And when she'd lain down awhile ago to sleep—as she lay now, after watching the Japanese painter seat his guest, but with a quilt over her—she had once again pictured the miniature swimmer heading toward the depths of the quarry pool, and at a tug in her interior she realized she was having a vision of the child; it would be a girl.

Now again the child drew her toward sleep, as if taking her by an ankle beneath the first layer of consciousness, and she heard a tiny voice saying in the high-pitched and warbling sound of someone speaking underwater, "Oh, thank you, Mommy, thank you, thank you."

It was midnight when she woke. She wrapped herself

in the quilt and sat in the alcove, on the settee. The lights at the Japanese painter's were off. Were those movements from his couch? She turned away from this, dismissing it, and stared out the window toward the street corner, as she had on Thanksgiving night. A new cold from the outdoors reached her now (the heat must be off for the night), and she felt frozen in place, immobile. The familiar pattern of the branches of the tree now seemed a permanent part of her memory, and after a while it was as if she hadn't moved from the moment she'd returned without Charles, her hair still wet from the rain. She touched it, and then ran her hand through it, and with the gesture saw Charles on the curb at the corner, waiting for a car to pass. His head, lifted and turned to the window where she sat, was held as if in expectation, although she knew he couldn't see her; no lights were on. He continued to stare after the car had passed, and then she noticed he was wearing only the cape to his raincoat; a wind lifted a corner of it to reveal the jacket he'd pulled on in the haste of leaving. The raincoat itself was gone.

She stood with chills winding down from her hair and threw the quilt on the bed. She stepped over to her vanity— she was barefoot—and leaned forward to see herself in its oval mirror, purple-green from the lamplight. There had been a plump and sated look about Charles as he stood there, as though he'd spent his time feeding on someone, Joyce or Gail, or both, or any of the dozen others he knew in the Village—it made little difference now. He was alive. There was another tumbling sensation below her heart and she placed her hand over it, convinced that this was indeed quickening which had begun.

Her heart took on harder strokes that she could hear in her breathing as she picked up a brush and brushed out her hair, sending down cascades of sparks, and then she leaned farther in, to apply cursory makeup, hurrying in order to be ready when he rang their buzzer, and the purple-green immobility of her face in the mirror held, she saw with her painter's eye, a new and untraceable geography of weighty beauty it had never held before.

S H E

She is an Indian. Tonight my mind is so filled with her my body also feels filled up, and outside it's raining so hard I've had to walk through the house several times to make sure a faucet isn't turned on somewhere and running, as if I'm overflowing. Her name is Estrelaria. Her wideset dark eyes, tipped up in a shapely turn of nature, like certain sumac leaves, rest on me in her open stare, as if her wakan or maya enables her to overcome the miles between us. She's gone back to Guatemala with her husband, an American who has something to do with printing presses or the printing process, and was working in Guatemala when he met her.

She wouldn't let me drive her to the El station to see her off, as if a final ride would leave her indebted to us in a way she didn't wish to be, and when she turned from her last goodbye to my wife she seemed to diminish even more (she's not quite five feet) as she went out the house and down the street into that vanishing point that eventually claims everyone we love. Though we enter the world (and often the lives of others) full of the weight of ourselves, we exit thin as air.

"How can she leave?" I said to my wife.

"It isn't as if she's leaving us. Guatemala is her home."

"But Guatemala is always in turmoil—coups, earthquakes, something. Why go back?"

"From what she's said, I believe it's partly her husband."

"The CIA, you think?"

"Oh, no," she said, ignoring my conspiratorial tendency. "They can probably live at an entirely different level there on his salary. Estrelaria says he doesn't like it here anymore, after Guatemala. She said his company offered to send him back."

There's been an unsettled atmosphere in the house since Estrelaria left, and not only because its usual ordered pattern of light and shadow over shining surfaces isn't apparent, or because the spirit of her parting has entered the place, or anything equally arcane; it's that I can't look forward to her moving among us anymore. At first she came only once a week, on Tuesdays, and we organized ourselves around that day; I was always shaved and wearing a suit jacket after her first visit, when she stepped into our bedroom to clean and found me turning to her from the covers, naked.

We discovered that we needed her twice a week and then sometimes more, and, to be forthright, I would almost have paid to watch her walk. She had the balanced, straightforward carriage of someone built for bearing loads—great earthen jugs of water, baskets of wet clothes—but with a buoyancy to it now that the loads were gone, along with a roll to her rounded hips that wasn't North American or provocative but like the revolving of power around an axis that wouldn't give. She moved in tune to an ancient time, with padded cheekbones as much ensigns as features: a native Guatemalan. Or I feel I almost would have paid to watch her walk, which was surely apparent in my relationship to her. She was the first woman I'd engaged for work, housecleaning or any other kind, and I don't enjoy being a master or overseer; I function best as a servant. I'm an interviewer for public radio.

But because my wife is so much a blonde in every respect, I find myself attracted to women exactly her opposite—or I used to be, until I started turning the corner toward forty. Now I've begun to search for the blonde who will epitomize the young woman my wife was when we met. She was sitting in a bar . . .

•

Here is where these pages broke off nine years ago. I was working then on an apologetics in the manner of Pascal, a presumption I was able to indulge myself in, I'm sure, only because the work was fragmentary, built up from notes, and drew on incidents out of actual life. These incidents began to interconnect and take on a growing (as I viewed it) eschatological bite, because of my mother. She died when I was nine and most of the incidents were concerned with her, or with the continuing aftereffects of her death, and I came to conclude that no truth could be perceived without the end of all things shining through from the other side. This seemed her legacy to me.

I had received a share in my father's estate and was able to set aside a year from my interviewing to complete the apologetics. It was then that Estrelaria arrived and began to invade that work. I kept at it, however, for a year beyond the time I'd allotted myself, until we had to leave the house Estrelaria had helped us set in order and move to a farmstead in the barren semi-badlands of western

North Dakota. We began to till the alkaline soil of this arid countryside, we had another child, our third, and (as these things go) my apologetics to this day remains undone. "We run carelessly to the precipice," Pascal says, "after we have put something before us to prevent us seeing it."

When I began those broken-off pages as if to exorcise Estrelaria, I must have sensed that the new relationship that was beginning between my wife and me and might not be able to bear up under their weight. We had been separated for two years, and were trying to start our marriage over, and I knew that I would have to deal, at least in one sense, with betrayal, a word that might well describe our age (at the mere sound of it my consciousness starts closing down), and I'd lived with enough betrayals to set this aside for nine years. I'm not sure I'd be returning to it even now if my wife wasn't away.

·

She is an Indian. Her poise and even-shouldered momentum through the spaces of that house continue to tug at me in the way that a story's annealed and wordless core tugs at you even after most of the details of the story have dimmed. My wife and I, working together, couldn't move ahead with the house as we'd hoped to. It was one of those two-story wood-frame affairs in a west-Chicago suburb, with one porch too many, trimmed with too much gingerbread scrollwork, and it kept me busy simply with painting and repairs. We put an ad in the newspaper, and Estrelaria interviewed for the job with her husband, who came along to make sure that her duties and wages were kept aboveboard and clear, and said, more than once, that there were certain things she would not do. She would not iron clothes, he said, or get down on her hands and knees and scrub a floor.

We soon learned that my wife was pregnant, with our first son, as it turned out—we have a daughter who was then seven—and over that year Estrelaria took on more and more of the housework. When she cleaned out a cupboard, she removed all the clutter and utensils, as you might expect, and then scoured every inside inch of wood, including the undersides of all the shelves, as if she saw into things in a way that we'd forgotten to, and then she washed and polished everything before she put it back—more than merely thoroughgoing in her attention to detail.

We had a hutch in the kitchen and on one of its shelves was a brass ashtray where the detritus of the house gathered—a cabinet catch that no longer worked, screws that had appeared on the floor, pennies, a marble, a beaver's curved, yellowish tooth from a trip to Canada— and one day I came down from the upstairs where I worked and found Estrelaria polishing every object in the ashtray. Her heavy black hair, which was usually in a single long braid down her back, lay over her shoulders like a mantilla (the first I'd seen it undone) and hung, after its curve over her shoulders, to her buttocks. She turned and looked at me from her wide, upturned eyes with the fear of a cornered animal, and I saw that the object in her hand was a woven-leather button from one of my suit jackets. She looked down at it, then at me, as if to see whether I'd dare imagine that she was trying to steal a valuable from our kitchen shrine—a moment of utmost delicacy. She couldn't read, her husband had said, as if to warn us not to take advantage of her, and I usually spoke to her in my classroom Spanish, although she often answered in English. Now I sensed that neither language could ease us through this.

Finally I said, with a formal bow, "Perdóneme," and turned and walked off.

"Do you think it's my accent?" I asked my wife, late that night. "I mean, she seems so skittish of me."

"It's probably about as good as mine."

"My attitude, then?"

"No. I don't think I've ever seen you as considerate as you are with her."

"Oh?" I said. "Not condescending?" Which is how my wife sometimes interprets my attempts to be considerate to her.

"Not that I've noticed. It might be that you're more considerate to her than you are to me."

Was this a warning? I rolled my weight off her and stared up at the ceiling, noticing, in the light from next door, the delicate fissures that meant it would have to be repainted. Estrelaria's cleaning had caused imperfections to appear all over, although visitors seemed to notice only the surfaces already attended to, as if Estrelaria had a way of directing their eyes, and we kept receiving compliments on the place. And it did have a look to it that sometimes made me sigh and sit in an easy chair to take it in.

"I think I know why her husband said he didn't want her to get down on her knees," I said.

My wife turned in a sea-wash of fresh sheets and propped her chin in one hand, letting the bedspread slide away from her plump nakedness. "You mean, you think that was his idea?" she asked.

"Didn't he say, when you interviewed them, that she'd use a mop to scrub but never get down on her hands and knees?"

"But Estrelaria also said to me, 'Not down on the knees?'"

"Oh." So this is why my wife had been so upset when

Estrelaria had done precisely that a week ago. "Well, she might have been echoing her husband. Didn't you say you walked in and saw her scrubbing as if she'd been doing it all her life?"

"I said, 'No, please, don't, get up, I'll do that,' and she smiled and shook her head. I feel awful!"

She let her face fall into the pillow and I pictured Estrelaria standing and staring up at her with a fervent look, her hands clasped at her waist, in the attitude she often took with my wife, and then I saw her go down on her knees, as we do before someone we love. Because it was clear that she loved my wife and that her love had magnified as my wife became more clearly pregnant.

"I'm sure she realizes you'd never take advantage of her, so she's doing what she wants. I figure it's her husband's idea, because he's afraid she might be used. Or he feels she could get so involved in a crack in somebody's linoleum—you know, the way she carries things through—that there's a sense in which her real self could disappear. Look how primitive people are about their souls—not even a photograph. I bet she won't let you take her picture."

"No! I've asked!" My wife is a photographer, but polite about where she points her camera. I put a hand on her back, to let her know I appreciate her discretion, and she was up over my chest so fast I had to lift her hair aside and shove strands of it out of my mouth with my tongue.

"She's also been *ironing*," she said, hiding her face against my shoulder, and there was a sudden scent of milk as her breasts shifted like armor over me. She kissed my shoulder and I was flooded with the sadness animals are supposed to feel at these times. I thought of the people crowded into the blocks of houses across Chicago—all of them settled into jobs to support a way of life that the lives of their neighbors suggested was normal when the jobs themselves, so far removed from the actuality of existence, raising crops for food, might be viewed by somebody like Estrelaria as insane. She came from the other side and had probably seen literal starvation. She said that her parents lived in a house with dirt floors.

I never thought I'd ask a special favor of her, but one day I came across a box of encyclopedias (after a year in the place, we were still getting unpacked) that had sprouted mildew on their covers. I asked my wife if it would be all right to ask Estrelaria to clean them, and then asked Estrelaria if she would mind cleaning them, and then demonstrated how to clean one, using a vinegar solution and finally rubbing the covers with Victoria and Albert Museum dressing. An hour later I found her on the third volume. After she removed the mildew, she wiped the dusty top stain with a rag, and then picked at the headband and groove of the binding with her nails—tough ivory against ginger-colored skin—and only then began to rub the dressing in, and the two that she'd finished and set up spraddle-legged on the living-room carpet to dry were like steps of bronze in the afternoon sun. She sat on her haunches on the carpet beside them, and at my sounds of approval she looked up and the padding over her cheek-bones altered—it was the first time she'd smiled at me, a flash in the sun—and I was surprised, or shocked or chagrined, at how wholly I was aroused.

Now my wife slid to one side—sleepy, to judge from her movements—and held my upper arm as she does when she senses my distance. She'd told me that when Estrelaria caught me in bed, she'd had to explain why I was home at all hours (the apologetics, of course), which was why I would clean my own room upstairs, as I'd always done, and now I realized that Estrelaria must have thought that the books she was polishing were mine. What a bulky uniform edition that would have been! But it must also have meant to her that I was one of the makers of words that enabled her husband to use his machines to print books: a true employer.

"I'll miss her when she goes," my wife whispered, nearly asleep, as if I'd spoken my thoughts of Estrelaria aloud.

"Yes," I said, and heard in my voice the tone of my father at his end (it was only the winter before that he'd died)—like an aggrieved patriot speaking out of the center of the country he'd always trusted in, which was now giving way. His entire body had been invaded, via his blood vessels, by cancer. It was the year of the Bicentennial, and the potential for America seemed to hold a particular promise then, even as I stood over him; though he was dying, there was a larger hope.

"Yes," I said again, and pictured him lying on his back in the bed where he'd died, as I was lying on my back on this one, and felt afloat on a river running under me.

•

When Estrelaria was in the house, she expected to serve lunch, and didn't believe it was proper to eat at the same table with us. But when my wife said that we would have lunch in the kitchen, as usual, rather than the dining room, and asked Estrelaria to join us, she did. I would try to keep the table conversation in Spanish and Estrelaria would try to answer in English, or, if this became too difficult when I asked a direct question, she would give the answer in Spanish to my wife. She never seemed purposely evasive, nor overly curious either; indeed, her circumspection was the quality in her I admired most.

She would keep her eyes on me in her fervent, open look as we ate, and before I realized I didn't have a knife, she would be up at the cupboard and then back in her chair, and a knife lay beside my spoon. Or she would be over at the stove to offer more food before I'd finished what was on my plate, or at my side, pouring coffee. This left me so uneasy I sometimes waited on her and my wife. One week she begged us to let her bring the lunch, as though to make restitution, and she arrived that day with a lump of tortilla dough and a bag of groceries. Her preparations resounded so much through the house I kept looking up from my work as I do at thunder, to learn what I might from its conjunction with a thought, and finally I went downstairs.

She showed us how to hammer out tortillas with our hands, and heat them till they barely browned. Then she fashioned a kind of taco, which she filled with a homemade sauce bubbling on the stove—actually she made about a dozen of these, and then merely nibbled at one, content to watch me eat, and then my wife eat, and then me, and I noticed her complexion taking on a red-gold sheen, with honey-colored highlights over her cheekbones, as though the semitropical sun she'd absorbed most of her life was stored below her skin and could be released at will. And then I thought, She hardly has an inkling of our culture.

•

When I speculate about my work, I begin to pace, half-blind with abstraction, at the mercy of every associative flight, and after our communal meals had begun, I noticed that these flights were ending, more and more, with me in the same room as Estrelaria. Or if I wandered into the kitchen to douse under the faucet the cigarette that had started to burn my fingers and then went to drop it into the sack inside the wastebasket under the sink (a nasty habit I'd developed during the separation from my wife, although it was meant to keep me from burning down the many makeshift apartments I had lived in)—if I went into the motions to accomplish this, it seemed that Estrelaria was also on her way to the sink, or already there, turning to me in surprise from the dishes.

"*Perdóneme, por favor*," I would say, unable to keep from carrying the action through, as it is with these rituals we become involved in, as though the tenor of the rest of the day depended upon my getting that butt into the bag, and as she backed away from the cabinet doors below the sink so I could get this over with, we sometimes bumped. She was as solid as a tree. Or we would meet in the house, going in opposite directions, and would have to engage in those evading maneuvers that are sometimes necessary when you gravitate toward a stranger on the sidewalk and you both find yourselves stepping in the directions that only make the encounter worse, as if a compass in each had swung toward the other's true north.

One afternoon during lunch Estrelaria became more animated than usual, with that curious orangy light entering her irises and her face, and in her outpouring of language all I was able to understand was something about beds and a grand day. Later I asked my wife what this was about—my first sense of how it feels to need an interpreter.

"She said that in Guatemala, in the spring, there's some kind of cleaning festival, when people take the mats and bed covers and clothes out of houses or huts and hang them out to air. Everything gets washed and scrubbed and it becomes a kind of holiday, apparently."

"Under which regime, I wonder."

My wife studied me with level green eyes. One of the advantages of turning forty is the latitude you have to express every reservation you've felt about anything. But perhaps I'd been exercising that prerogative too often. My wife turned back to the camera she was cleaning; everything in the house was being cleaned.

"I understand it's more of a traditional event," she said. "It's something that's gone on in Estrelaria's village for as long as she can remember, she said. You should have stayed around to hear how she described the dancing, and how drunk the men get." She gave a low laugh. "You left the table without a word. I meant to say something to you. Are you that distracted?"

"Involved, I'd call it. New ideas keep recurring."

"Recurring? Well, Estrelaria asked if maybe we couldn't do that here."

"A festival? In this house?"

"I have a feeling it's mostly for Becky." Our daughter.

"In the spring, Estrelaria said. Well, it's nearly spring now. Late spring, say."

I raised my eyebrows and went back to work. And later, in the midst of that work, my head came up and I made a vow: For the cleaning festival, which would be a minor one, I would crank up a bucket of homemade ice cream. But after that I would not go downstairs when Estrelaria was in the house.

·

"What?" I asked.

"Estrelaria wants to give Becky a birthday present," my wife said.

I sat down at the kitchen table. "What next?" Estrelaria called our daughter *"mi rubia mía"* and would sometimes stand in her bedroom, off the kitchen, wringing her hands and surveying everything as if perfection hadn't been attained, quite. Or she would absently wipe a dustrag over our daughter's vanity as she stared into its mirror, and then would sit on our daughter's bed and polish all of the model horses on the shelf I'd built for our daughter's model horses, and then all of the model horses that had overrun this shelf onto the windowsill; and she would look so dreamily absorbed I was sure she must be imagining what it would be like to live with us, which of course caused me to wonder the same thing.

"If her parents still live in a house with dirt floors, where did she learn to clean?" I asked, out of the silence that overtook the house whenever Estrelaria left for the day.

"I'm sure you have to be even more industrious to clean bamboo, or thatch, or whatever," my wife said. "And certainly dirt. She said she sends her money to her parents. To have a refrigerator there, apparently, is tantamount to being royalty. She's working on that now."

"Good," I said, and was sorry for my suspicions about Estrelaria's husband—that he was using her to bolster his income. Then I had a vision of our wages making their way through a Central American rain forest to a jungle village: an Amana on a shadowed earth floor.

My wife said, "She has an uncanny ability to see into everything."

"Ah," I said, and nodded, still in the distance. "I see."

"I'm not sure you do." She was across from me at the table, sewing a button on a coat that lay bulged over her lap, as if a body were beneath; I sometimes forgot that she was pregnant. She hated sewing, and I couldn't imagine why she was at it in the middle of the day. "She seems concerned about my pregnancy, and lately she's mentioned something I can only translate as 'women's trouble.' From what I can understand, I believe she's had a D & C." My wife bit off the end of the thread and spat it out. "I have a feeling they want children but aren't able to have any."

"Ah," I said again, and nodded, which is what I do when I can't think of anything to say.

•

Estrelaria wasn't able to explain what she was making for our daughter, and my wife begged her not to be extravagant. I knew my wife felt that my gifts to our daughter during our separation, such as the model horses, had been too much. She didn't want that sort of currency to continue. A week later Estrelaria came in carrying something packed between flats of cardboard—a large sheet of tinfoil she had crinkled and then pressed flat and used as a base for painting. Glittering enamels rayed out from a black stallion standing at attention.

"Oh, horses are so difficult to do," my wife said, and I heard a note of disappointment in her voice. We had suspected Estrelaria would sew an article of clothing out of native materials. To my eyes her picture was not only a horse seen whole, but with the rainbow array of enamels emanating from it like a projection of its lights and vitals, it seemed the essence of horse.

Estrelaria tried to explain, at least partly, how carefully it would have to be framed, to keep the crinkles from giving, so the figure wouldn't be ruined. She had noticed the work I did with wood in the basement, she said, and turned to me. I took the painting down to the basement and started the frame that hour. There was a slowdown when the wood had to be varnished, and then I broke the piece of glass I was cutting to fit the frame, which I saw as a bad omen. I got so shaky about this I didn't have the picture hanging in our daughter's room until the next week, and when Estrelaria arrived she hurried across the kitchen, still in her coat, to the door of the room, and then breathed out as if she'd been holding her breath for a block. *"Bueno,"* she said. Which was how I felt. I turned to my wife, who was easing herself into a chair at the table, and saw that she looked worn out.

•

Soon after this our son was born, and everybody's attentiveness to him added to the daily shuffle. Estrelaria had prepared the house for him, as she saw it, and at the first sight of him she cried out and held her hands over her breasts, as if the accomplishment of birth were hers. Then she gave us her gift to him and stood over me as I unwrapped it. His first pair of shoes. A comment on my pacing? She let us understand that she expected to spend some time with him when she was there, and the living-room couch became her territory. She would place him in her lap and lean over him, outlined by the picture window looking out on our porch (the only photograph my wife took of her is in this attitude, all dark and light, her features obscured), bending over his white-blond head, and play with his hands and ears as she spoke to him in a language even my wife couldn't understand.

Once, when I forgot my vow and my pacing drew me to the living room, I paused at the door and saw him pawing at her breasts. The red-gold suffusion colored her face. Another afternoon I heard him, all the way downstairs, crying as if he'd been abandoned, and went down to our bedroom to pick him up. Suddenly Estrelaria was between us as quick as a cat.

"No, no, no!" she said, and put a hand to my chest.

No, what? I thought. She was being more possessive than his mother.

"No cigarillo," she said, pointing at me, then at my son, and shook her head.

I'd forgotten I had a lit cigarette in my mouth. I went to the kitchen sink, doused it, and dropped it into the bag. Then I started looking for my wife.

•

Estrelaria spoke to me in Spanish the week before she left. I was composing a formal speech of farewell to her, in Spanish, which I planned to deliver at lunch, so it wouldn't be buried in the moment of her actual leaving, but when I went downstairs it was late. In the kitchen, my wife and Estrelaria were holding each other's arms at the elbows, as if they'd just embraced. They were silent, but I felt fields of force like magnetic fields between them and Estrelaria's face was so altered it looked as if she'd been crying.

No.

I started my speech and Estrelaria held up a hand.

"Will you drive her to the station?" my wife asked, and walked off.

Estrelaria sat all the way across the seat from me in our wide convertible, a tattered old Bonneville she preferred to our new Duster, glancing up at the sky and placing a hand over her hair, as though the braid of it might unfurl, and I was aware again of her size—a child. I tried to put the finishing touches on my speech. I wanted to say that she'd become a necessary member of the household, and to thank her for the way she'd helped to pull the house, if not our family, together, and then, as if she'd picked up the tumble of Spanish in me, she said she didn't like *los morenos*. She was so afraid of them, she said in Spanish, that she . . . But she didn't go on; her eyes were wide with fear, I saw in a quick glance: a confession. I figured I was dark enough to be considered a *moreno*, or dark one (with the connotation of swarthy darkness more than brunet), since I certainly wasn't the *rubia* my wife and children were. But if there was ever an epitome of the *moreno*, it was Estrelaria, with her crow-black hair and her complexion now copper-gold in the sun.

"Here, they are not like in Guatemala, but frighten you," she said, again in Spanish. "They purposely do this. This is why I don't like it here."

An explanation for leaving? Then as we pulled up to the El station, constructed of that awful oatmeal-yellow brick, I saw some teenagers jiving around with portable radios on their shoulders, and thought, Just when you believe you understand somebody, a door is opened on their weakness. She was afraid of blacks. She wouldn't let me walk her to the El platform, and as I watched her go, with that weight-bearing steadiness to her back and hips, I was sure we wouldn't see her next week. This was goodbye.

•

At home, my wife was lying face down on the unmade bed, on both pillows, as she does when she's upset. I tiptoed over to the window and looked at our son below it, lying in the wooden cradle I'd built for him, flushed with sleep in the afternoon light. He'd nearly outgrown the cradle by the time I'd finished it; I'd forgotten how fast infants grow. His head was pressed against one end in an uncomfortable tuck, with dewy beads like a sweat of exertion over his fatty neck, as if he were straining to break free. Estrelaria would run a finger over his features and then point at me, smiling, to indicate how he'd inherited them, and it never occurred to me to translate her look into love.

I touched the back of my hand to my son's cheek, passing on my fears to him, I felt, when I should have been passing on a promise, then worked a blanket between his head and the end of the cradle. Finally I stepped over to the bed and put a hand on my wife's shoulder.

"I don't know how we'll manage without her!" she cried into the pillows with a force that startled me.

"I know," I said, and sat on the edge of the bed.

"And I don't mean work! It isn't the work!" she cried.

"It's *her!*"

"I know," I said again, staring out the sunlit window at the blaze of an empty parking lot, and felt that a crowd at my back, which my apologetics seemed to set in place, was dropping over the bed around her.

•

Estrelaria arrived on time the next week, my wife told me. I slept in late and woke thinking of her, of her retreating back at the El station, and of the texture she'd brought to our new home, like a lunar light I could taste, and then of the texture of her hands, gingery brown, with polished, rose palms. I dressed and started up the stairs with my head so low I could see the treads behind my heels, daunted by the work ahead, and stepped onto the landing. Estrelaria was there, on her knees, her backside to me, her bare feet crossed at the ankles, scrubbing the landing floor. Her toes, so close, looked prehensile, gripping, curved at their ends from her walk, and the angle of her legs in her rolled-up blue jeans, this pose, reminded me so powerfully of something I felt my mind about to give with a seizure that would catapult me down the stairs. She turned to me and smiled, exposing glittering teeth, and, as if to keep my equilibrium, I thought, Her family must be terribly primitive. She's never had sugar.

Then she sat back on her legs and reached over her shoulder to her single braid, as thick as my wrist, and drew it with a hand over one breast, and a lighted space opened above us, as if the ceiling were gone and the roof swept away. Clouds were pouring across the open rafters in a bright-blue sky. I could feel the heat of an equatorial sun. If I looked away from her smile, which was a mere lifting of her lips, I would see foliage opening out from the landing, I was sure. The green at our edges was the grass of a mesa we were settled upon—she half-reclining, I standing—with the land spreading off in gray and green undulations to a roll of buttes in the distance, and above us and all about us was the openness of a Western sky.

This woman at my feet had worked for us as perhaps no other woman ever would, and her expression as she stared up at me conveyed more than the dignity of her womanhood. She was aware that there was little to fear in me; I was a dreamer, and she had released me into my dreams as only my mother could. Matters with my wife were too sexually complicated for her to be my mother, and though there had been times when I'd felt that this would be convenient—what an absurd thought, I saw now, a boy's thought!—I knew I never could have accepted her above me or under me in that role. My mother had appeared instead in Estrelaria.

How many times had I seen my mother's legs drawn together in this way as she sat back to rest from scrubbing a floor, running an arched wrist over her forehead, shaking back her hair?—and now it occurred to me that she was Estrelaria's size, no taller, and a sudden physical incursion of height through my limbs readjusted me. It wasn't a tropical landscape I had glimpsed but the country of my childhood. These were the fields and the hills and the turtle-green buttes of North Dakota. That was the hilly mass of Hawk's Nest in the distance, its creased and shimmering slopes piling over one another toward the sky. This was my mother's gift to me, a vision of this land in its endless configurations from the center of a faithful family. As long as I retained the vision I was in touch with her, and I felt sure that I would walk across a place of my own in this countryside someday.

"*Perdóneme*," she whispered, and moved her feet.

"*Perdóneme*," I said. And then I shook my head at her and walked on by.

·

And now I feel the scroll and swirl of the topography I've recently passed through, and I'm dropped back a further notch, into the present, at this desk where I work on interviews when I'm not working the fields of this farm. My wife and I are separated again, not in that parlance of lawyers, but by two thousand miles. We've spent the winter in the East and I've returned early, to prepare this place for her and our children. During the drive back, every mile of highway reminded me of her, and I realized that everything I was seeing I'd seen several times with her, so that I wasn't able to take in any of the landscape as separate from her—or I saw details of it, or the panorama surrounding these details, at least partly through her eyes. There were moments when I felt that she was beside me, looking out, or lying with her head in my lap, or speaking with excitement about the potential for our lives that the vistas of a trip always opened up, as if in promise that we could become as renewable as the changing countryside. The physicality of her presence was so alarming at times I started to pull over. I saw her in different clothes, at different ages, with her hair in different styles, but always with the same spirit that was in her when she turned from her friend in the motorcycle jacket in that darkened bar where we first met, projecting herself all the way around me and a long way ahead with a smile as generous as any of Estrelaria's—as if she were traveling now in that spirit from the Pacific Coast to meet me in my journey westward, until the miles between us only extended her everywhere, so that she seemed the weaving of the landscape.

My love for this land is, of course, my love for a woman. She is this countryside, she is this continent, joined by Estrelaria's dark country to that shapelier continent extending south. She is my developed half, my fruitful auditor, my only faithful one, the one for whom this is spoken and for whom it remains speaking when all of the rest has fallen away to reveal that other side—my wife.